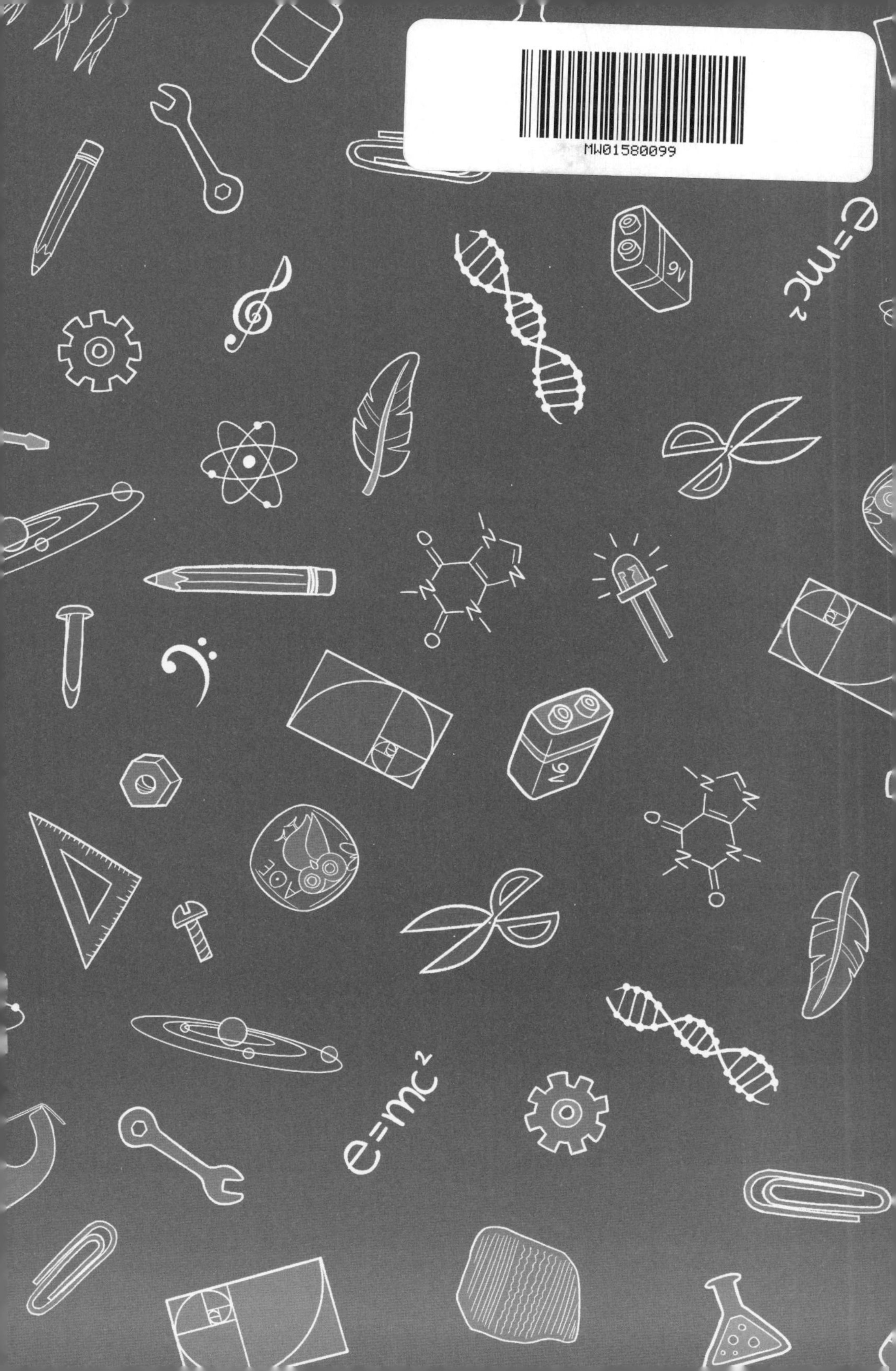
e=mc²
e=mc²

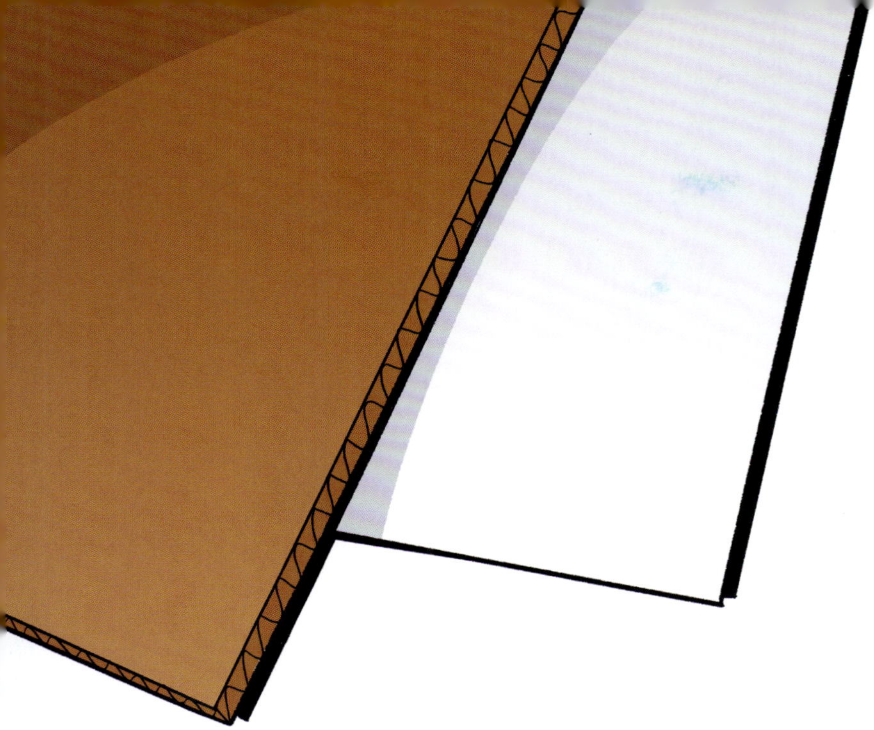

MAKER GIRL AND PROFESSOR SMARTS

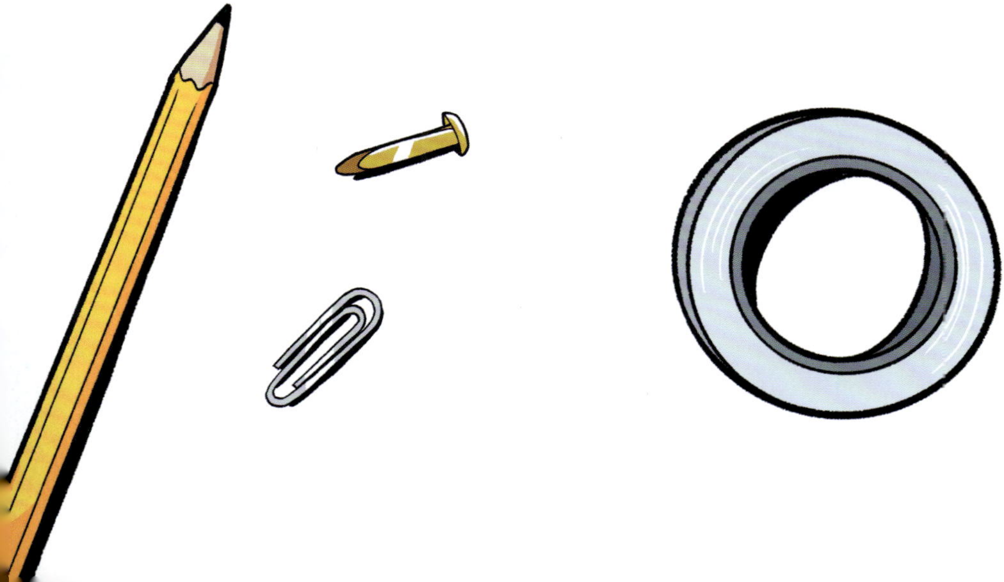

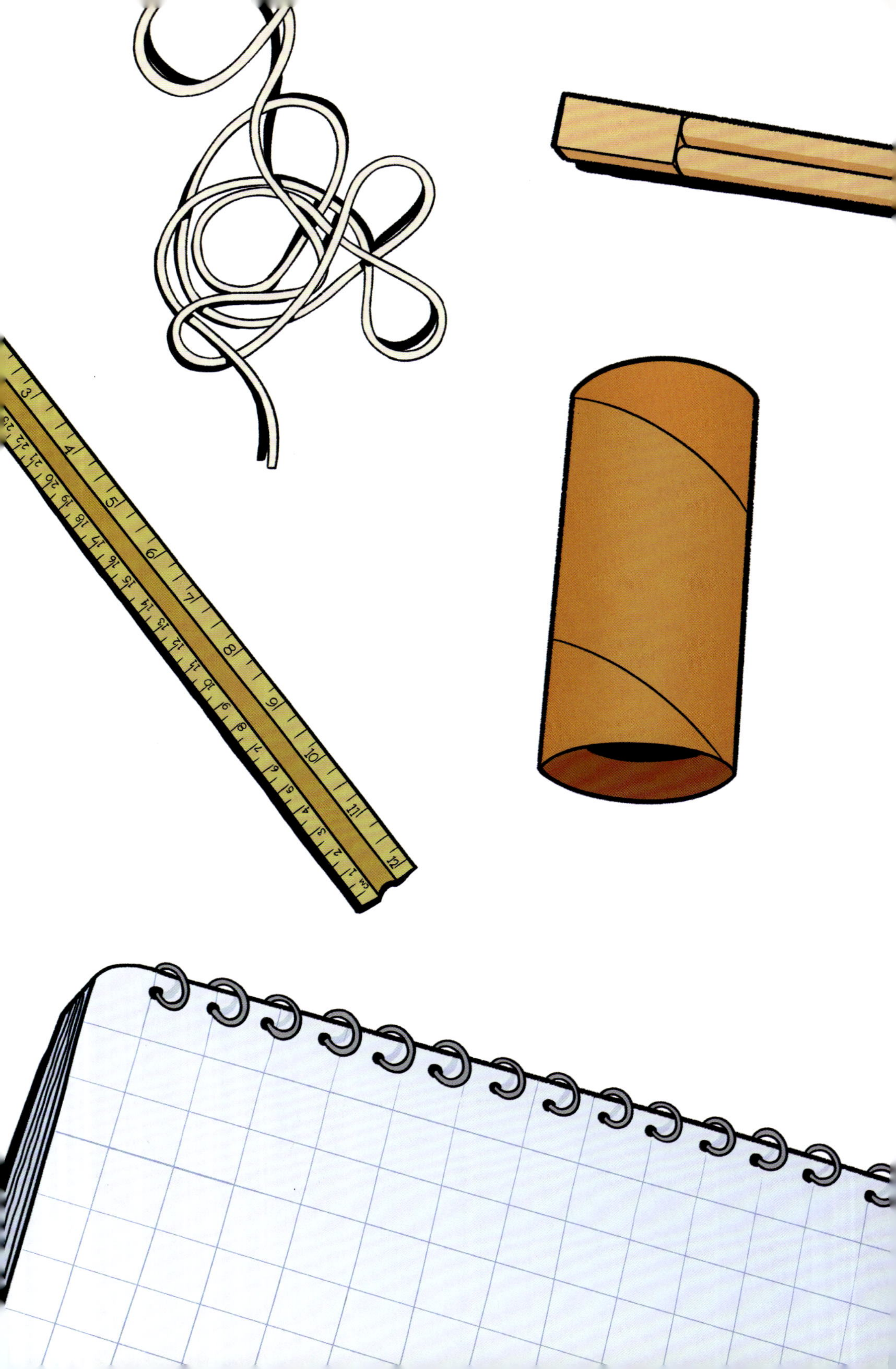

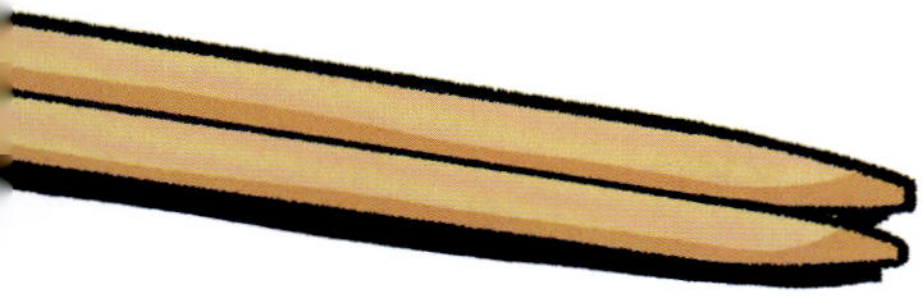

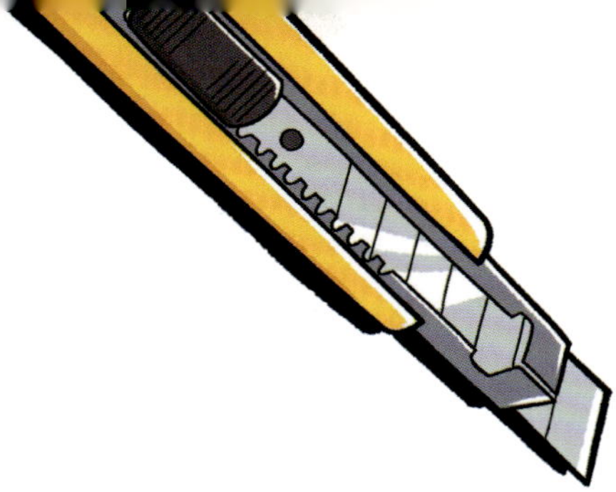

MAKER GIRL AND PROFESSOR SMARTS

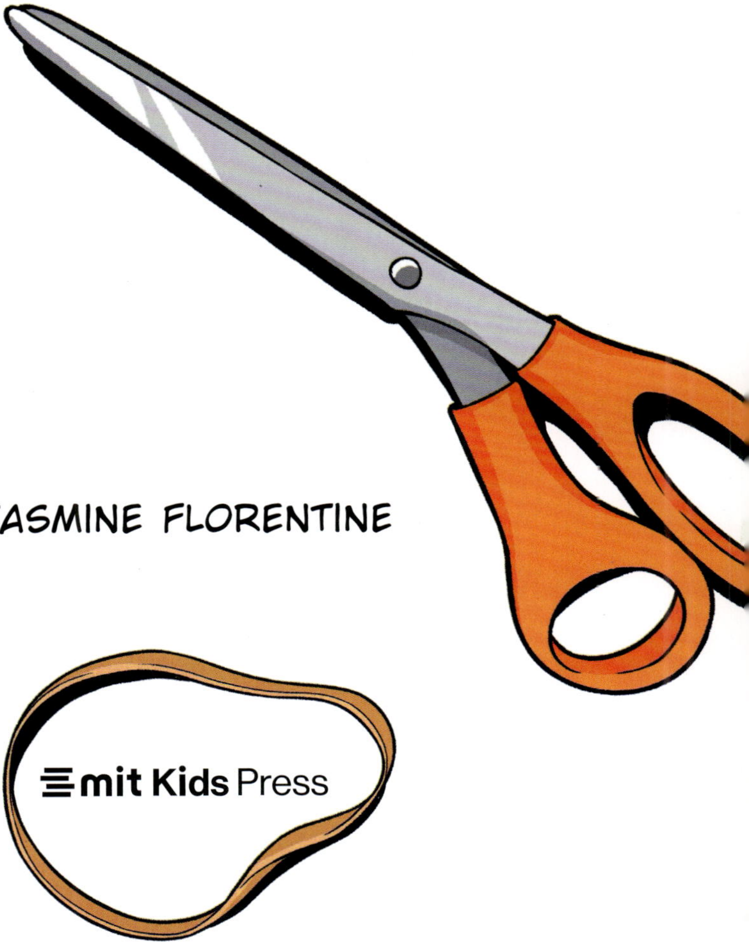

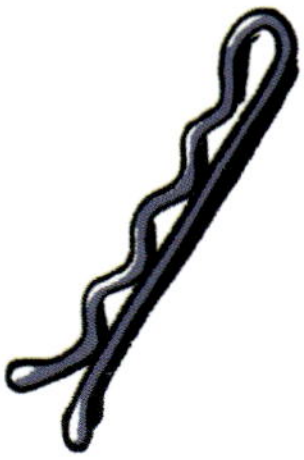

JASMINE FLORENTINE

mit Kids Press

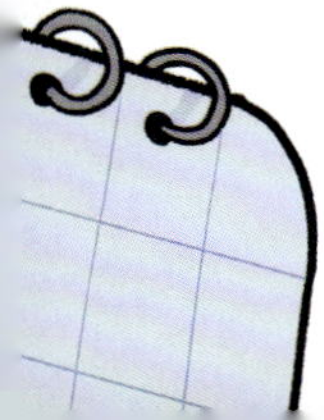

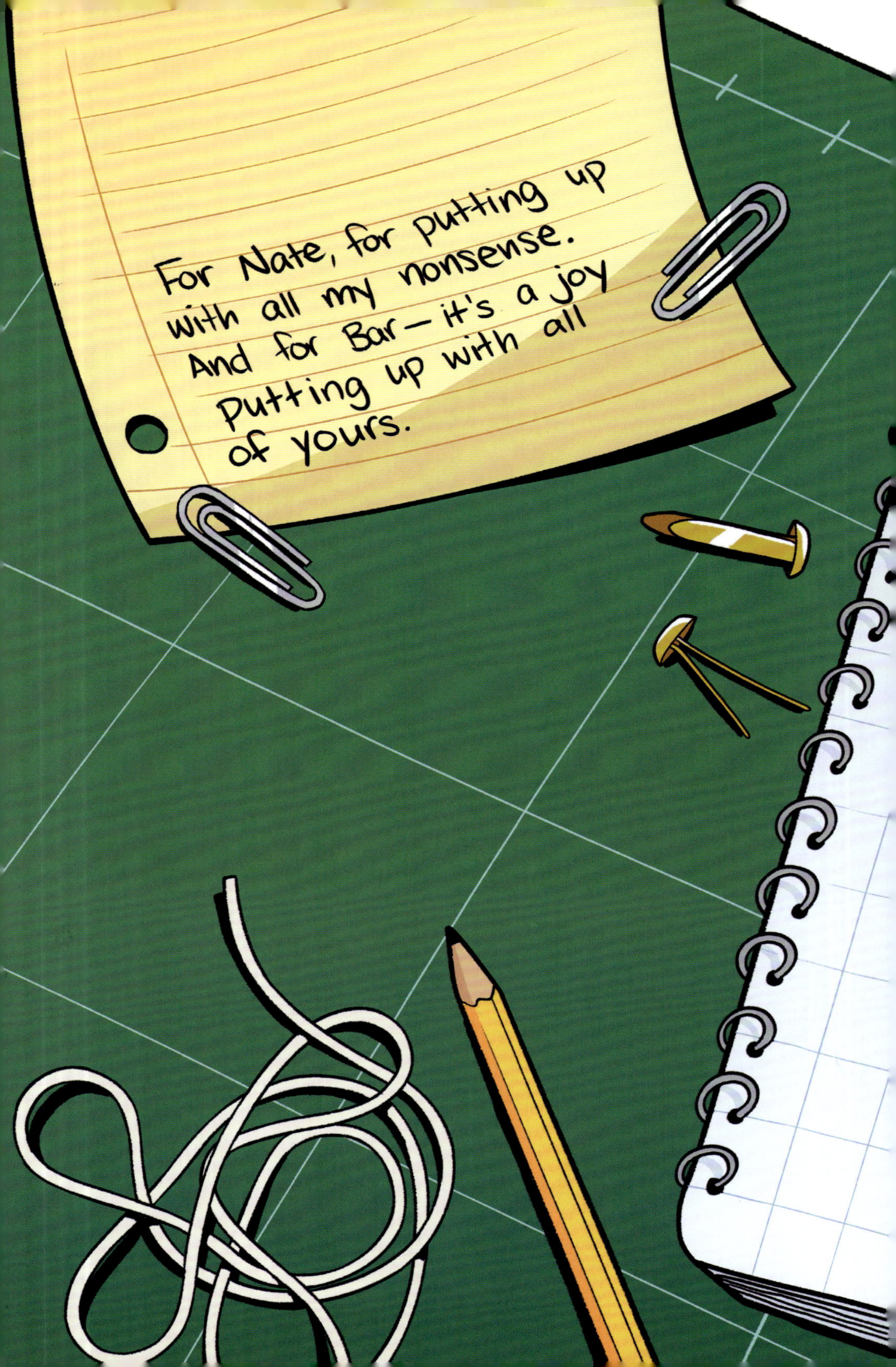
For Nate, for putting up
with all my nonsense.
And for Bar—it's a joy
putting up with all
of yours.

CONTENTS

INTRODUCTION
The story of how we didn't get superpowers 1

ICE SCREAM, YOU SCREAM 13
How to make a grappling hook 42
How to make sorbet 58

Book 2 sneak peek 72
Character sketches 82
Awesome resources 86
Acknowledgments 88

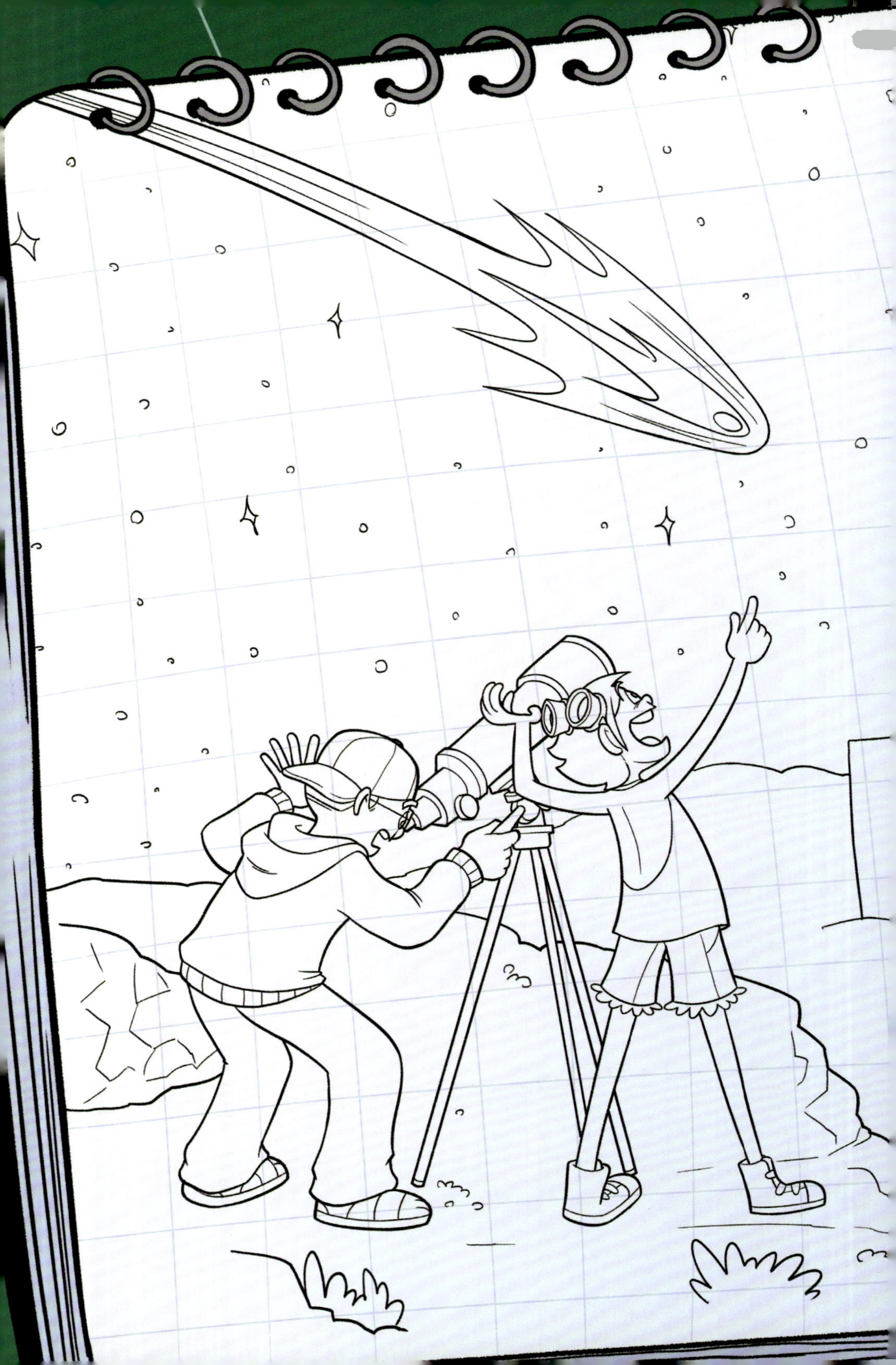

INTRODUCTION
THE STORY OF HOW WE DIDN'T GET SUPERPOWERS

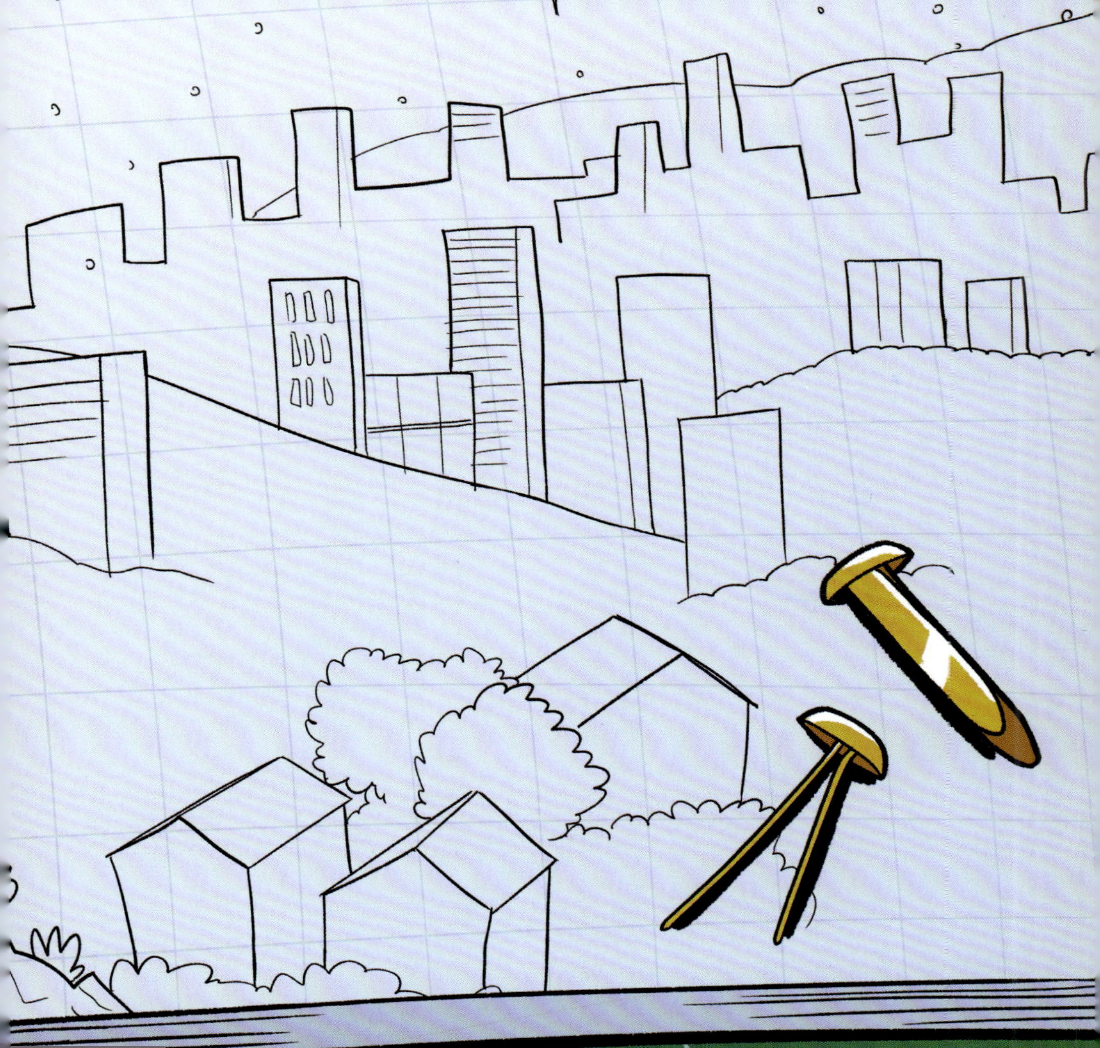

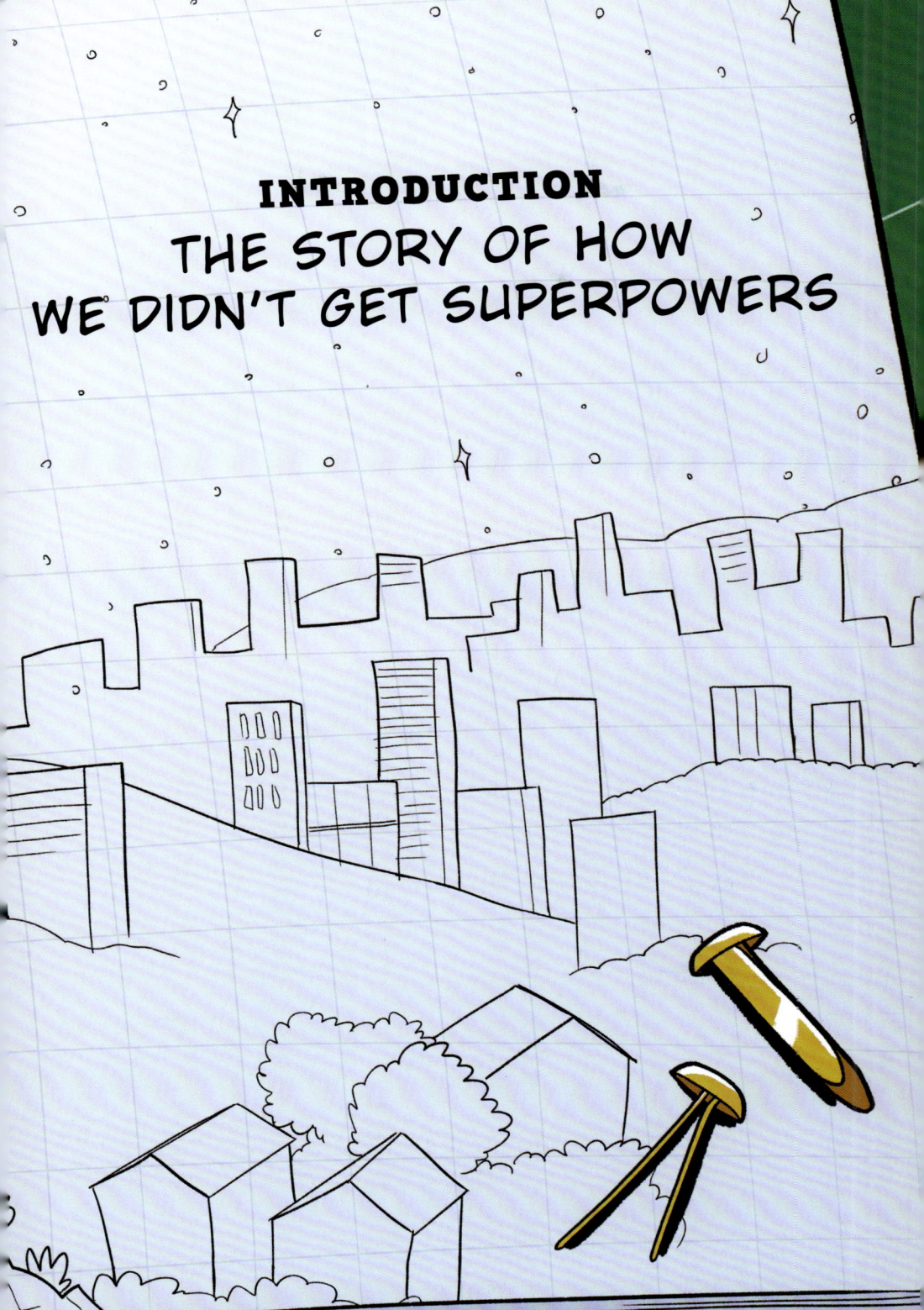

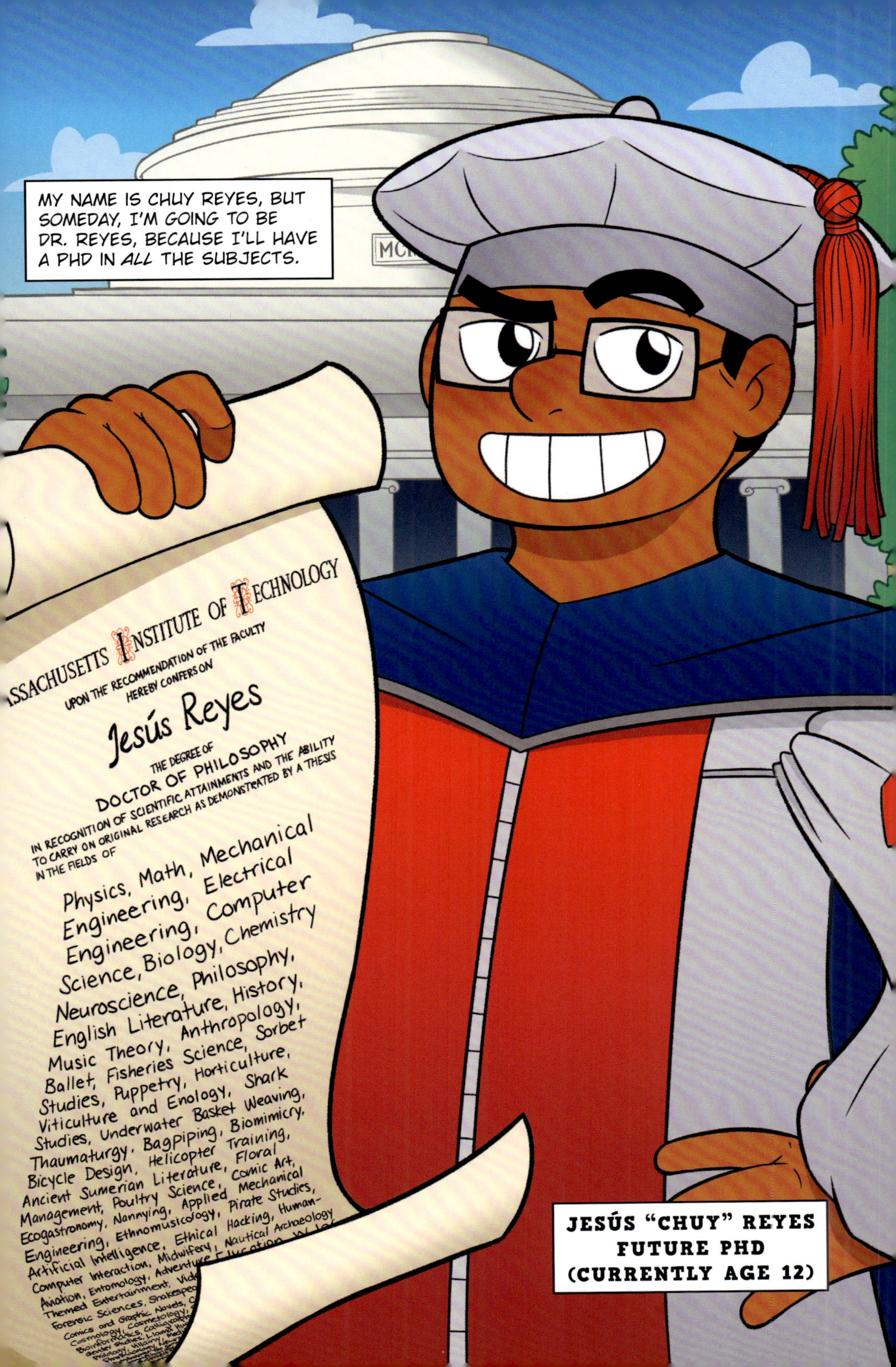
MY NAME IS CHUY REYES, BUT SOMEDAY, I'M GOING TO BE DR. REYES, BECAUSE I'LL HAVE A PHD IN *ALL* THE SUBJECTS.
ASSACHUSETTS INSTITUTE OF TECHNOLOGY
UPON THE RECOMMENDATION OF THE FACULTY
HEREBY CONFERS ON
Jesús Reyes
THE DEGREE OF
DOCTOR OF PHILOSOPHY
IN RECOGNITION OF SCIENTIFIC ATTAINMENTS AND THE ABILITY
TO CARRY ON ORIGINAL RESEARCH AS DEMONSTRATED BY A THESIS
IN THE FIELDS OF
Physics, Math, Mechanical
Engineering, Electrical
Engineering, Computer
Science, Biology, Chemistry
Neuroscience, Philosophy,
English Literature, History,
Music Theory, Anthropology,
Ballet, Fisheries Science, Sorbet
Studies, Puppetry, Horticulture,
Viticulture and Enology, Shark
Studies, Underwater Basket Weaving,
Thaumaturgy, Bagpiping, Biomimicry,
Bicycle Design, Helicopter Training,
Ancient Sumerian Literature, Floral
Management, Poultry Science, Comic Art,
Ecogastronomy, Nannying, Applied Mechanical
Engineering, Ethnomusicology, Pirate Studies,
Artificial Intelligence, Ethical Hacking, Human-
Computer Interaction, Midwifery, Nautical Archaeology
Aviation, Entomology,
Themed Entertainment,
Forensic Sciences,
Comics and Graphic Novels,
JESÚS "CHUY" REYES
FUTURE PHD
(CURRENTLY AGE 12)

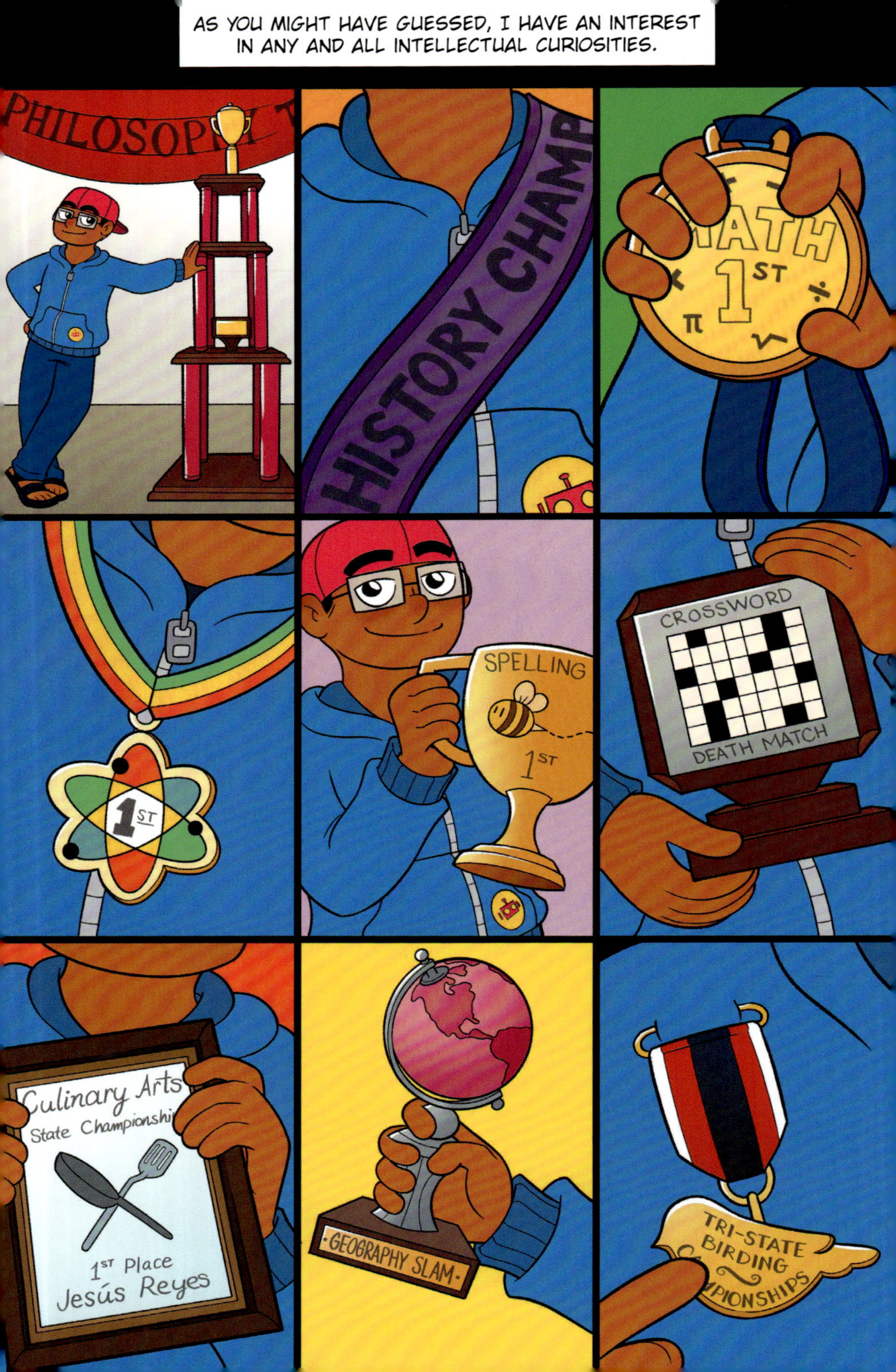

AS YOU MIGHT HAVE GUESSED, I HAVE AN INTEREST IN ANY AND ALL INTELLECTUAL CURIOSITIES.
HISTORY CHAMP
1ST
SPELLING
1ST
CROSSWORD
DEATH MATCH
Culinary Arts
1ST Place
Jesús Reyes
GEOGRAPHY SLAM
TRI-STATE
BIRDING

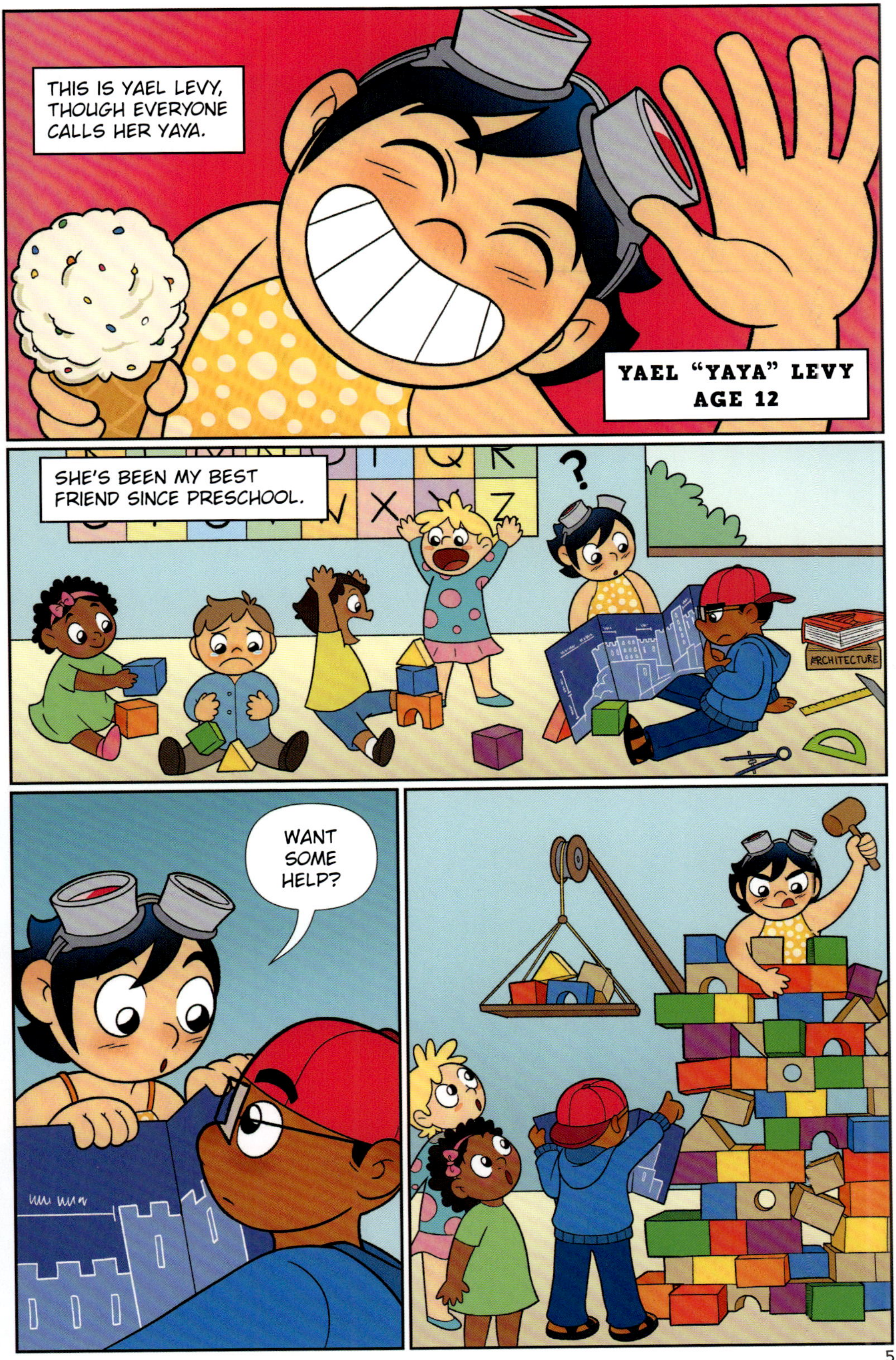

THIS IS YAEL LEVY, THOUGH EVERYONE CALLS HER YAYA.
YAEL "YAYA" LEVY
AGE 12
SHE'S BEEN MY BEST FRIEND SINCE PRESCHOOL.
ARCHITECTURE
WANT SOME HELP?

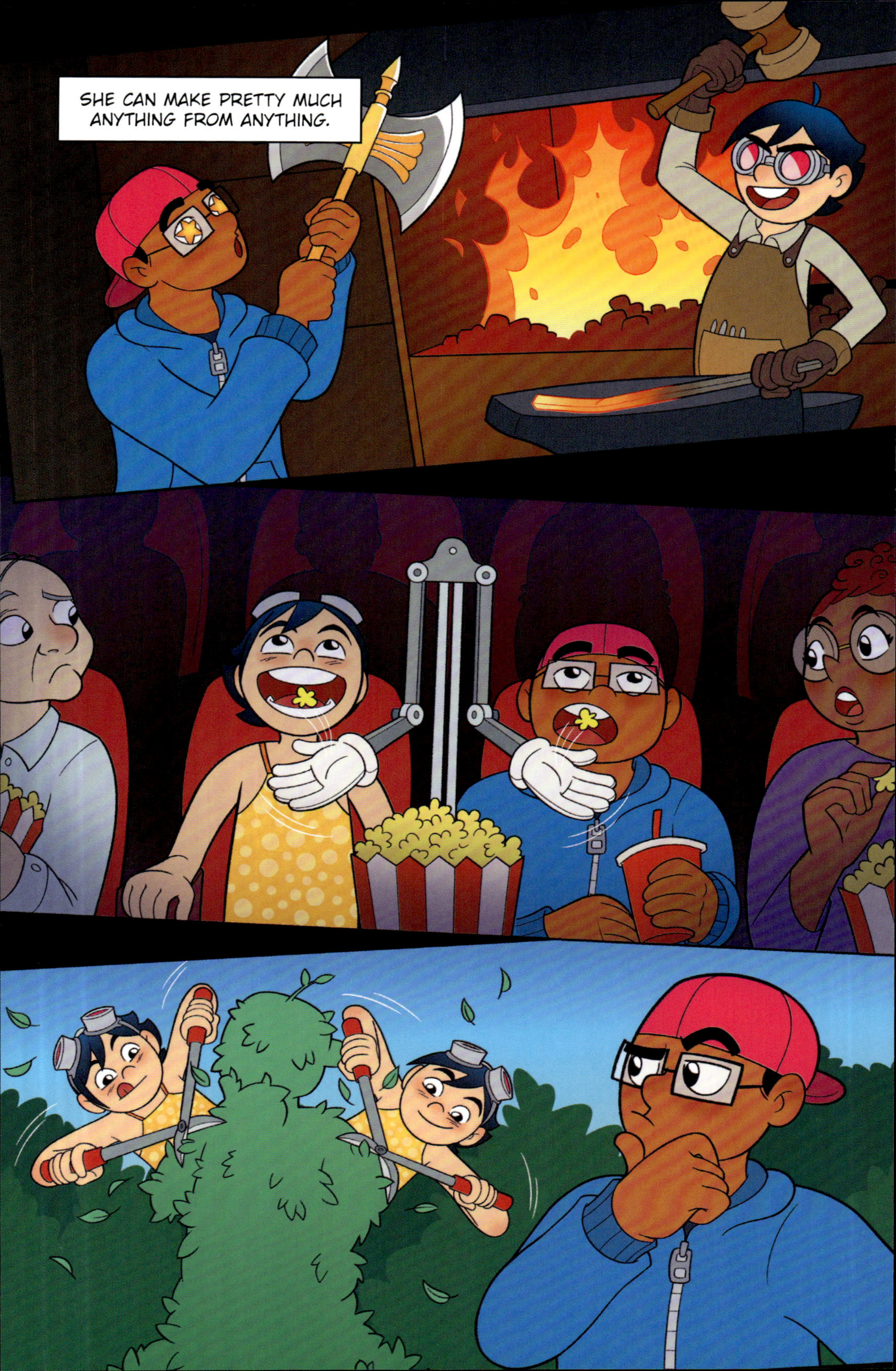
SHE CAN MAKE PRETTY MUCH ANYTHING FROM ANYTHING.

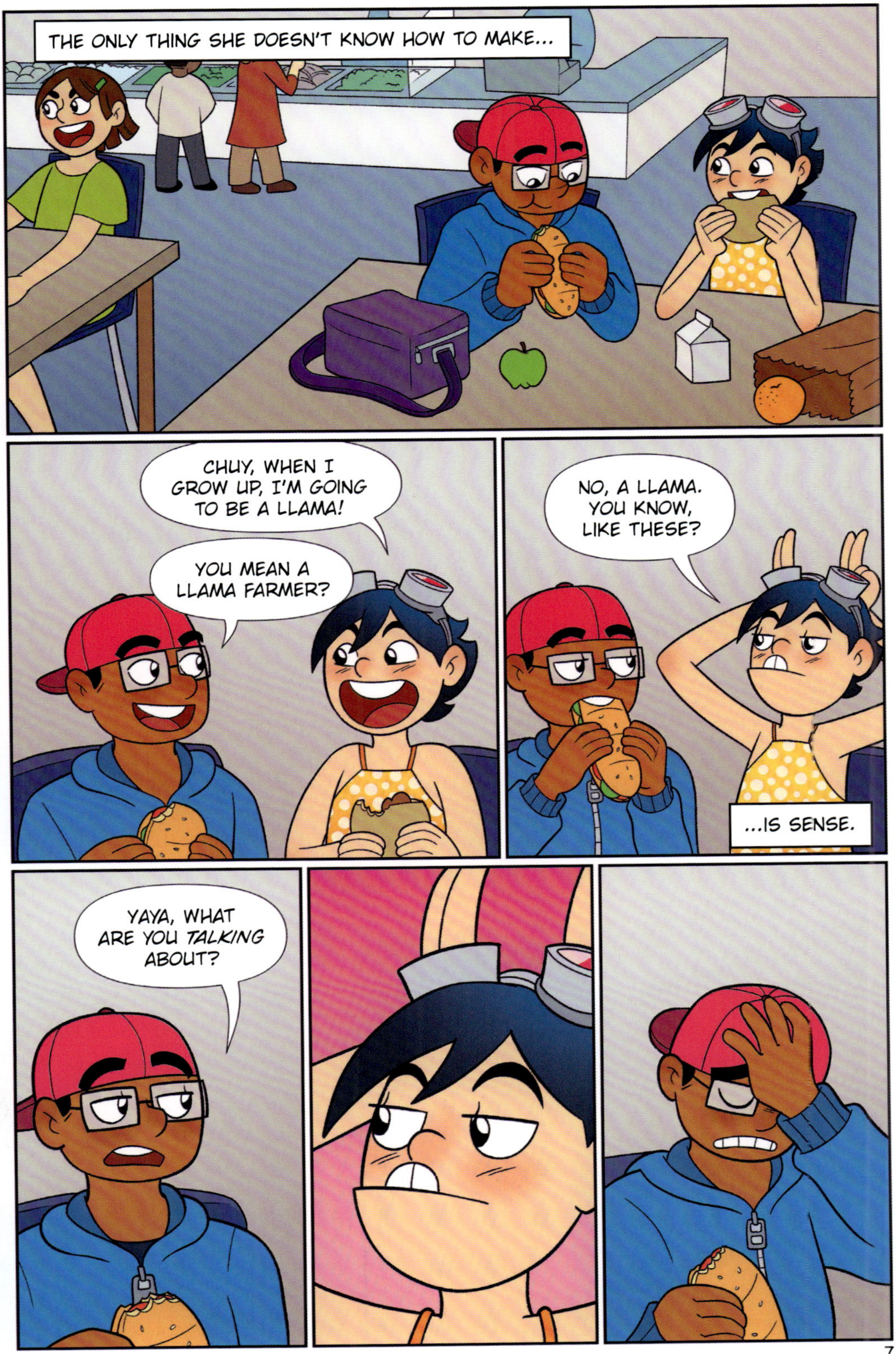
THE ONLY THING SHE DOESN'T KNOW HOW TO MAKE...
CHUY, WHEN I GROW UP, I'M GOING TO BE A LLAMA!
YOU MEAN A LLAMA FARMER?
NO, A LLAMA. YOU KNOW, LIKE THESE?
...IS SENSE.
YAYA, WHAT ARE YOU *TALKING* ABOUT?

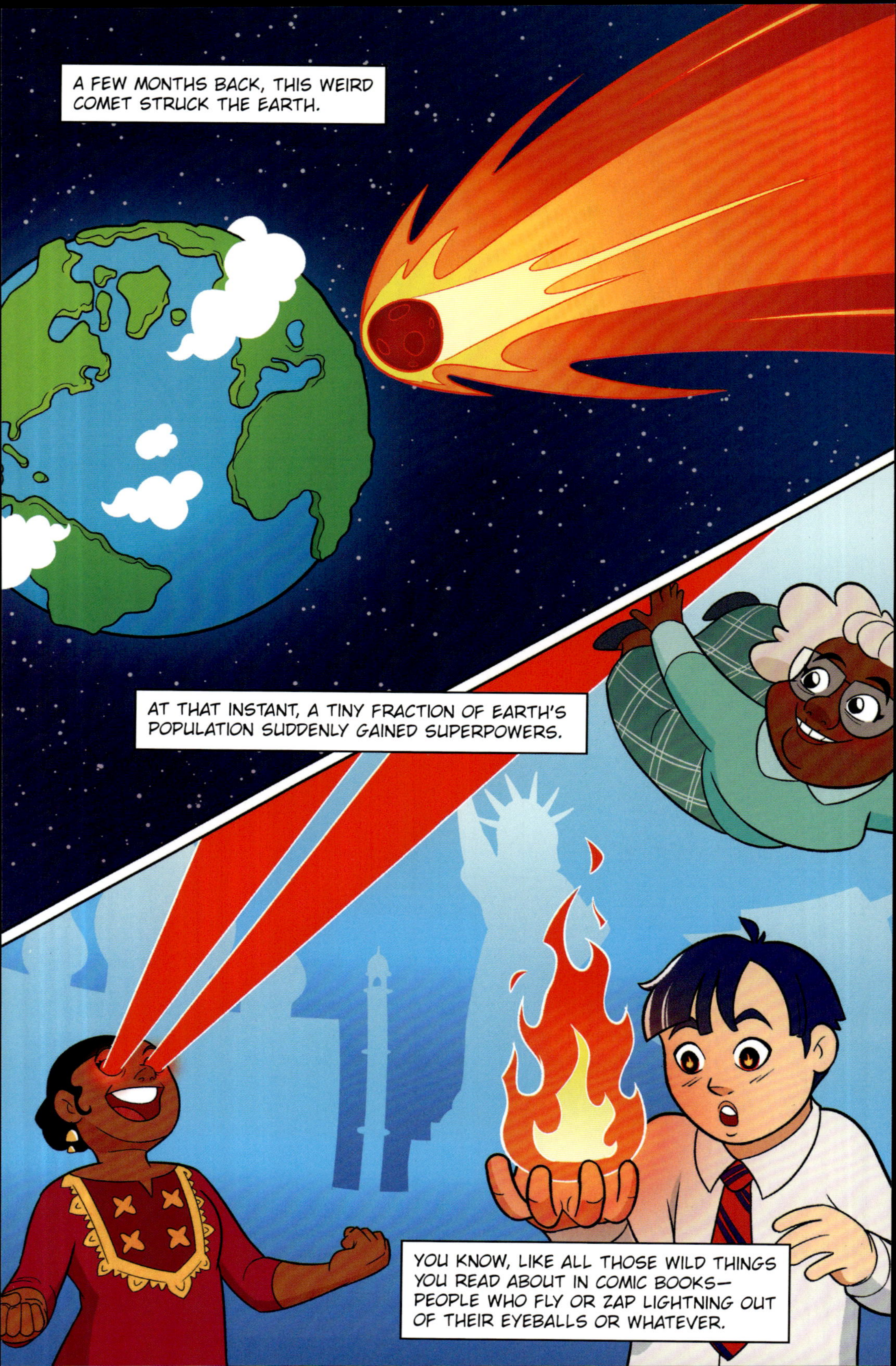
A FEW MONTHS BACK, THIS WEIRD COMET STRUCK THE EARTH.
AT THAT INSTANT, A TINY FRACTION OF EARTH'S POPULATION SUDDENLY GAINED SUPERPOWERS.
YOU KNOW, LIKE ALL THOSE WILD THINGS YOU READ ABOUT IN COMIC BOOKS— PEOPLE WHO FLY OR ZAP LIGHTNING OUT OF THEIR EYEBALLS OR WHATEVER.

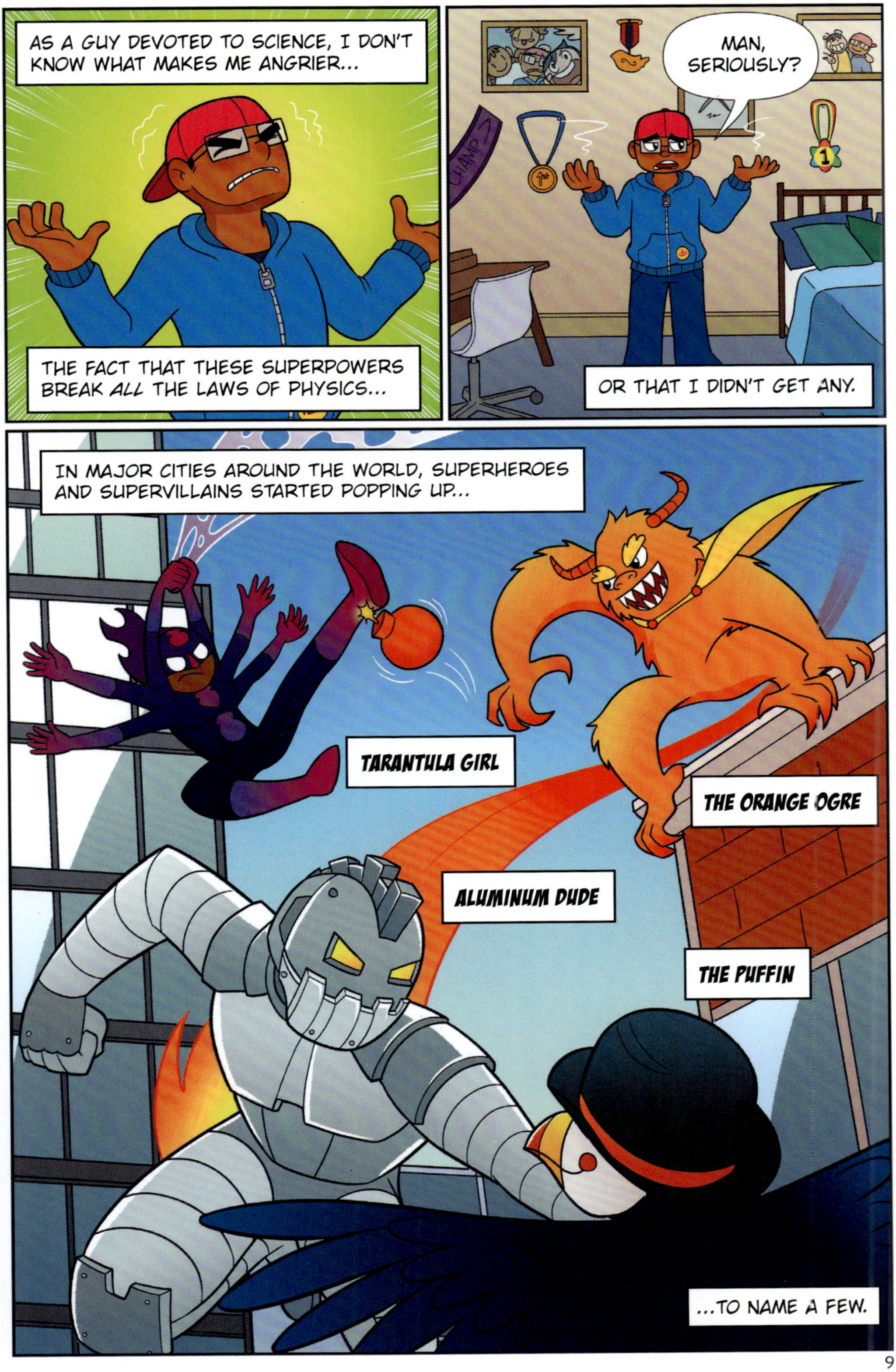
AS A GUY DEVOTED TO SCIENCE, I DON'T KNOW WHAT MAKES ME ANGRIER...
THE FACT THAT THESE SUPERPOWERS BREAK ALL THE LAWS OF PHYSICS...
CHAMP
MAN, SERIOUSLY?
OR THAT I DIDN'T GET ANY.
IN MAJOR CITIES AROUND THE WORLD, SUPERHEROES AND SUPERVILLAINS STARTED POPPING UP...
TARANTULA GIRL
THE ORANGE OGRE
ALUMINUM DUDE
THE PUFFIN
...TO NAME A FEW.

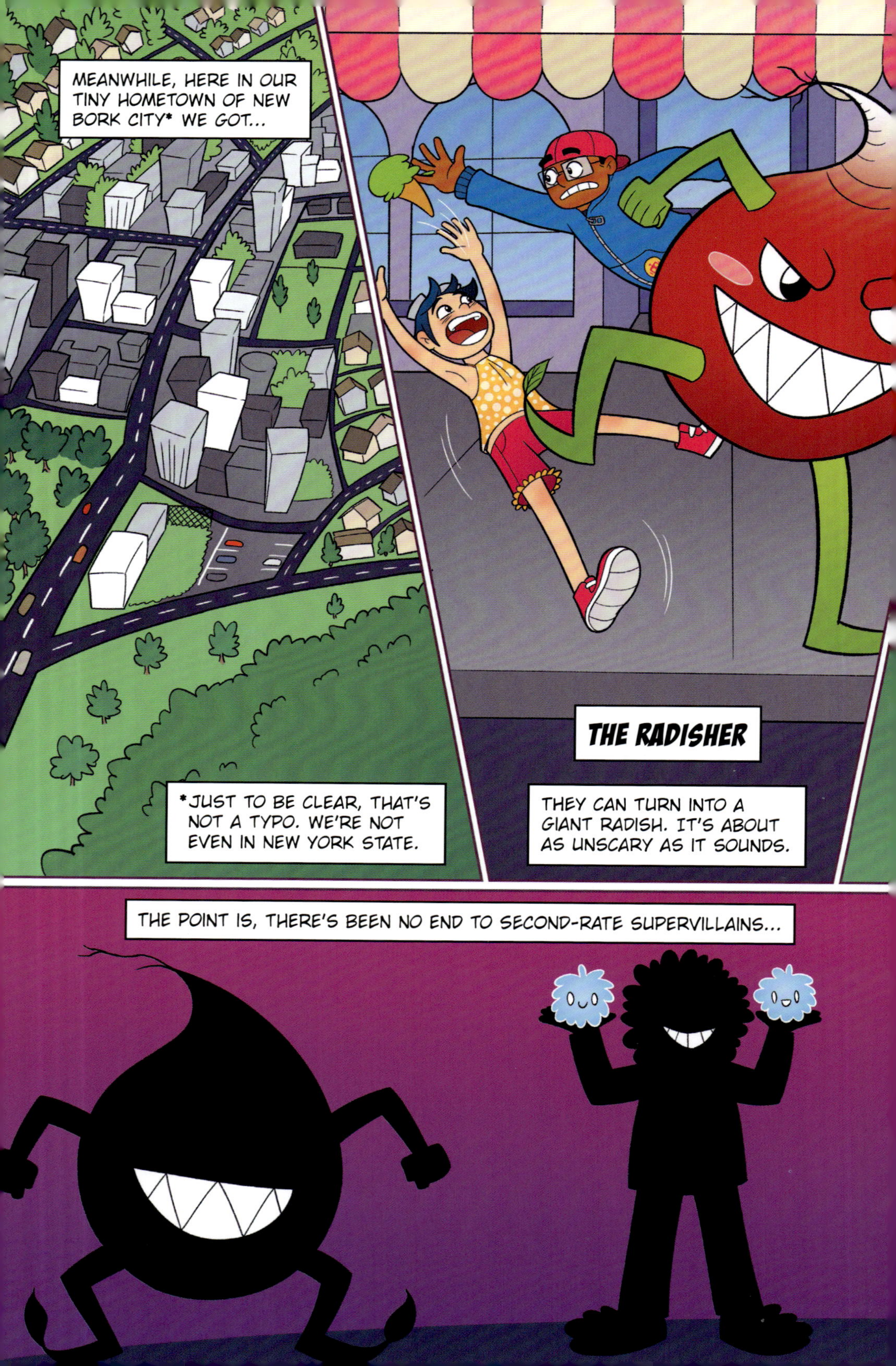
MEANWHILE, HERE IN OUR TINY HOMETOWN OF NEW BORK CITY* WE GOT...
THE RADISHER
*JUST TO BE CLEAR, THAT'S NOT A TYPO. WE'RE NOT EVEN IN NEW YORK STATE.
THEY CAN TURN INTO A GIANT RADISH. IT'S ABOUT AS UNSCARY AS IT SOUNDS.
THE POINT IS, THERE'S BEEN NO END TO SECOND-RATE SUPERVILLAINS...

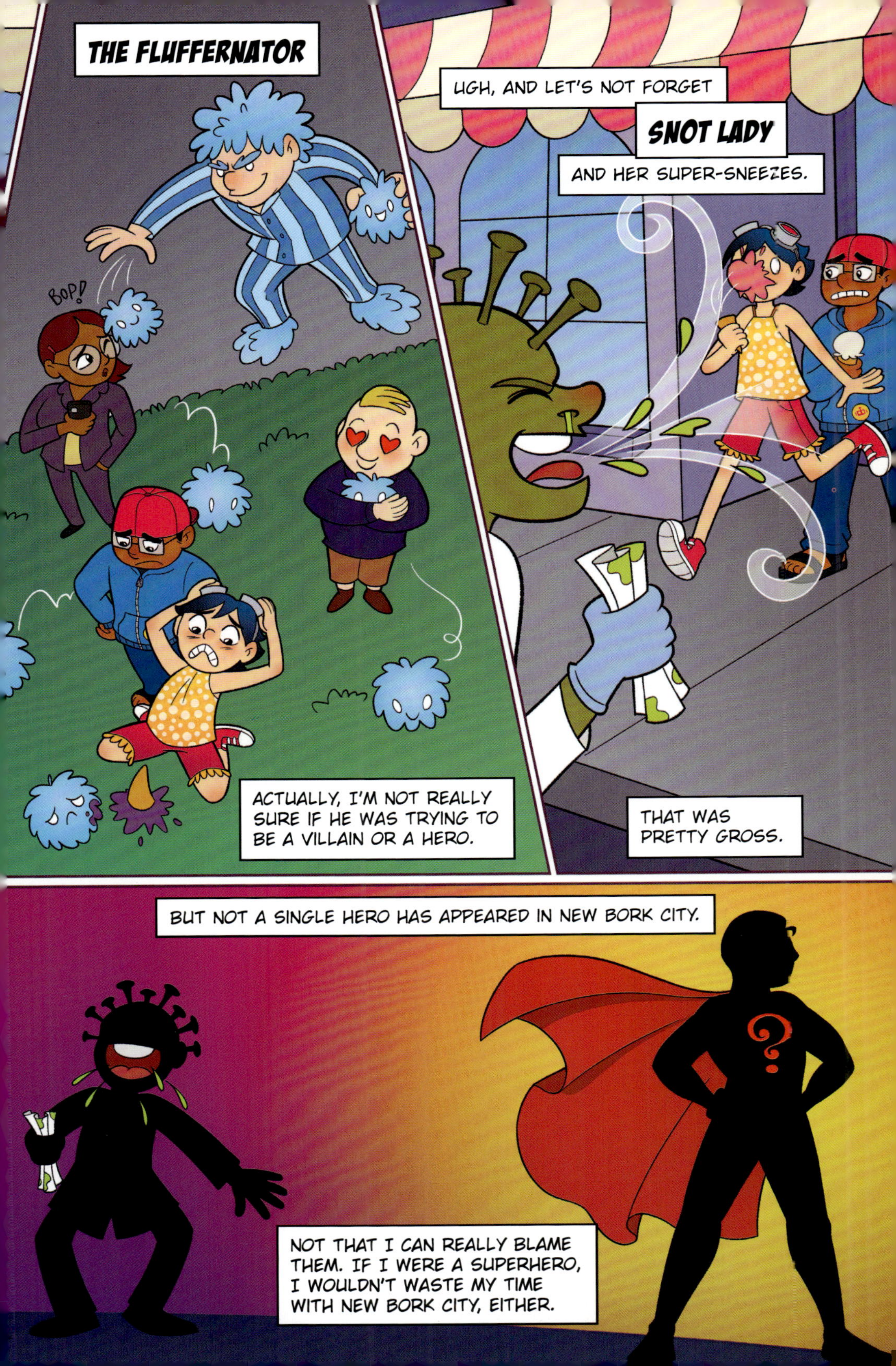
THE FLUFFERNATOR
BOP!
ACTUALLY, I'M NOT REALLY SURE IF HE WAS TRYING TO BE A VILLAIN OR A HERO.
UGH, AND LET'S NOT FORGET
SNOT LADY
AND HER SUPER-SNEEZES.
THAT WAS PRETTY GROSS.
BUT NOT A SINGLE HERO HAS APPEARED IN NEW BORK CITY.
NOT THAT I CAN REALLY BLAME THEM. IF I WERE A SUPERHERO, I WOULDN'T WASTE MY TIME WITH NEW BORK CITY, EITHER.

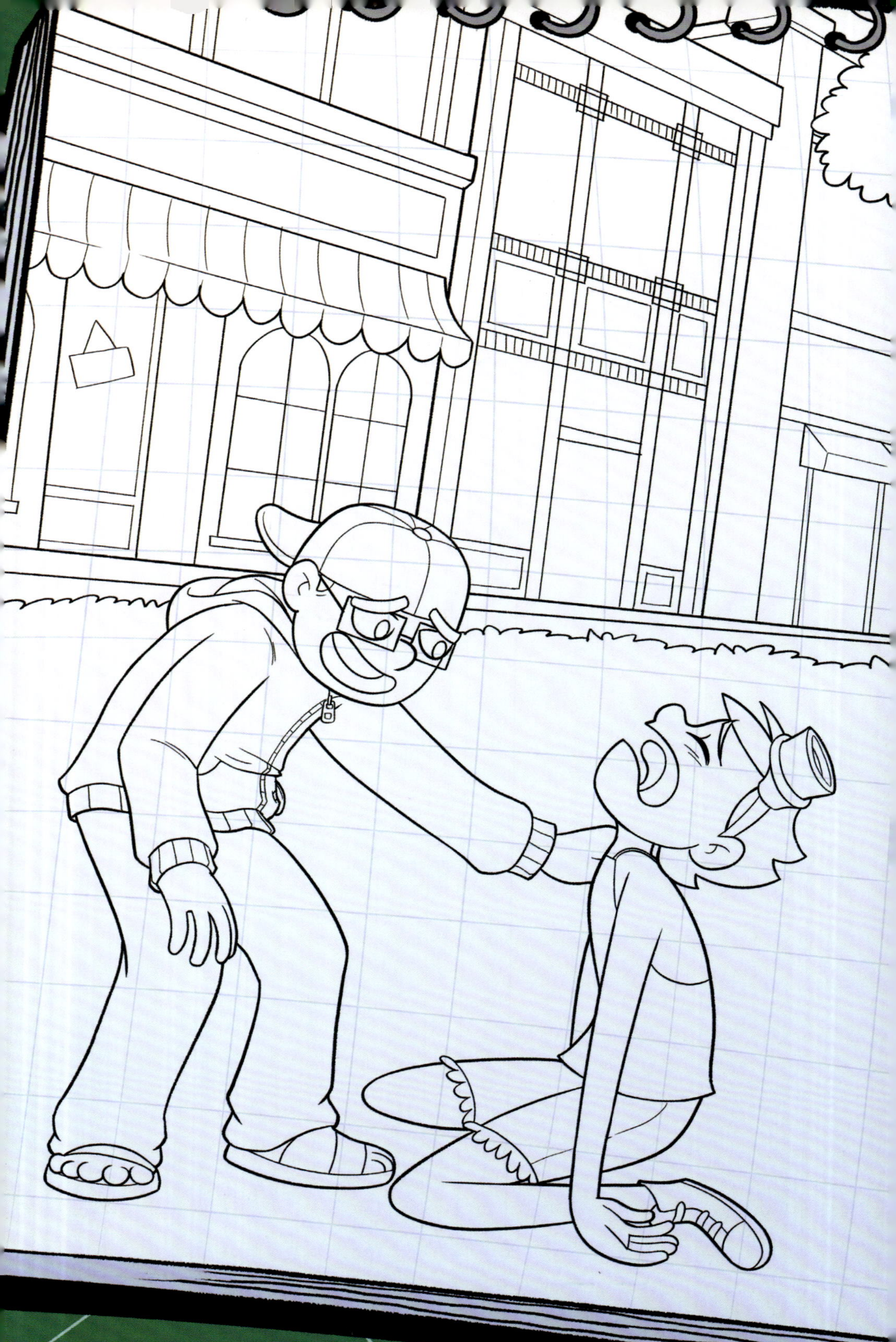

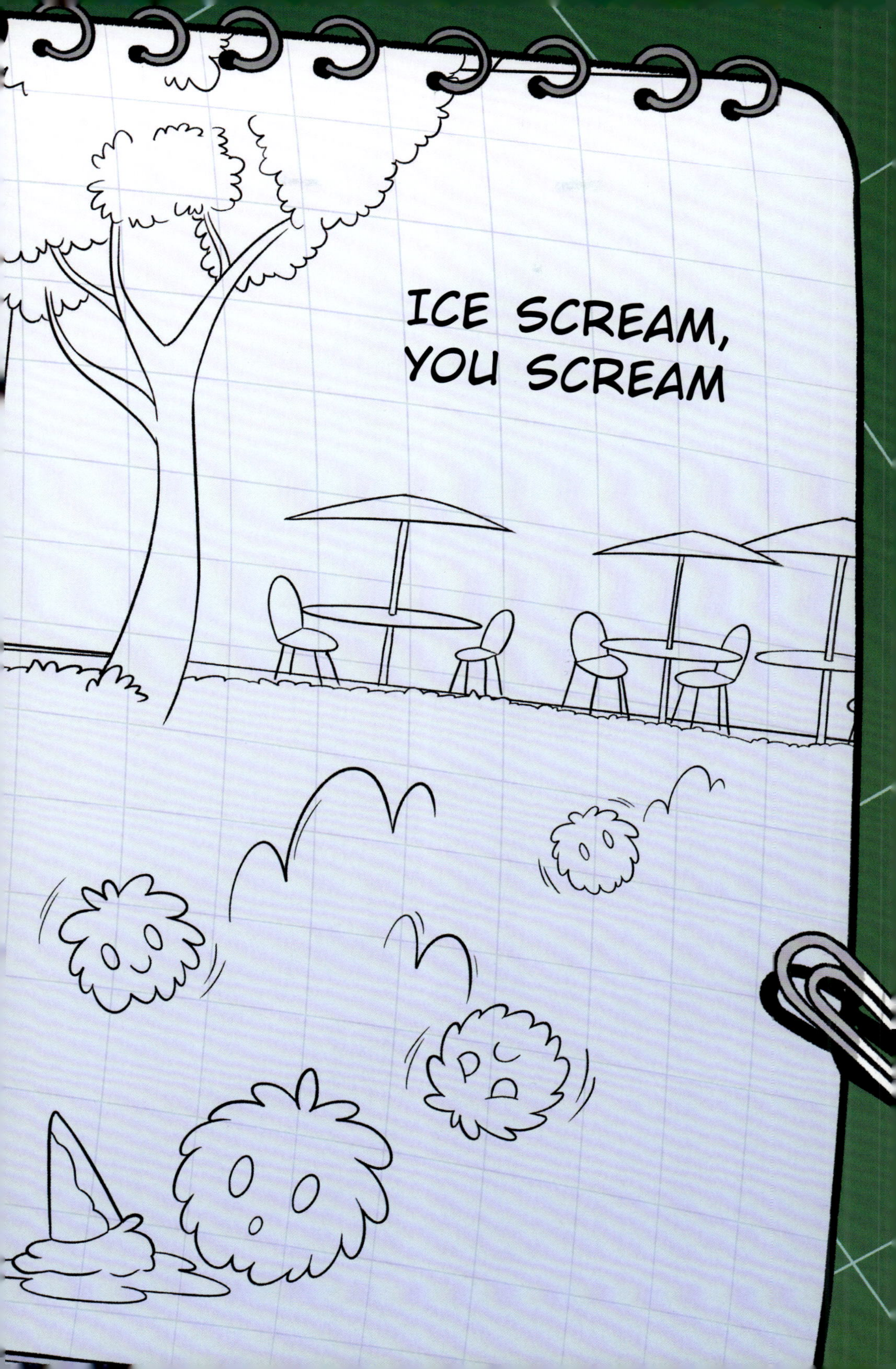
ICE SCREAM,
YOU SCREAM

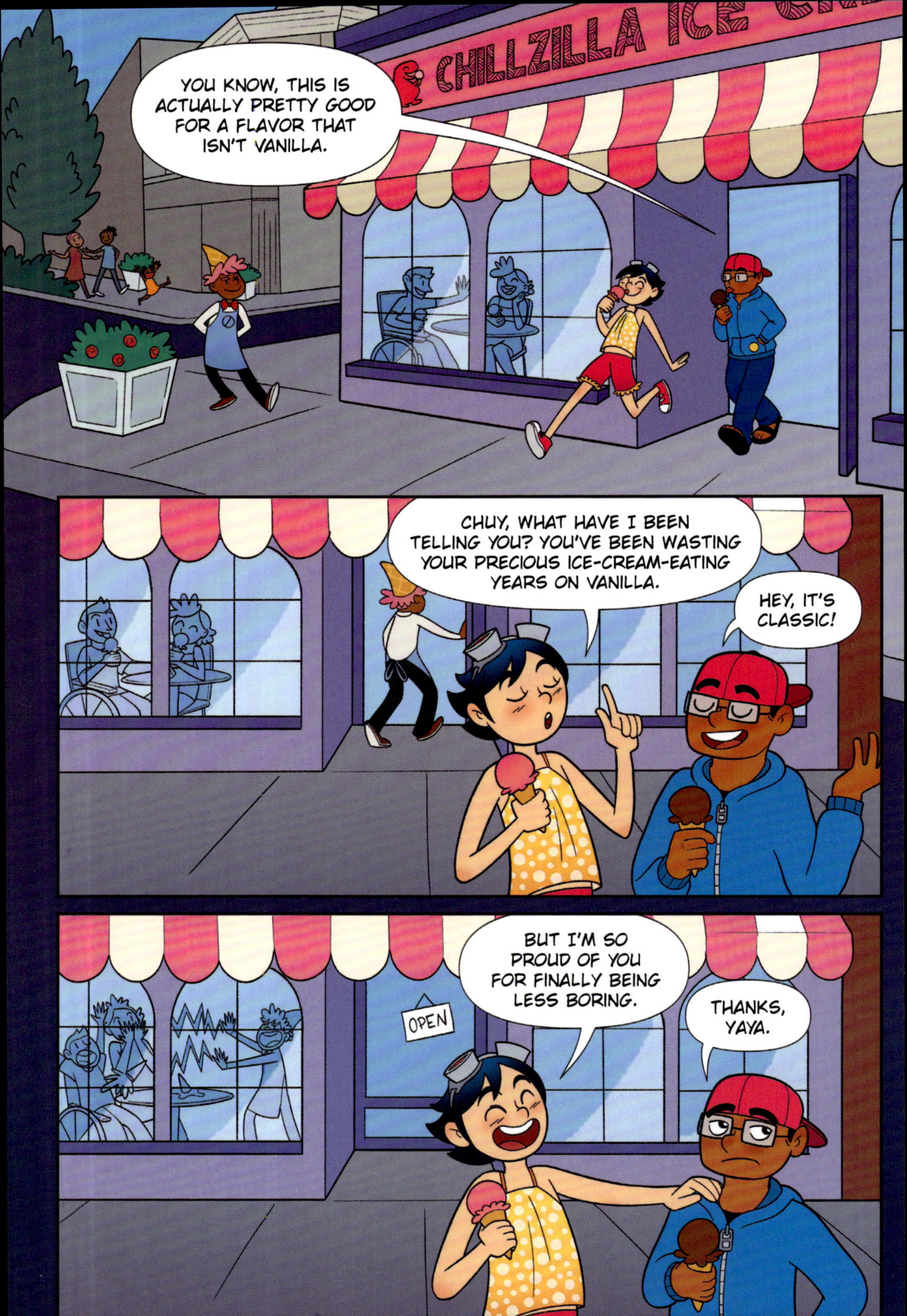
CHILLZILLA ICE CR
YOU KNOW, THIS IS ACTUALLY PRETTY GOOD FOR A FLAVOR THAT ISN'T VANILLA.
CHUY, WHAT HAVE I BEEN TELLING YOU? YOU'VE BEEN WASTING YOUR PRECIOUS ICE-CREAM-EATING YEARS ON VANILLA.
HEY, IT'S CLASSIC!
OPEN
BUT I'M SO PROUD OF YOU FOR FINALLY BEING LESS BORING.
THANKS, YAYA.

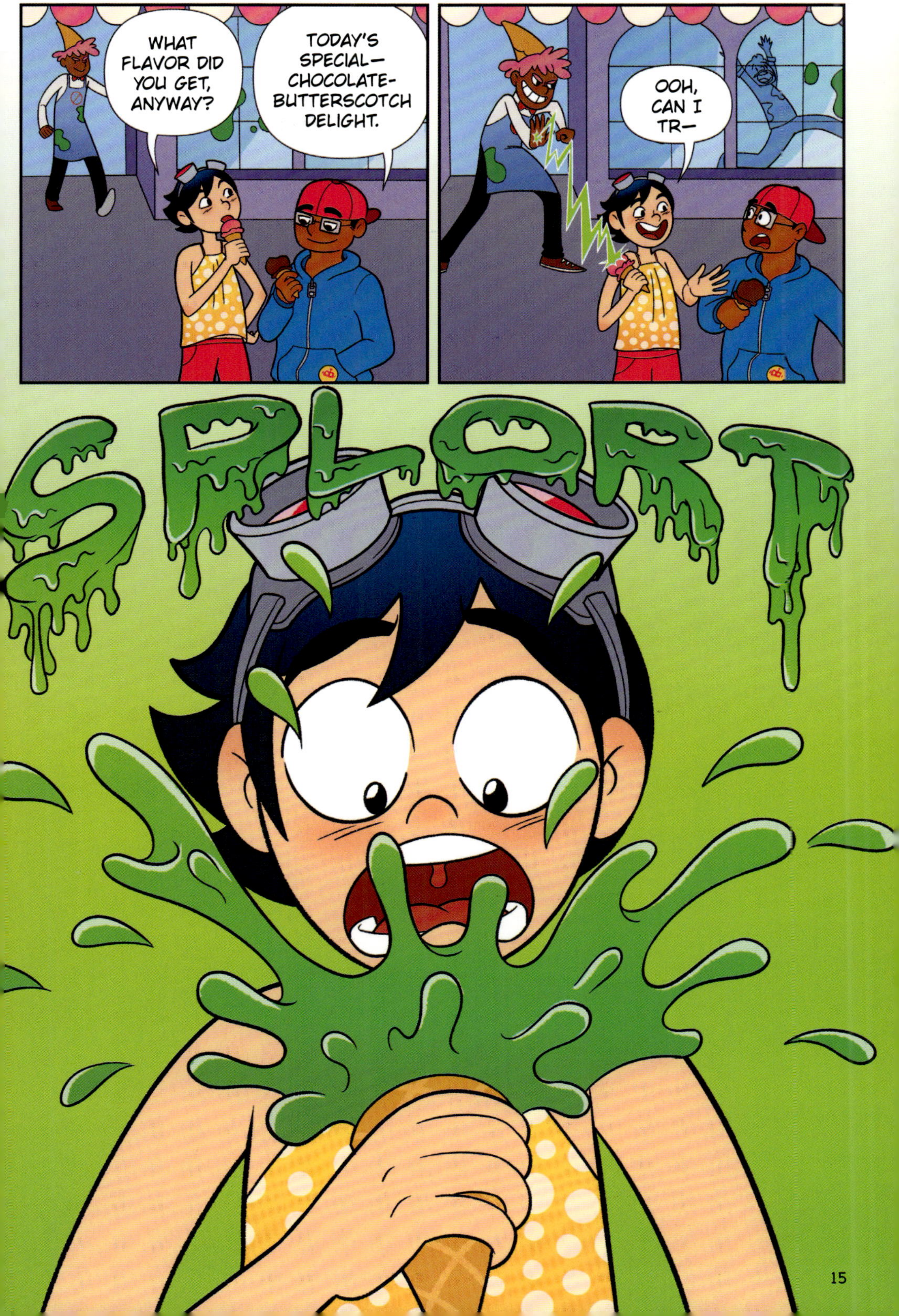
WHAT FLAVOR DID YOU GET, ANYWAY?
TODAY'S SPECIAL— CHOCOLATE-BUTTERSCOTCH DELIGHT.
OOH, CAN I TR—
SPLORT

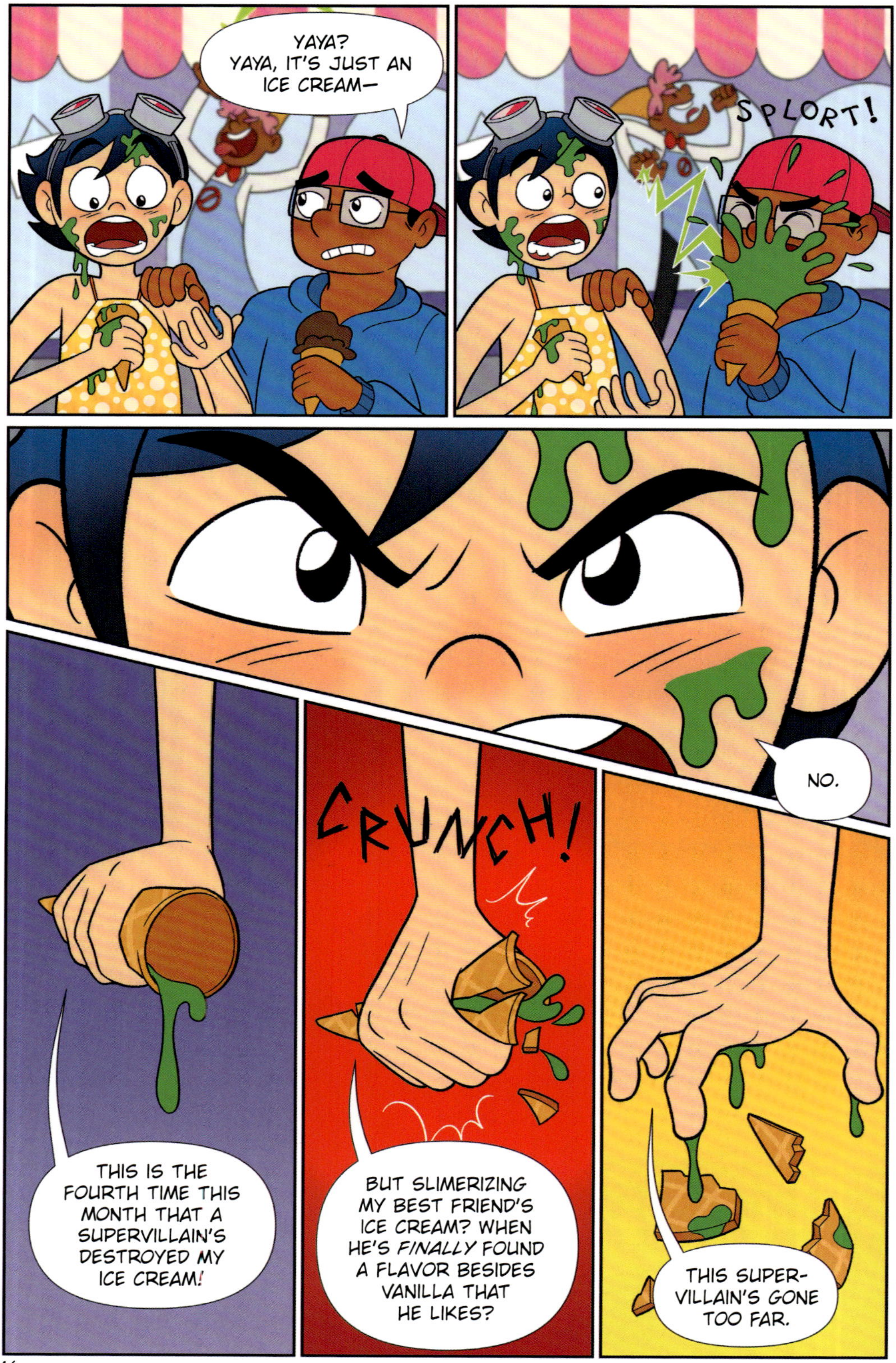
YAYA?
YAYA, IT'S JUST AN ICE CREAM—
SPLORT!
NO.
THIS IS THE FOURTH TIME THIS MONTH THAT A SUPERVILLAIN'S DESTROYED MY ICE CREAM!
CRUNCH!
BUT SLIMERIZING MY BEST FRIEND'S ICE CREAM? WHEN HE'S *FINALLY* FOUND A FLAVOR BESIDES VANILLA THAT HE LIKES?
THIS SUPER-VILLAIN'S GONE TOO FAR.

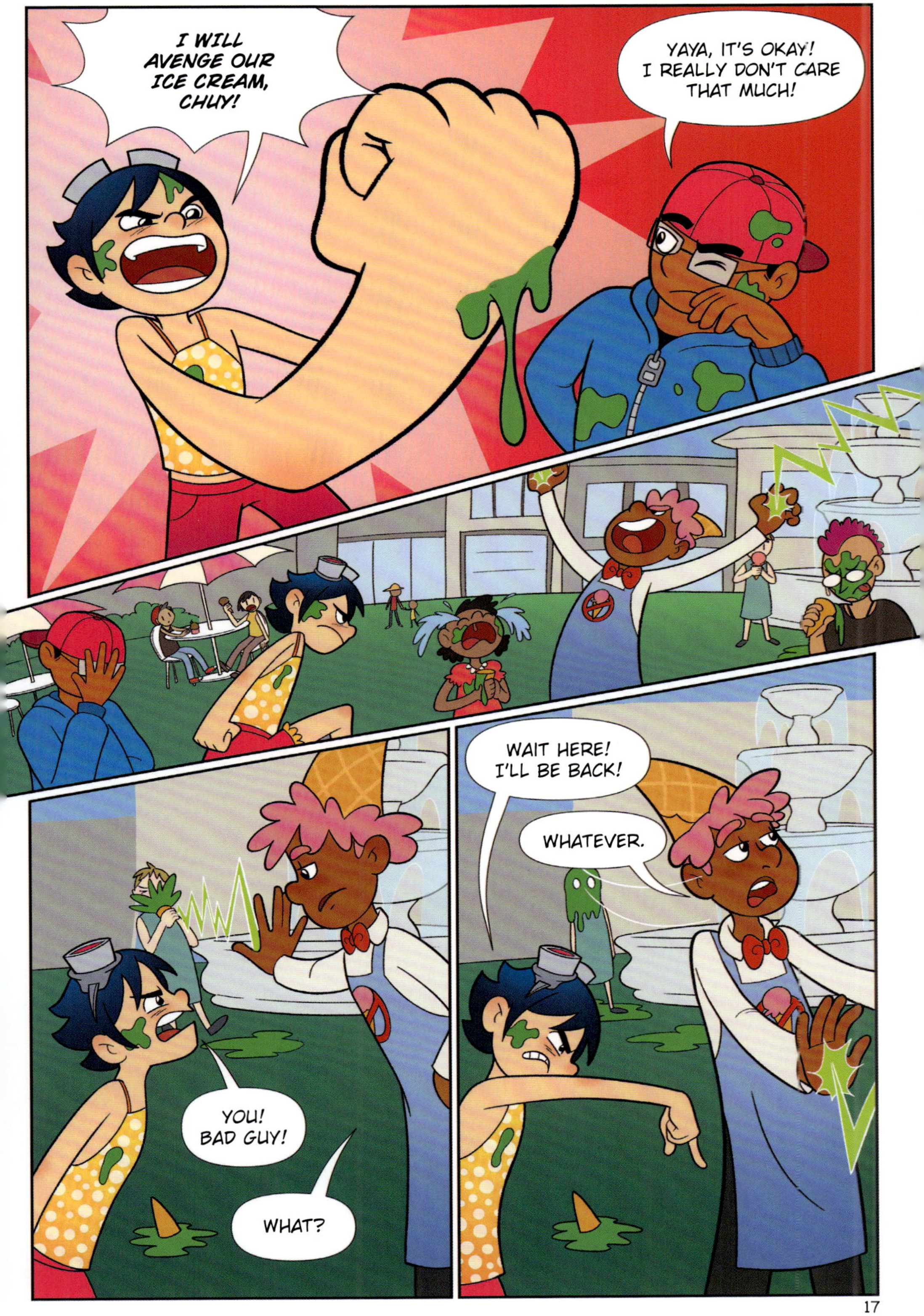
I WILL AVENGE OUR ICE CREAM, CHUY!
YAYA, IT'S OKAY! I REALLY DON'T CARE THAT MUCH!
YOU! BAD GUY!
WHAT?
WAIT HERE! I'LL BE BACK!
WHATEVER.

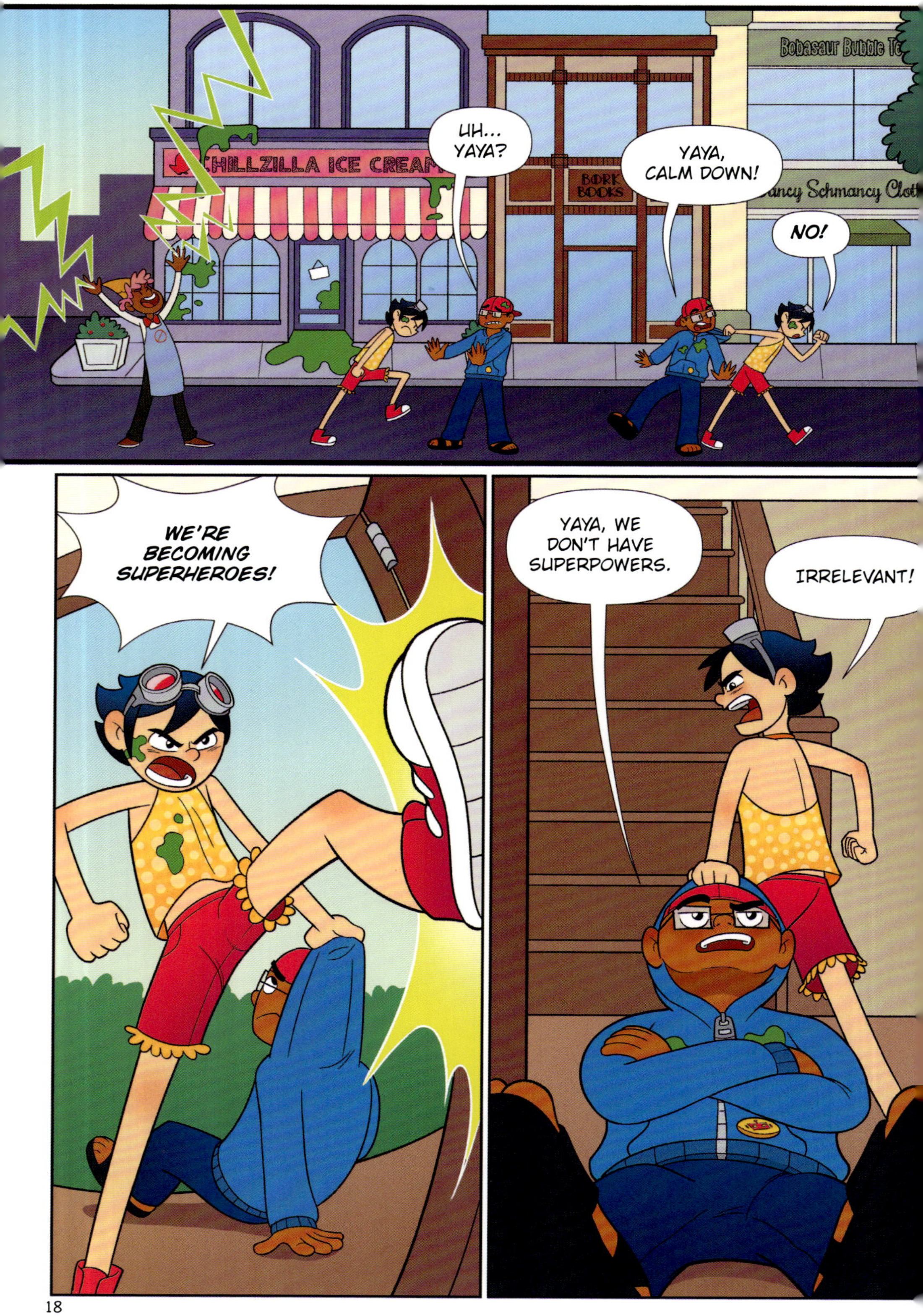
CHILLZILLA ICE CREAM
BORK BOOKS
UH...
YAYA?
YAYA,
CALM DOWN!
NO!
WE'RE
BECOMING
SUPERHEROES!
YAYA, WE
DON'T HAVE
SUPERPOWERS.
IRRELEVANT!

WHERE ARE YOU TAKING ME?
MY HOUSE! I HAVE A PLAN!
AY, GÜEY... I'M AFRAID TO ASK...
ROUGH DAY, HUH?
YOEL LEVY, AGE 10
YAYA'S LITTLE BROTHER
THAT'S RIGHT, THEIR PARENTS NAMED THEM YAEL AND YOEL. NO, HE DOESN'T THINK IT'S FUNNY. UNDER NO CIRCUMSTANCES SHOULD YOU CALL HIM YOYO.
YOU HAVE NO IDEA.
IF SHE GETS TOO OUT OF HAND, JUST DISTRACT HER WITH SOME CANDY.
HE GOT ALL THE COMMON SENSE YAYA DIDN'T.

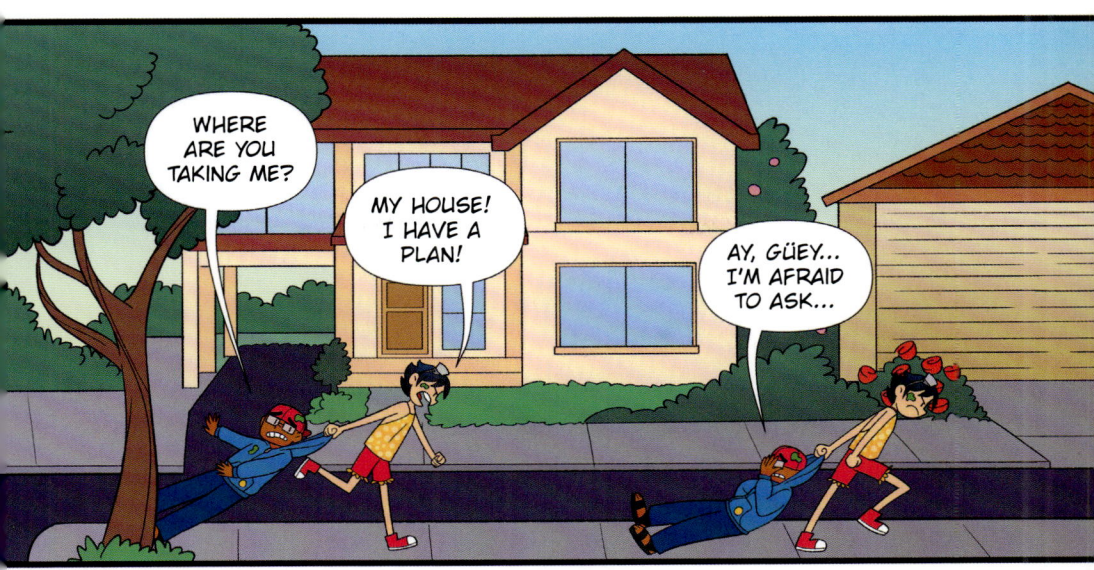

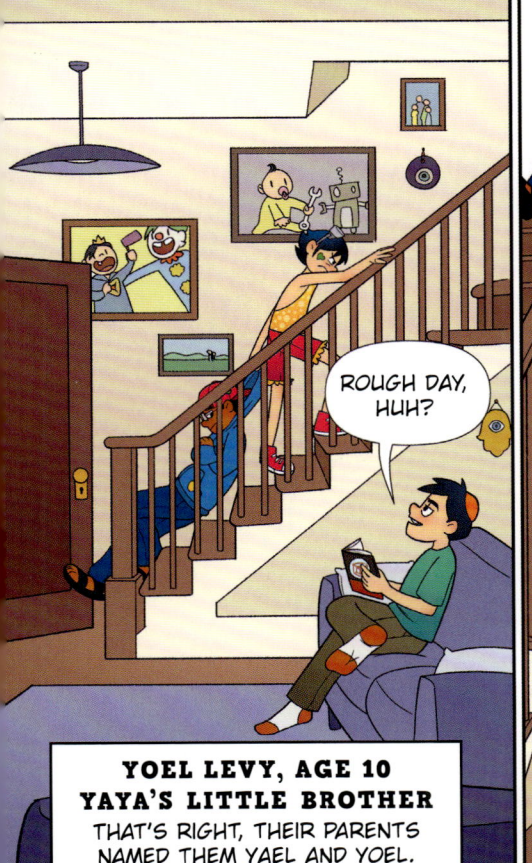

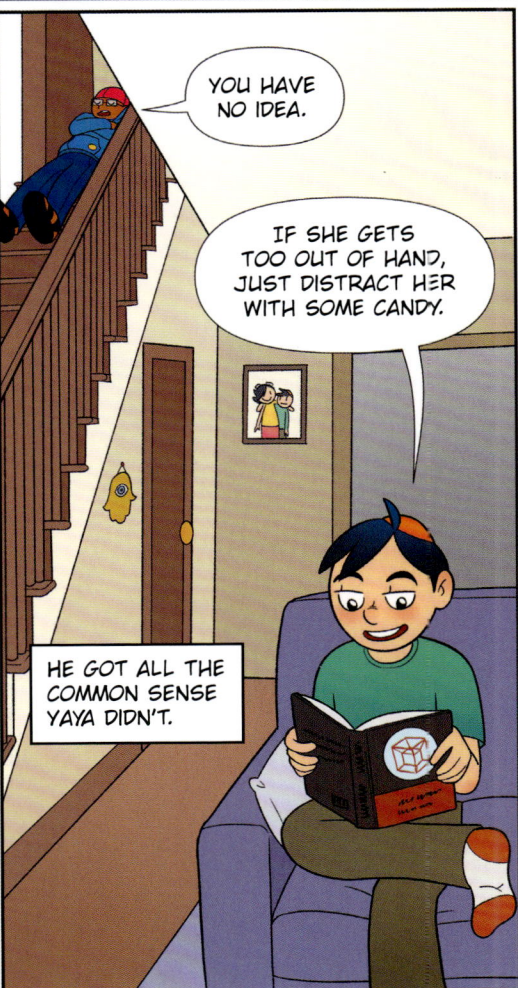

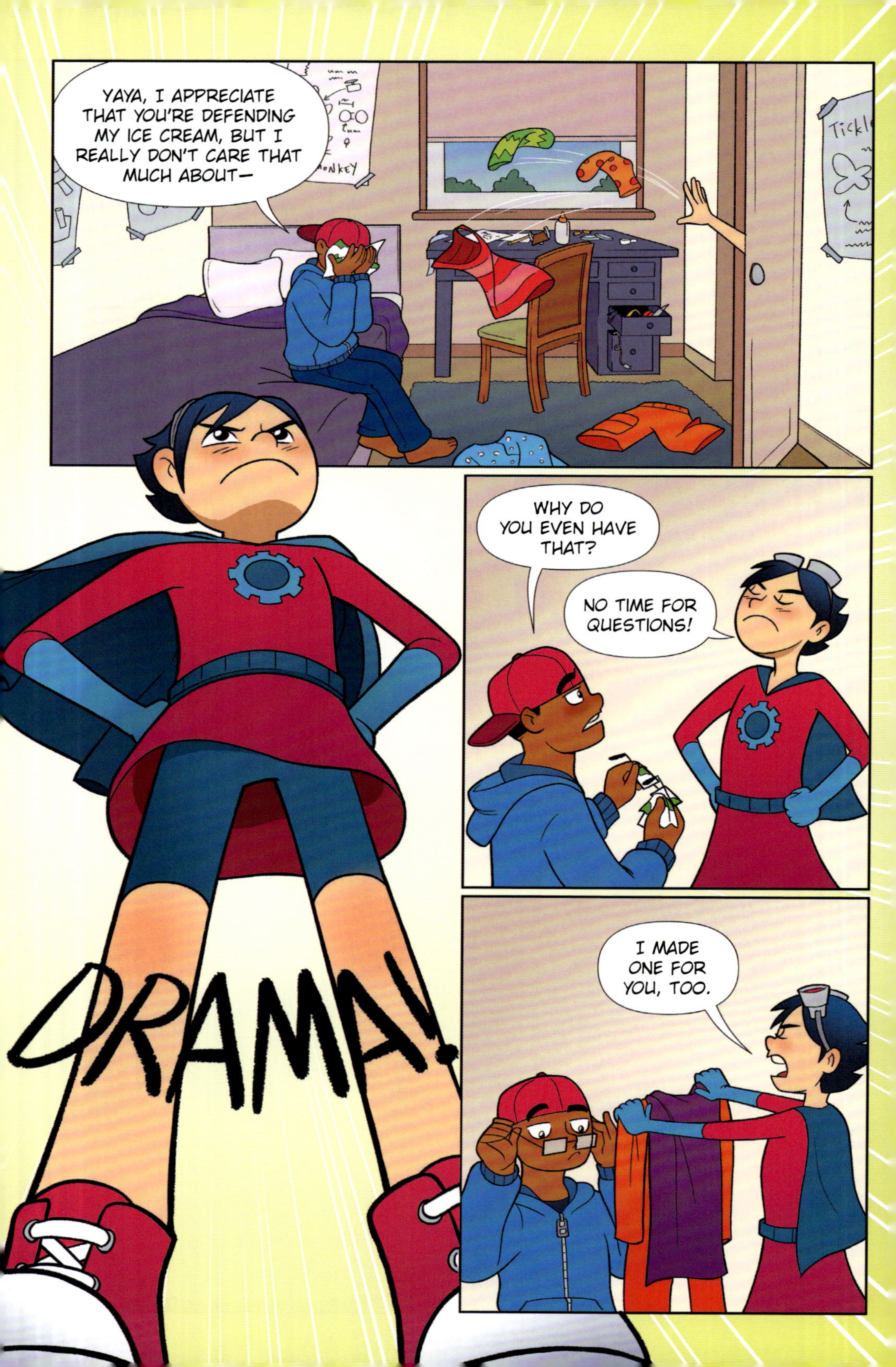
YAYA, I APPRECIATE THAT YOU'RE DEFENDING MY ICE CREAM, BUT I REALLY DON'T CARE THAT MUCH ABOUT—
DRAMA!
WHY DO YOU EVEN HAVE THAT?
NO TIME FOR QUESTIONS!
I MADE ONE FOR YOU, TOO.

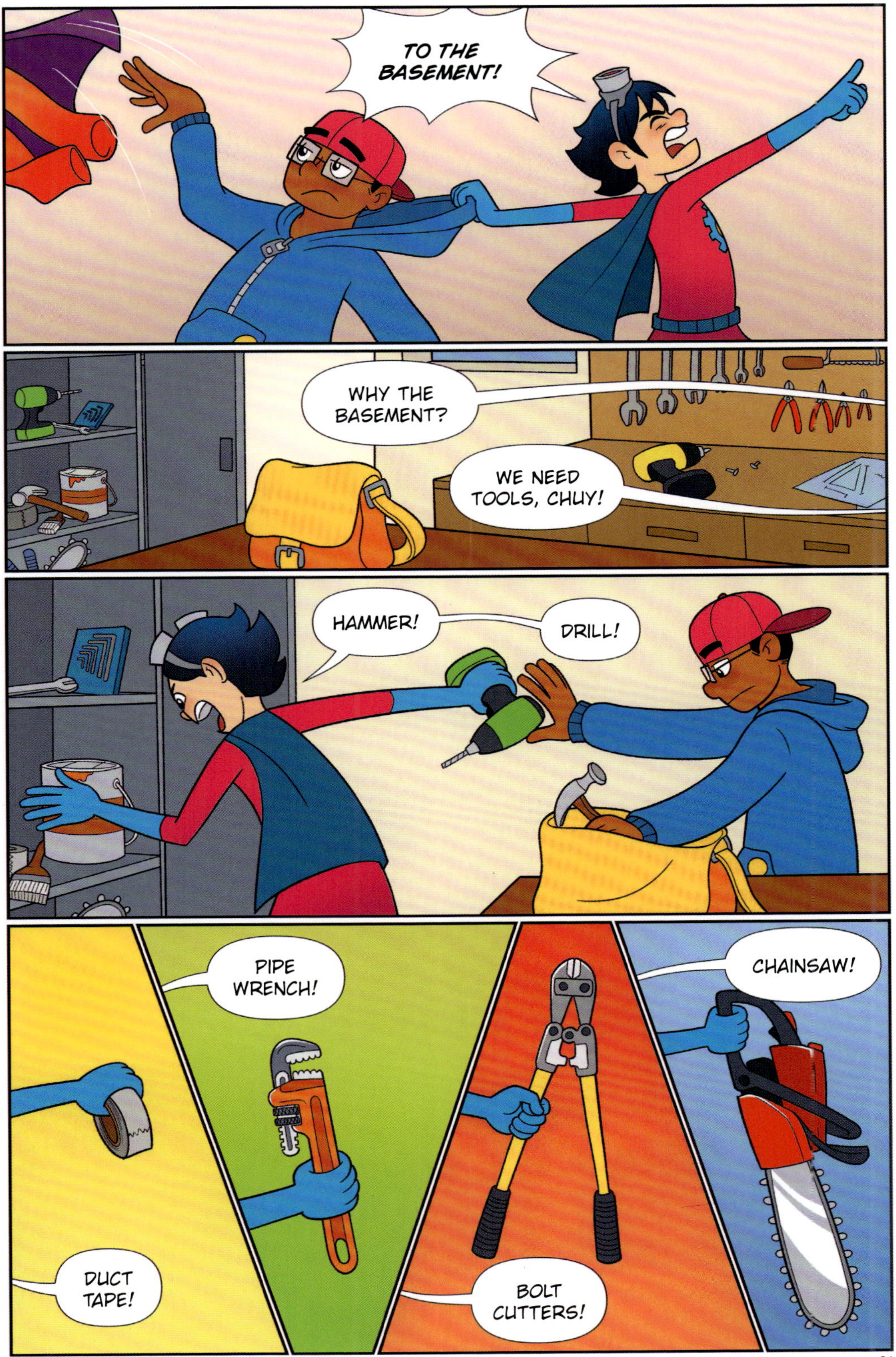
TO THE BASEMENT!
WHY THE BASEMENT?
WE NEED TOOLS, CHUY!
HAMMER!
DRILL!
PIPE WRENCH!
CHAINSAW!
DUCT TAPE!
BOLT CUTTERS!

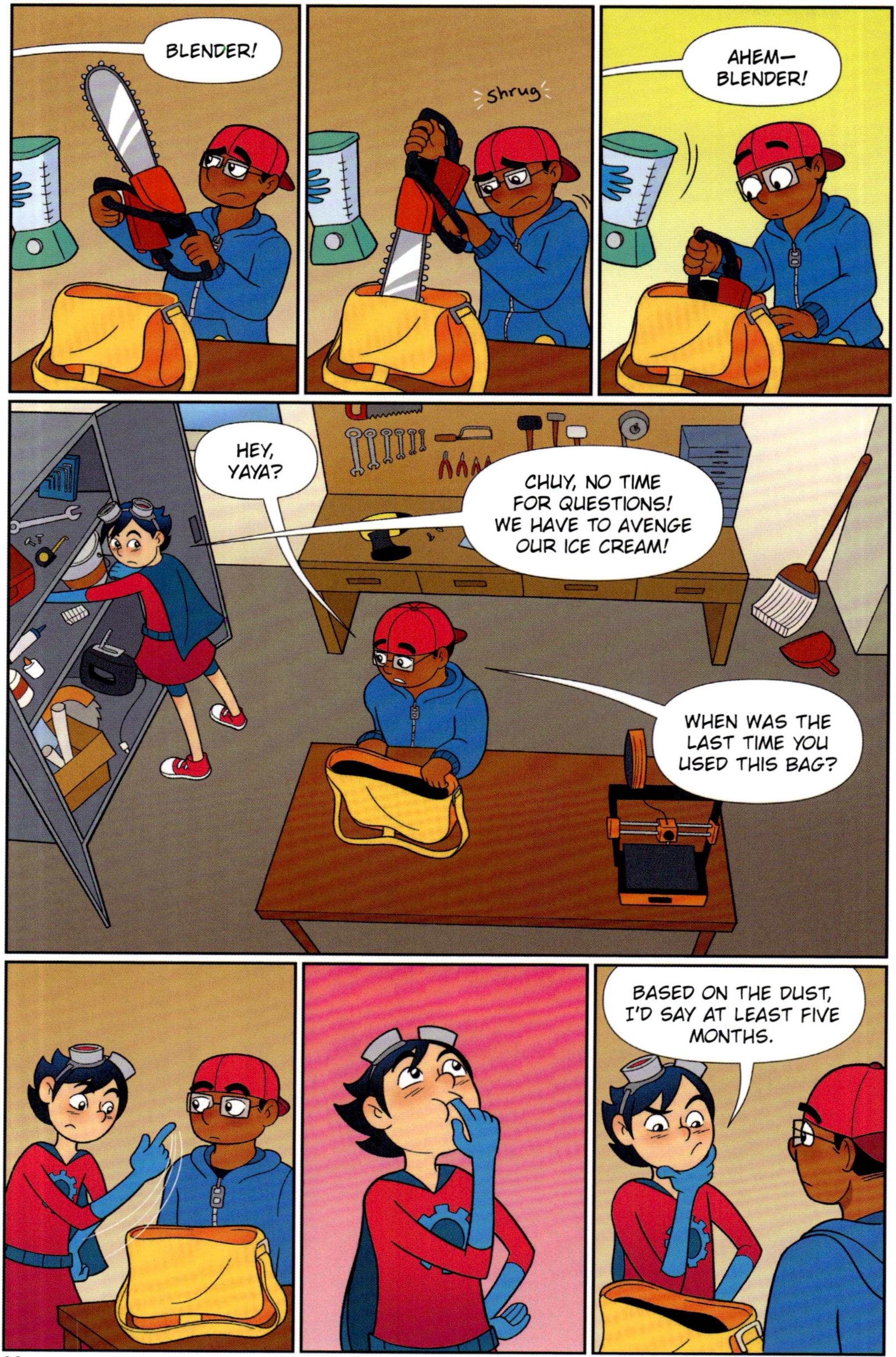
BLENDER!
shrug
AHEM—
BLENDER!
HEY,
YAYA?
CHUY, NO TIME FOR QUESTIONS! WE HAVE TO AVENGE OUR ICE CREAM!
WHEN WAS THE LAST TIME YOU USED THIS BAG?
BASED ON THE DUST, I'D SAY AT LEAST FIVE MONTHS.

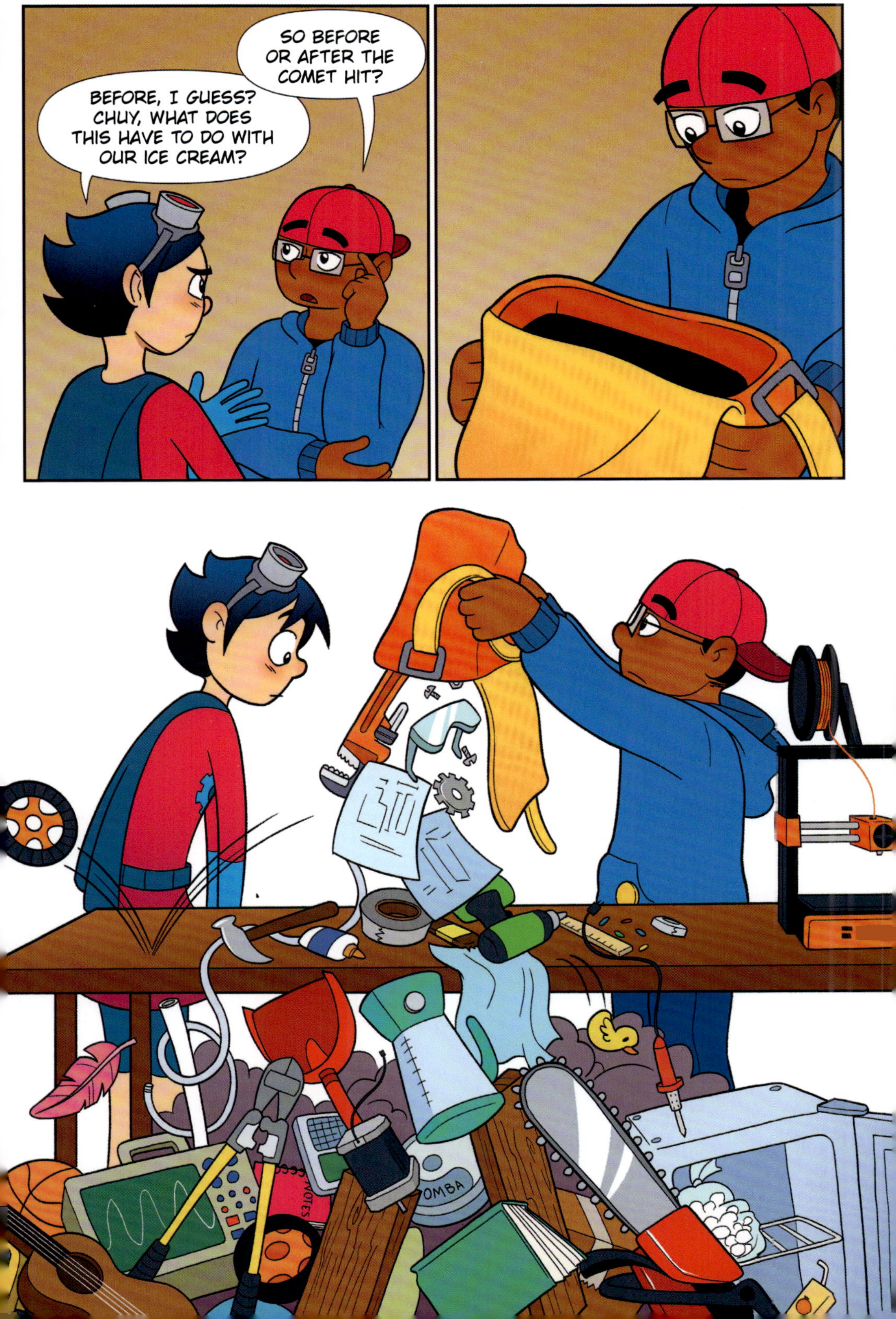
SO BEFORE OR AFTER THE COMET HIT?
BEFORE, I GUESS? CHUY, WHAT DOES THIS HAVE TO DO WITH OUR ICE CREAM?

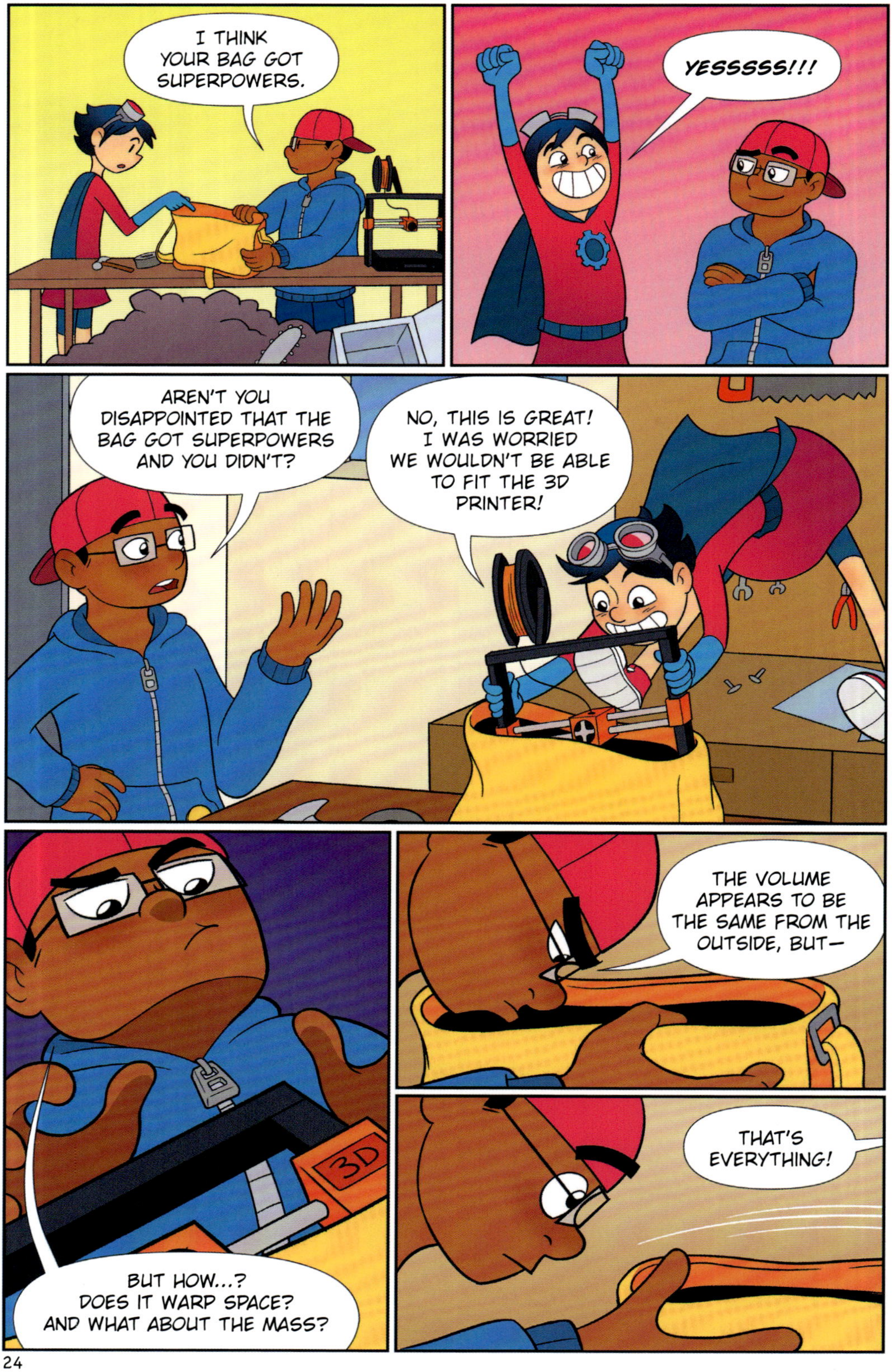
I THINK YOUR BAG GOT SUPERPOWERS.
YESSSSS!!!
AREN'T YOU DISAPPOINTED THAT THE BAG GOT SUPERPOWERS AND YOU DIDN'T?
NO, THIS IS GREAT! I WAS WORRIED WE WOULDN'T BE ABLE TO FIT THE 3D PRINTER!
3D
BUT HOW...? DOES IT WARP SPACE? AND WHAT ABOUT THE MASS?
THE VOLUME APPEARS TO BE THE SAME FROM THE OUTSIDE, BUT—
THAT'S EVERYTHING!

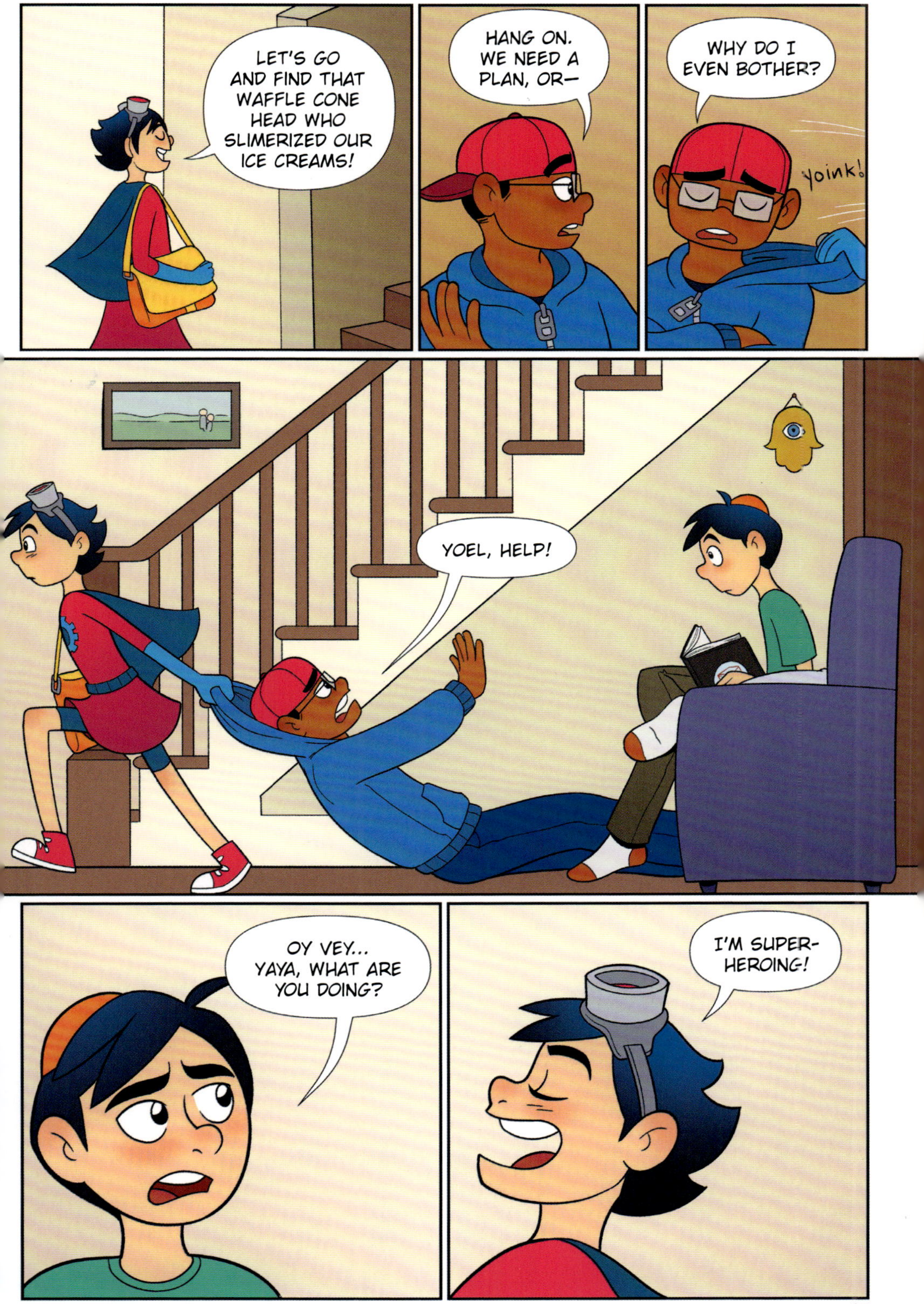
LET'S GO AND FIND THAT WAFFLE CONE HEAD WHO SLIMERIZED OUR ICE CREAMS!
HANG ON. WE NEED A PLAN, OR—
WHY DO I EVEN BOTHER?
yoink!
YOEL, HELP!
OY VEY... YAYA, WHAT ARE YOU DOING?
I'M SUPER-HEROING!

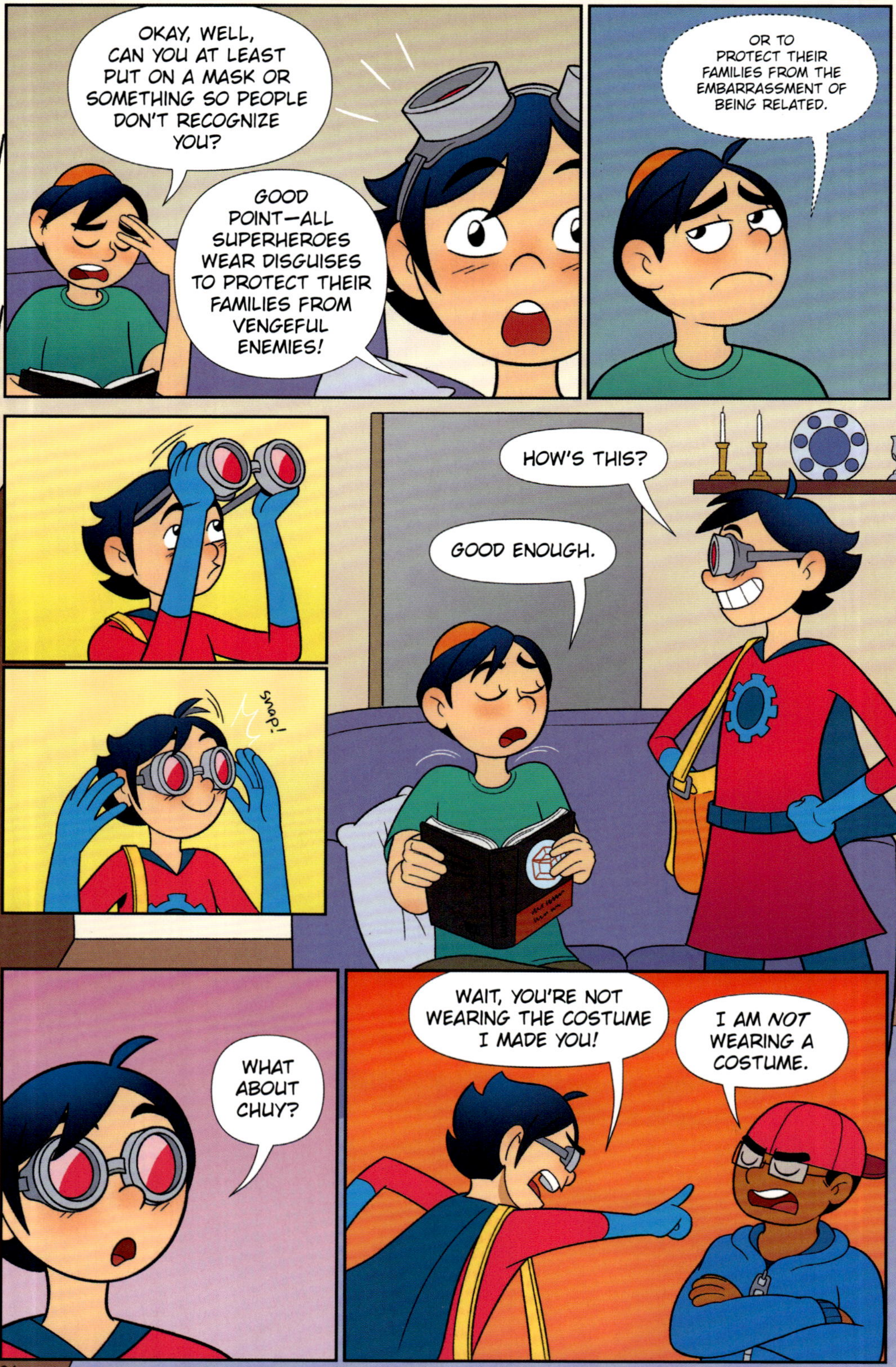
OKAY, WELL, CAN YOU AT LEAST PUT ON A MASK OR SOMETHING SO PEOPLE DON'T RECOGNIZE YOU?
GOOD POINT—ALL SUPERHEROES WEAR DISGUISES TO PROTECT THEIR FAMILIES FROM VENGEFUL ENEMIES!
OR TO PROTECT THEIR FAMILIES FROM THE EMBARRASSMENT OF BEING RELATED.
snap!
HOW'S THIS?
GOOD ENOUGH.
WHAT ABOUT CHUY?
WAIT, YOU'RE NOT WEARING THE COSTUME I MADE YOU!
I AM *NOT* WEARING A COSTUME.

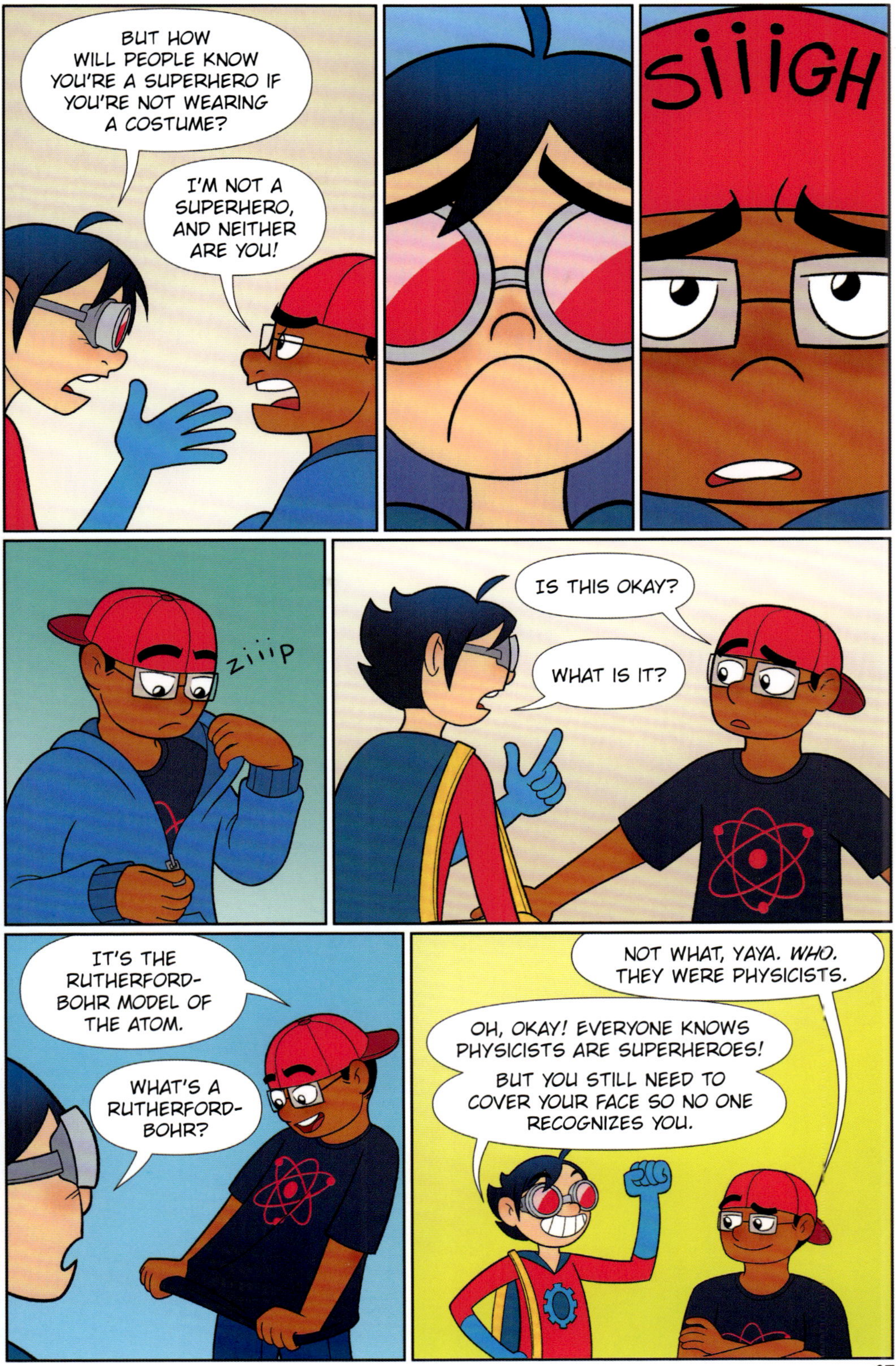
BUT HOW WILL PEOPLE KNOW YOU'RE A SUPERHERO IF YOU'RE NOT WEARING A COSTUME?
I'M NOT A SUPERHERO, AND NEITHER ARE YOU!
SIIIGH
ziiip
IS THIS OKAY?
WHAT IS IT?
IT'S THE RUTHERFORD-BOHR MODEL OF THE ATOM.
WHAT'S A RUTHERFORD-BOHR?
NOT WHAT, YAYA. *WHO.* THEY WERE PHYSICISTS.
OH, OKAY! EVERYONE KNOWS PHYSICISTS ARE SUPERHEROES!
BUT YOU STILL NEED TO COVER YOUR FACE SO NO ONE RECOGNIZES YOU.

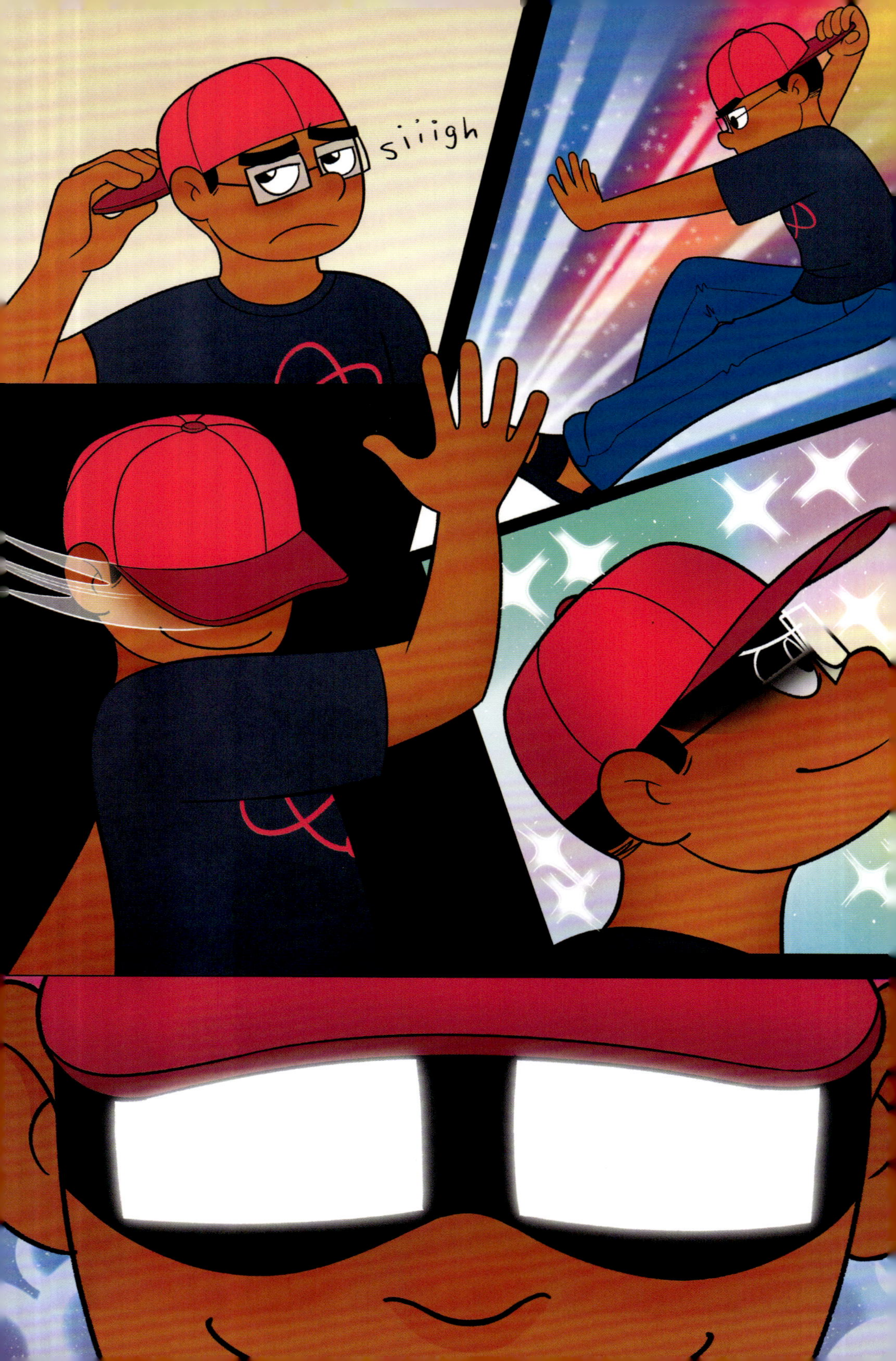
siiigh

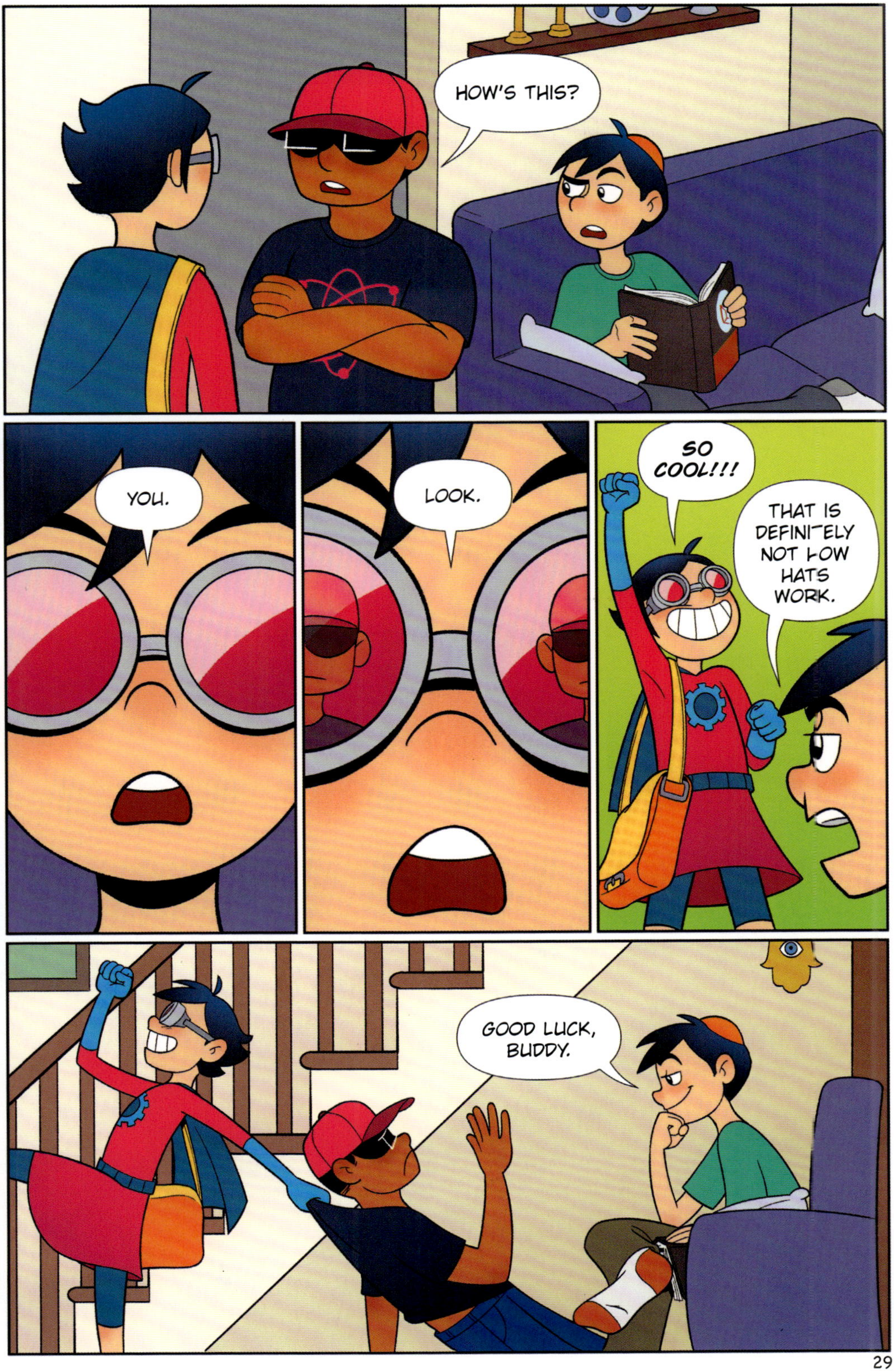
HOW'S THIS?
YOU.
LOOK.
SO COOL!!!
THAT IS DEFINITELY NOT HOW HATS WORK.
GOOD LUCK, BUDDY.

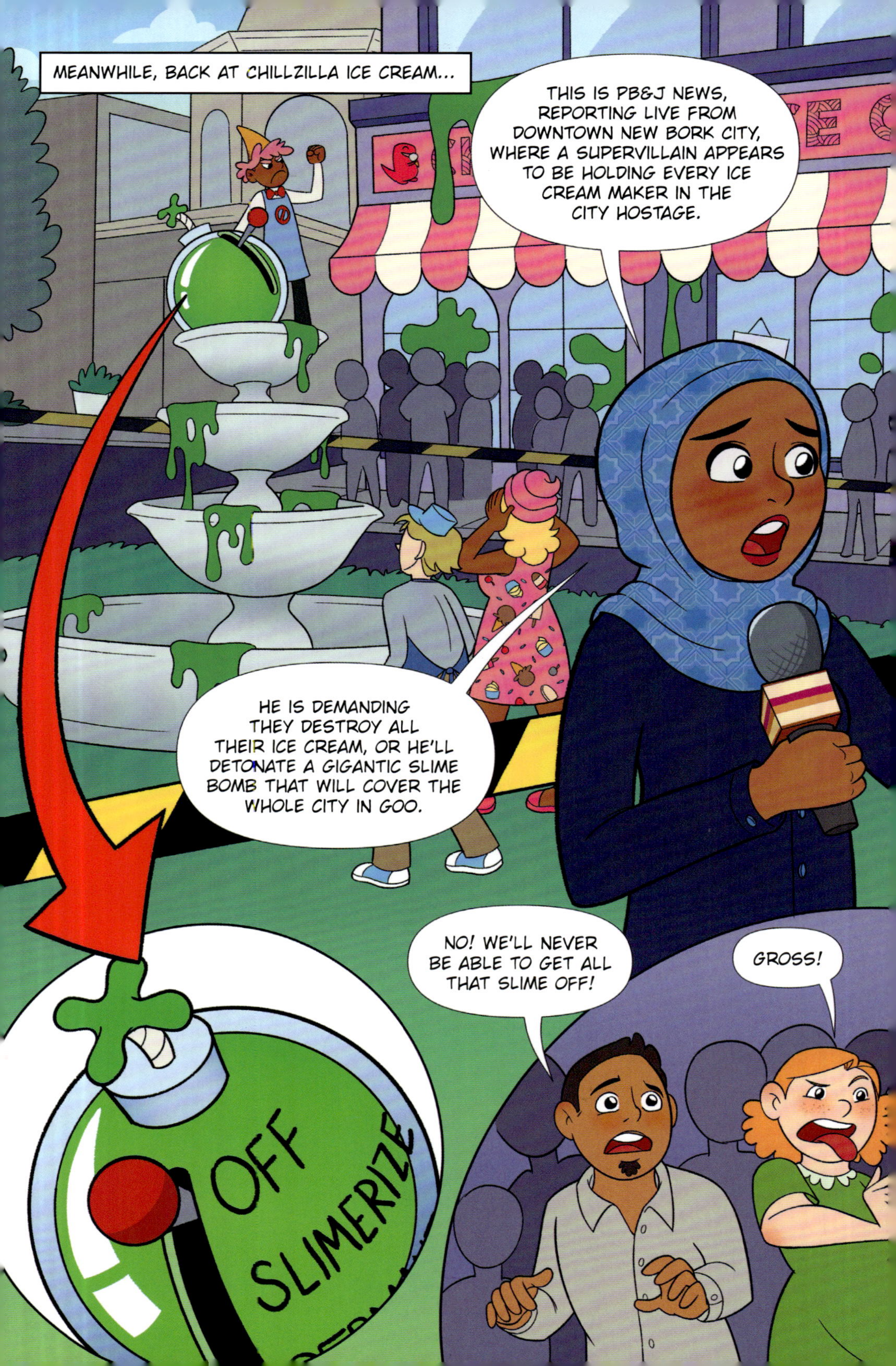

MEANWHILE, BACK AT CHILLZILLA ICE CREAM...
THIS IS PB&J NEWS, REPORTING LIVE FROM DOWNTOWN NEW BORK CITY, WHERE A SUPERVILLAIN APPEARS TO BE HOLDING EVERY ICE CREAM MAKER IN THE CITY HOSTAGE.
HE IS DEMANDING THEY DESTROY ALL THEIR ICE CREAM, OR HE'LL DETONATE A GIGANTIC SLIME BOMB THAT WILL COVER THE WHOLE CITY IN GOO.
OFF
SLIMERIZE
NO! WE'LL NEVER BE ABLE TO GET ALL THAT SLIME OFF!
GROSS!

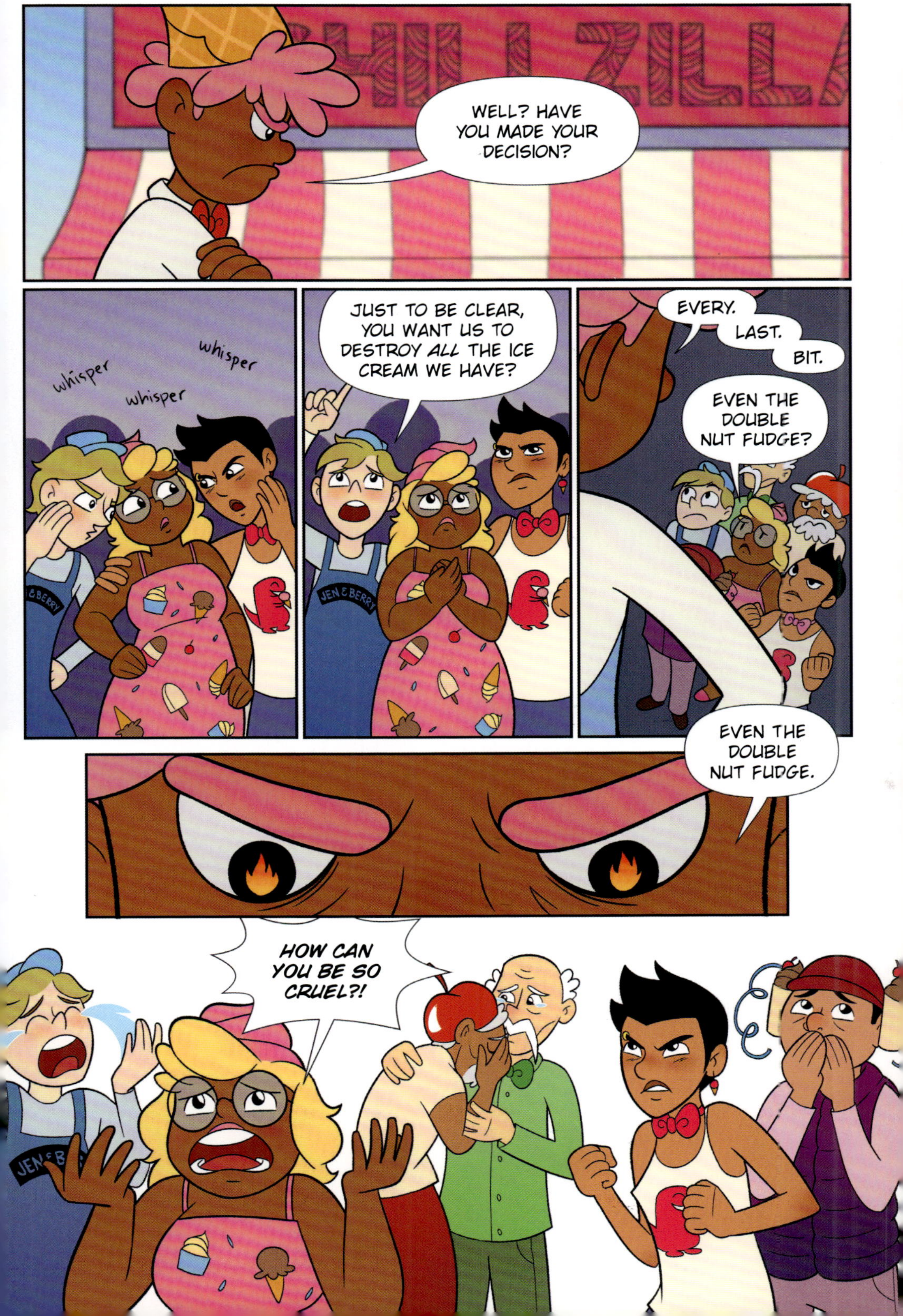

CHILLZILLA
WELL? HAVE YOU MADE YOUR DECISION?
whisper
whisper
whisper
JEN & BERRY
JUST TO BE CLEAR, YOU WANT US TO DESTROY *ALL* THE ICE CREAM WE HAVE?
JEN & BERRY
EVERY.
LAST.
BIT.
EVEN THE DOUBLE NUT FUDGE?
EVEN THE DOUBLE NUT FUDGE.
HOW CAN YOU BE SO CRUEL?!

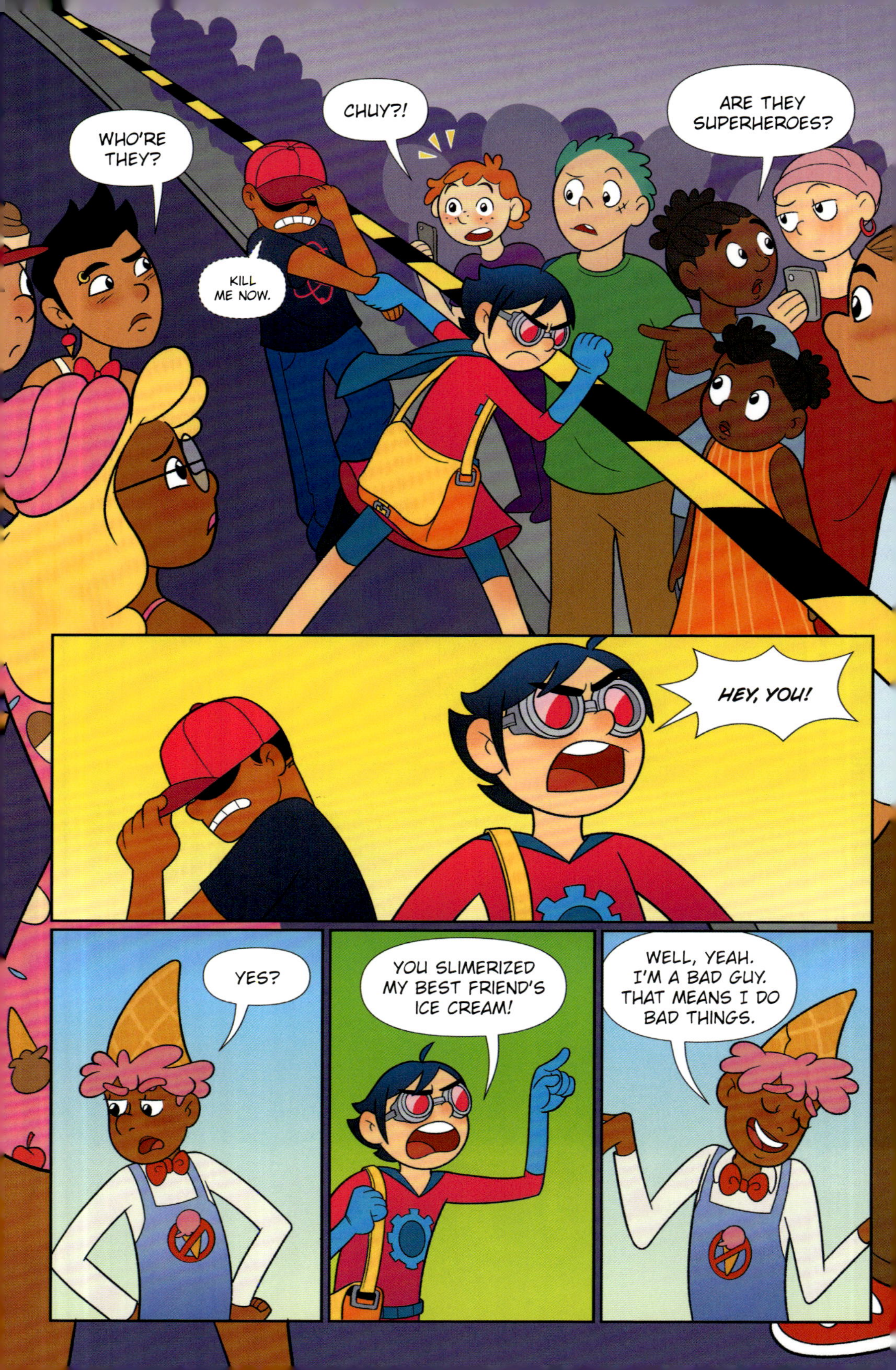
WHO'RE THEY?
CHUY?!
ARE THEY SUPERHEROES?
KILL ME NOW.
HEY, YOU!
YES?
YOU SLIMERIZED MY BEST FRIEND'S ICE CREAM!
WELL, YEAH. I'M A BAD GUY. THAT MEANS I DO BAD THINGS.

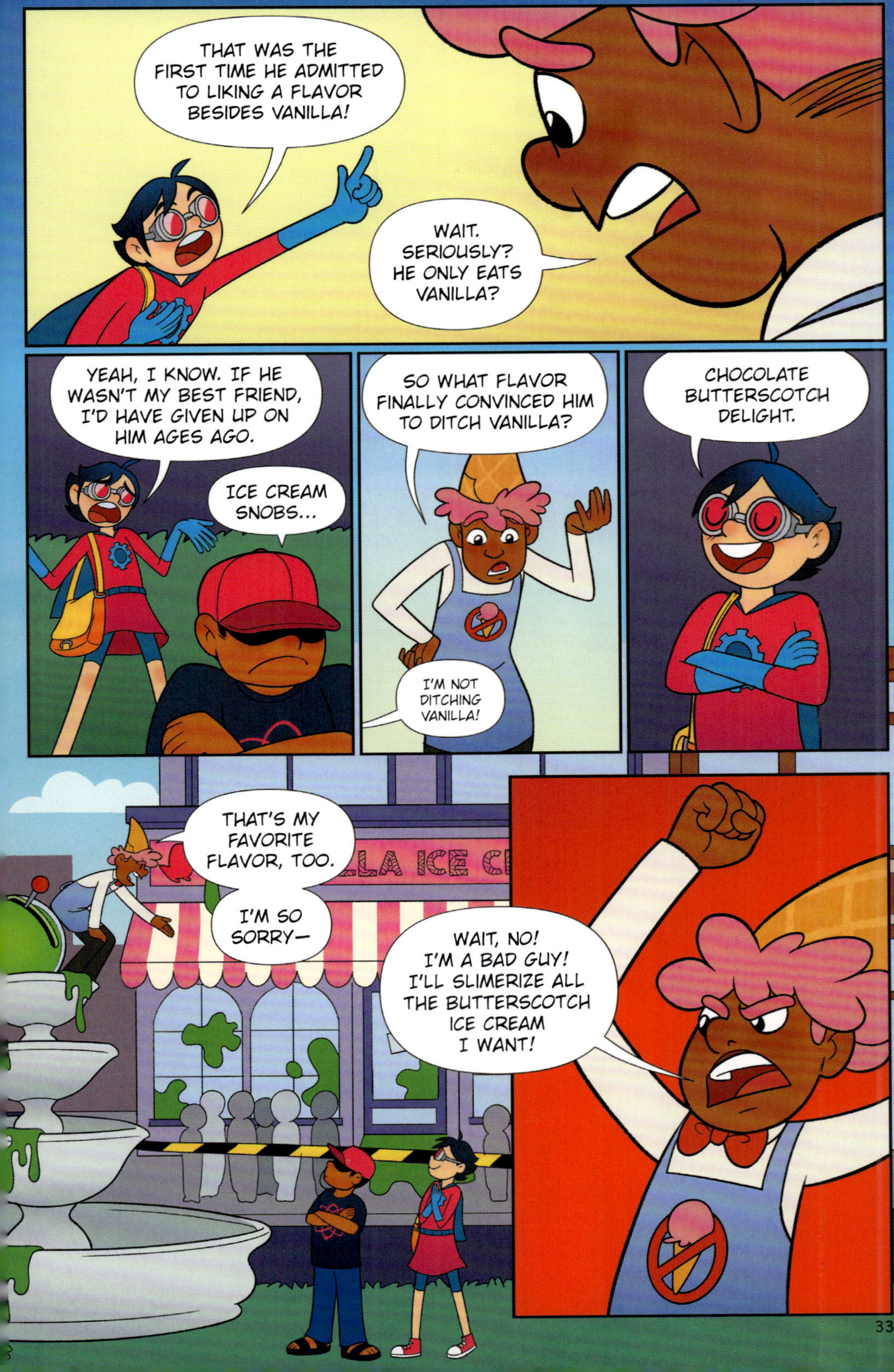

THAT WAS THE FIRST TIME HE ADMITTED TO LIKING A FLAVOR BESIDES VANILLA!
WAIT. SERIOUSLY? HE ONLY EATS VANILLA?
YEAH, I KNOW. IF HE WASN'T MY BEST FRIEND, I'D HAVE GIVEN UP ON HIM AGES AGO.
ICE CREAM SNOBS...
SO WHAT FLAVOR FINALLY CONVINCED HIM TO DITCH VANILLA?
I'M NOT DITCHING VANILLA!
CHOCOLATE BUTTERSCOTCH DELIGHT.
THAT'S MY FAVORITE FLAVOR, TOO.
I'M SO SORRY—
WAIT, NO! I'M A BAD GUY! I'LL SLIMERIZE ALL THE BUTTERSCOTCH ICE CREAM I WANT!

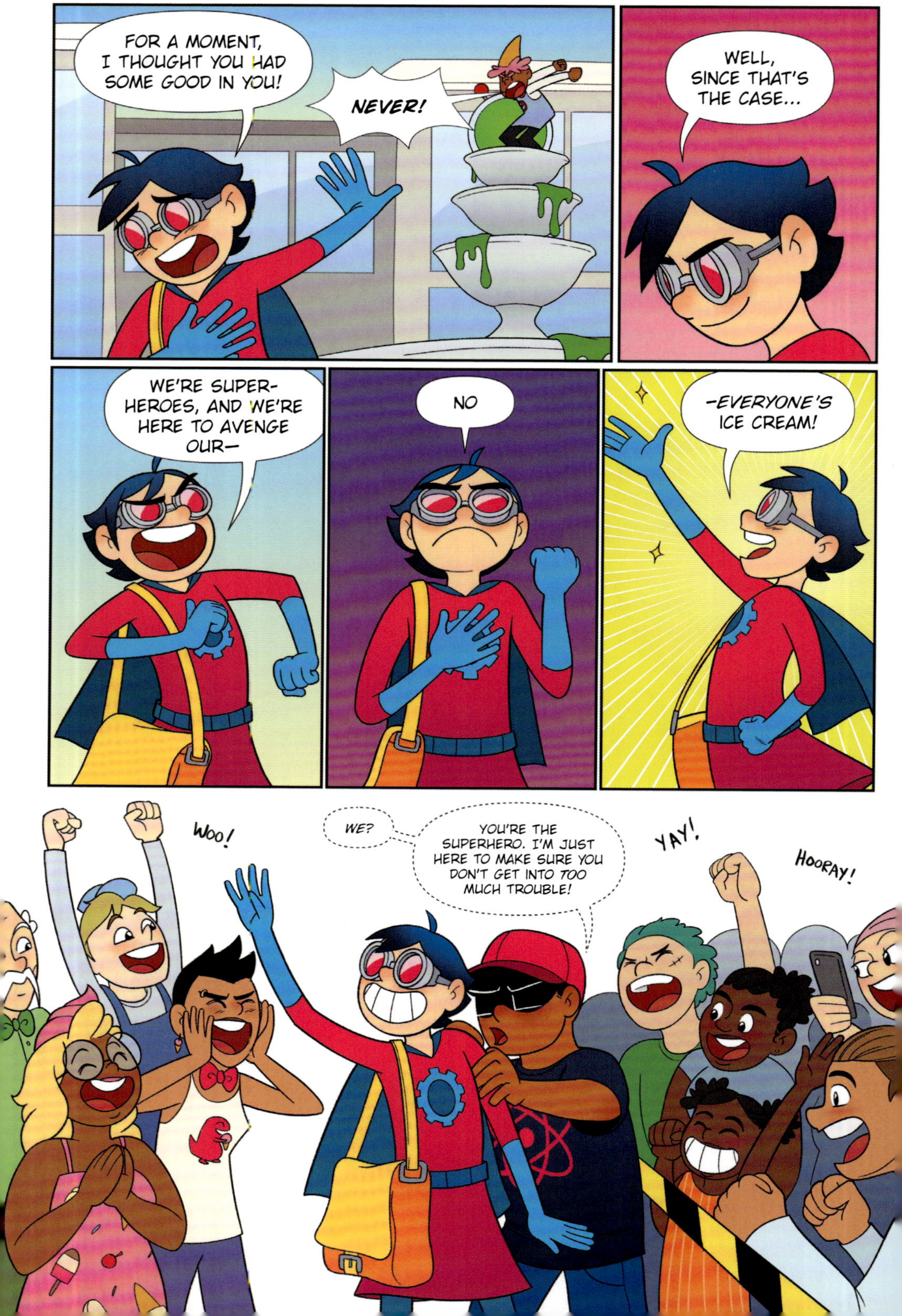
FOR A MOMENT, I THOUGHT YOU HAD SOME GOOD IN YOU!
NEVER!
WELL, SINCE THAT'S THE CASE...
WE'RE SUPER-HEROES, AND WE'RE HERE TO AVENGE OUR—
NO
—EVERYONE'S ICE CREAM!
WOO!
WE?
YOU'RE THE SUPERHERO. I'M JUST HERE TO MAKE SURE YOU DON'T GET INTO *TOO* MUCH TROUBLE!
YAY!
HOORAY!

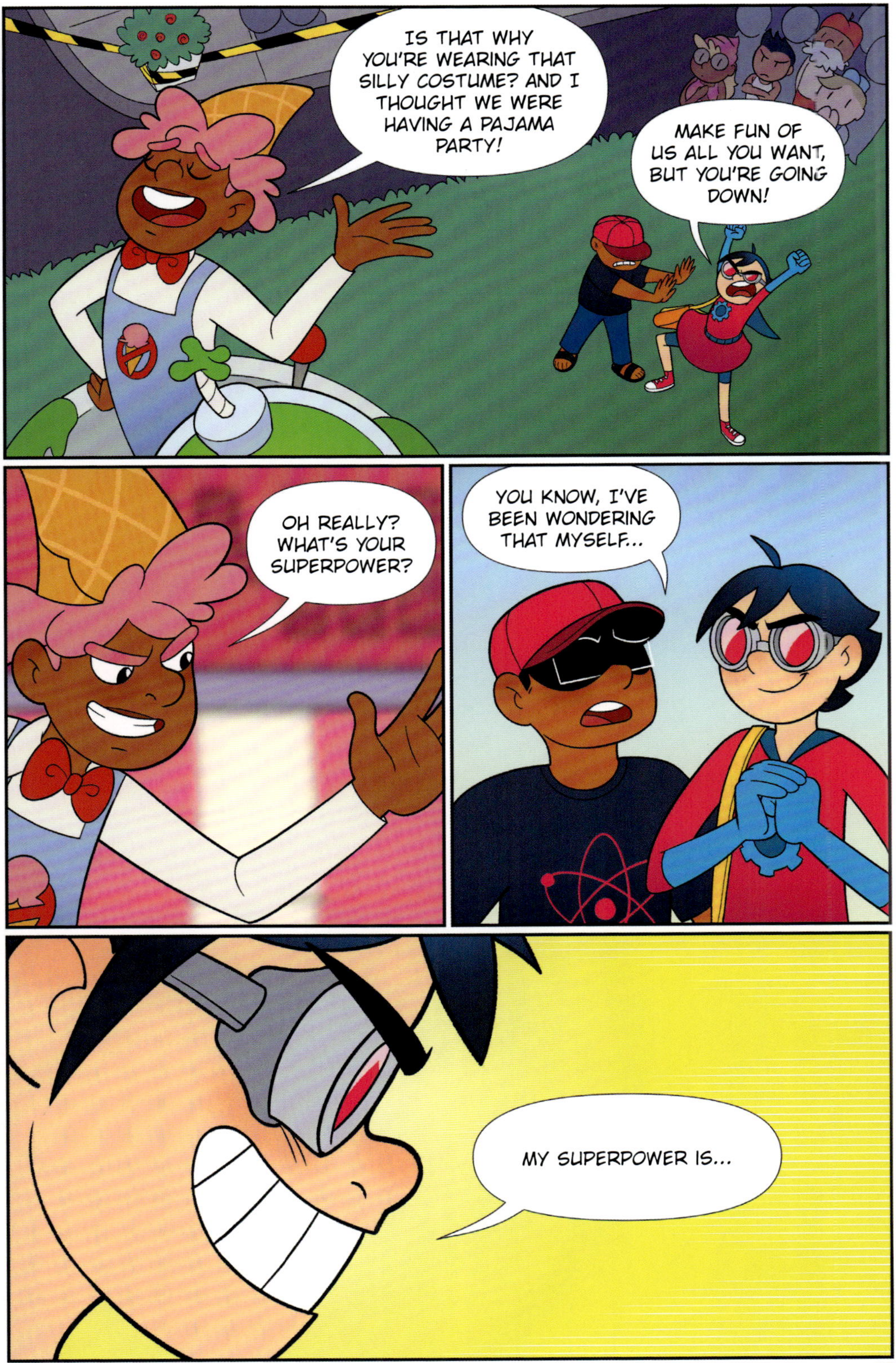
IS THAT WHY YOU'RE WEARING THAT SILLY COSTUME? AND I THOUGHT WE WERE HAVING A PAJAMA PARTY!
MAKE FUN OF US ALL YOU WANT, BUT YOU'RE GOING DOWN!
OH REALLY? WHAT'S YOUR SUPERPOWER?
YOU KNOW, I'VE BEEN WONDERING THAT MYSELF...
MY SUPERPOWER IS...

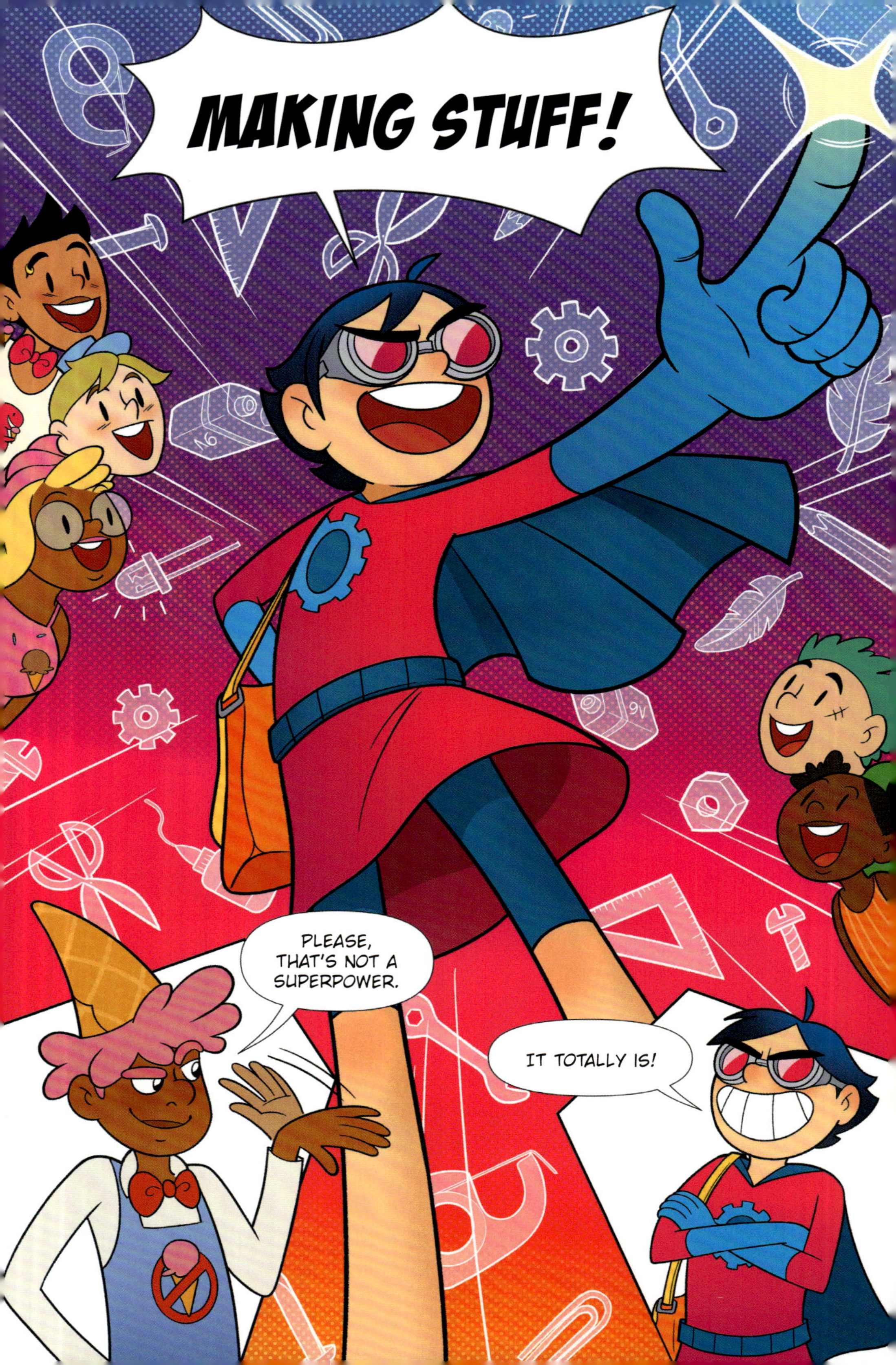
MAKING STUFF!
PLEASE, THAT'S NOT A SUPERPOWER.
IT TOTALLY IS!

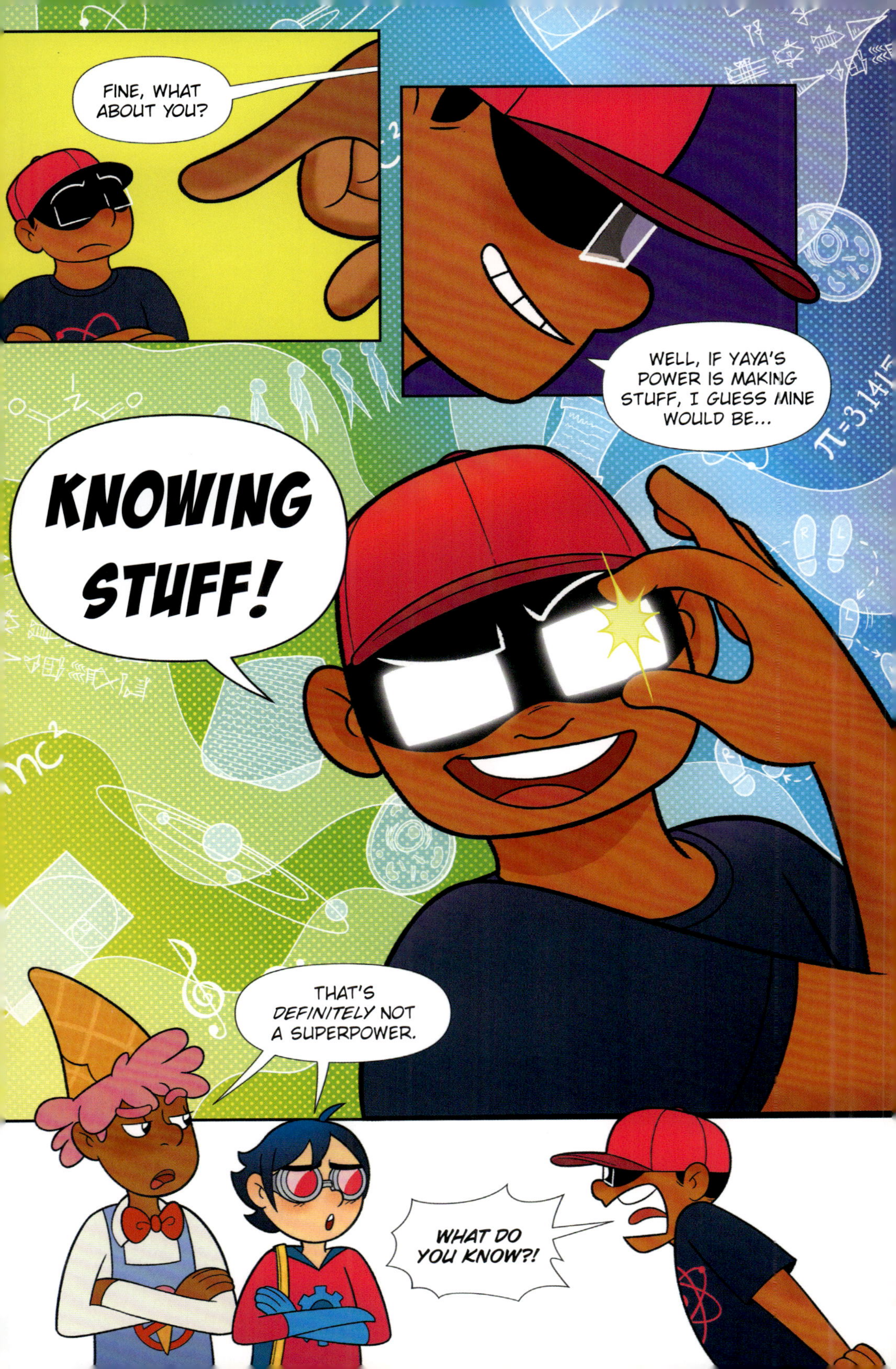
FINE, WHAT ABOUT YOU?
WELL, IF YAYA'S POWER IS MAKING STUFF, I GUESS MINE WOULD BE...
KNOWING STUFF!
THAT'S *DEFINITELY* NOT A SUPERPOWER.
WHAT DO YOU KNOW?!

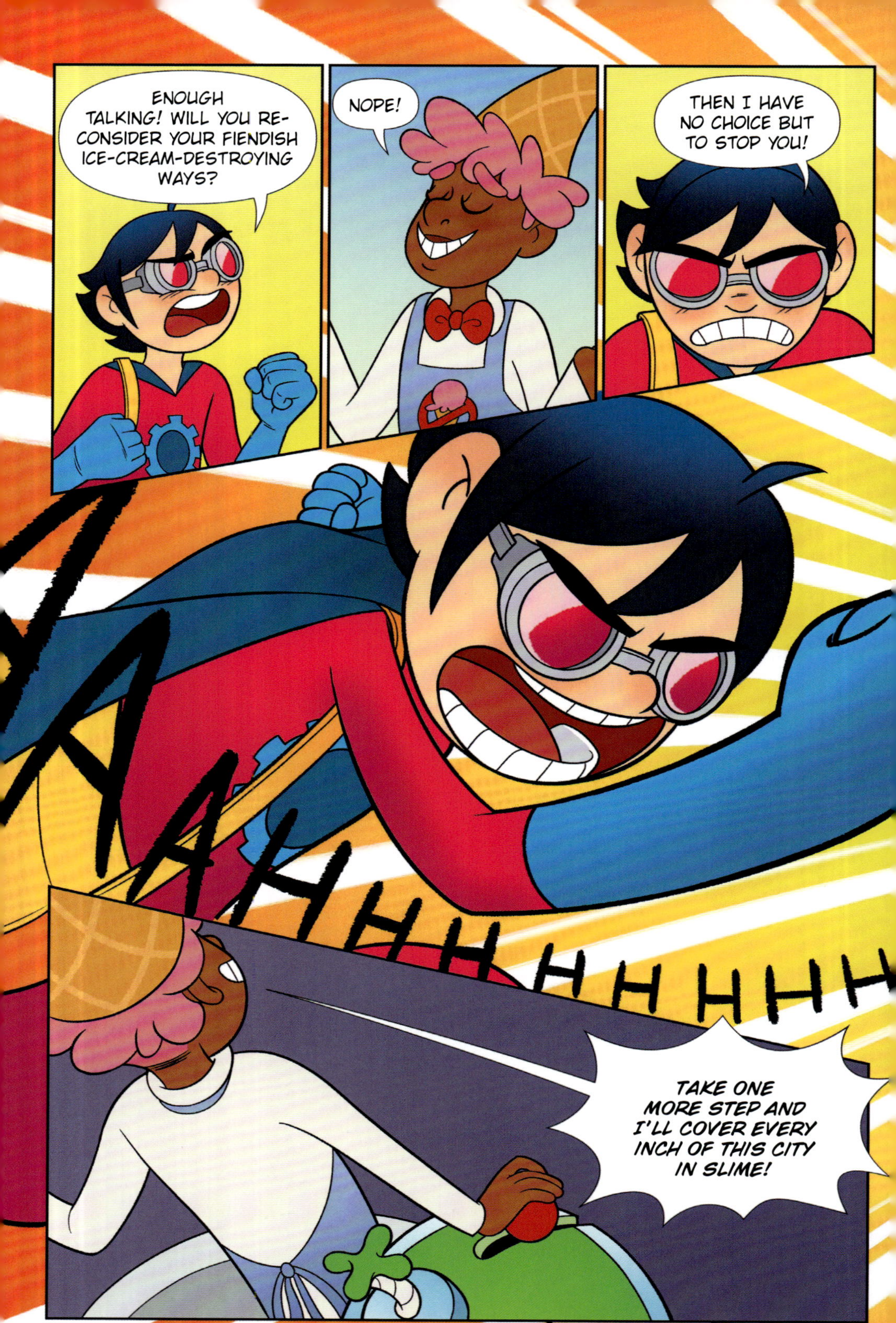
ENOUGH TALKING! WILL YOU RE-CONSIDER YOUR FIENDISH ICE-CREAM-DESTROYING WAYS?
NOPE!
THEN I HAVE NO CHOICE BUT TO STOP YOU!
AAAHHHHHHHHHHH
TAKE ONE MORE STEP AND I'LL COVER EVERY INCH OF THIS CITY IN SLIME!

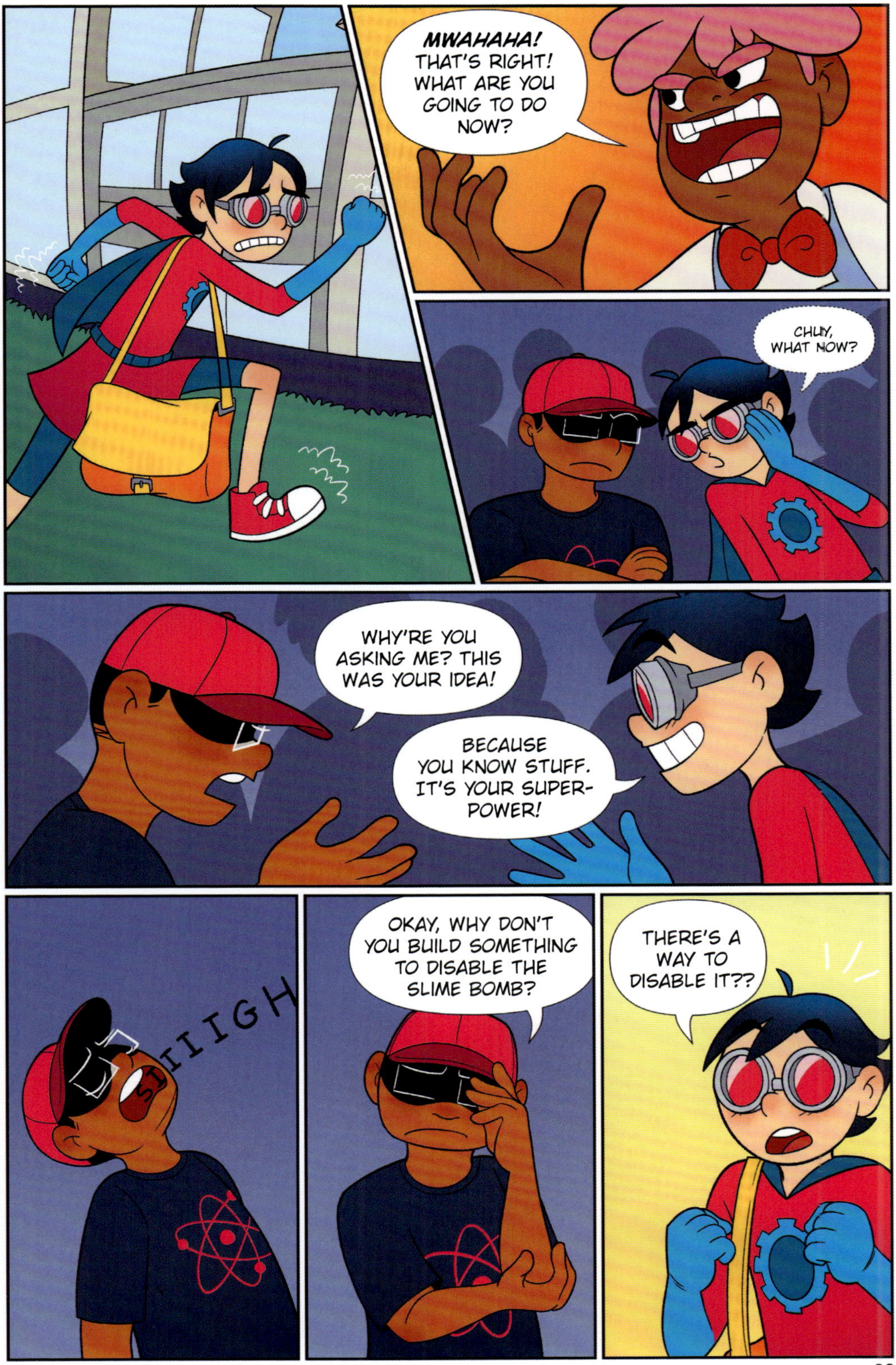
MWAHAHA! THAT'S RIGHT! WHAT ARE YOU GOING TO DO NOW?
CHUY, WHAT NOW?
WHY'RE YOU ASKING ME? THIS WAS YOUR IDEA!
BECAUSE YOU KNOW STUFF. IT'S YOUR SUPER-POWER!
SIIIIGH
OKAY, WHY DON'T YOU BUILD SOMETHING TO DISABLE THE SLIME BOMB?
THERE'S A WAY TO DISABLE IT??

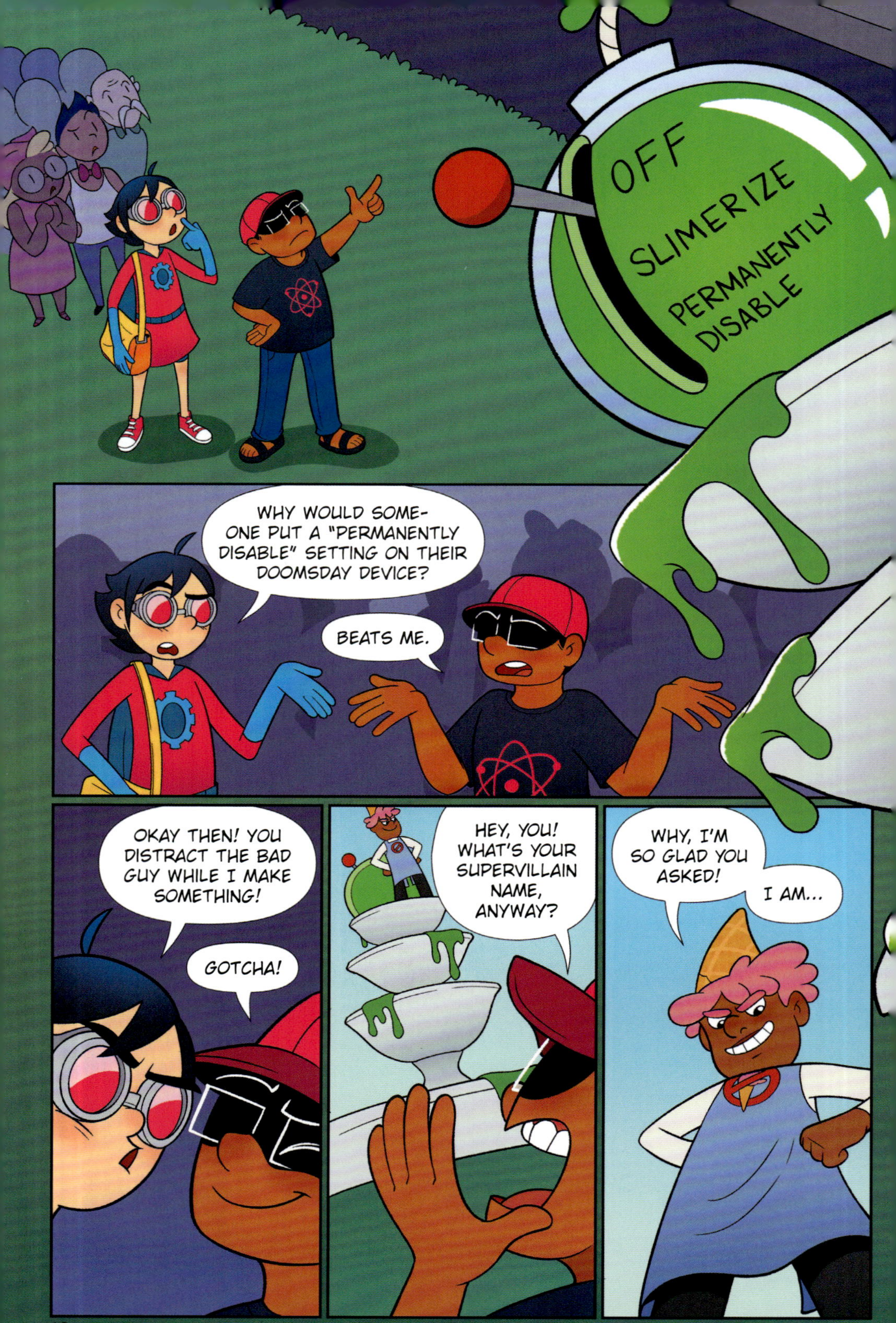
OFF
SLIMERIZE
PERMANENTLY DISABLE
WHY WOULD SOME-ONE PUT A "PERMANENTLY DISABLE" SETTING ON THEIR DOOMSDAY DEVICE?
BEATS ME.
OKAY THEN! YOU DISTRACT THE BAD GUY WHILE I MAKE SOMETHING!
GOTCHA!
HEY, YOU! WHAT'S YOUR SUPERVILLAIN NAME, ANYWAY?
WHY, I'M SO GLAD YOU ASKED!
I AM...

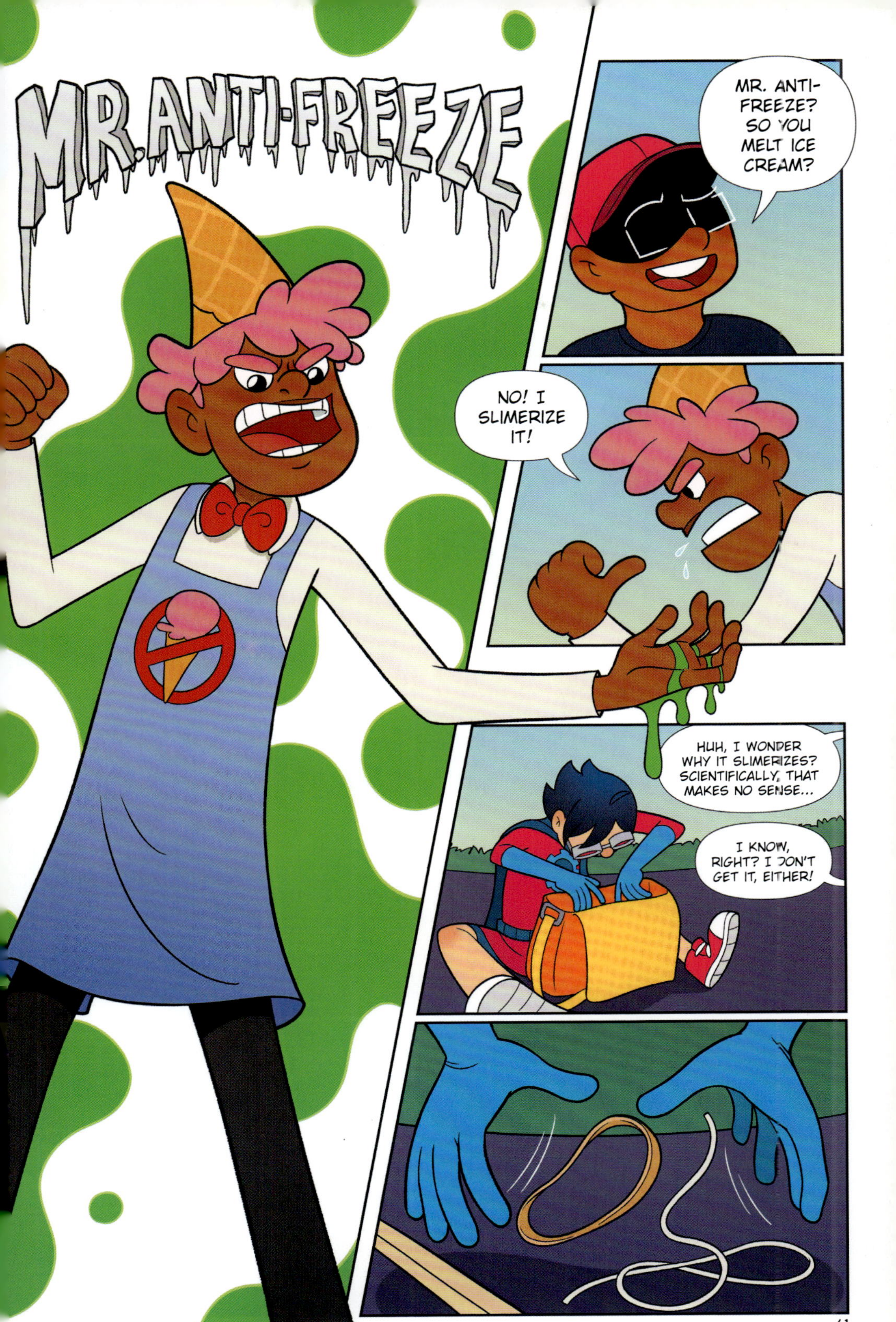
MR. ANTI-FREEZE
MR. ANTI-FREEZE? SO YOU MELT ICE CREAM?
NO! I SLIMERIZE IT!
HUH, I WONDER WHY IT SLIMERIZES? SCIENTIFICALLY, THAT MAKES NO SENSE...
I KNOW, RIGHT? I DON'T GET IT, EITHER!

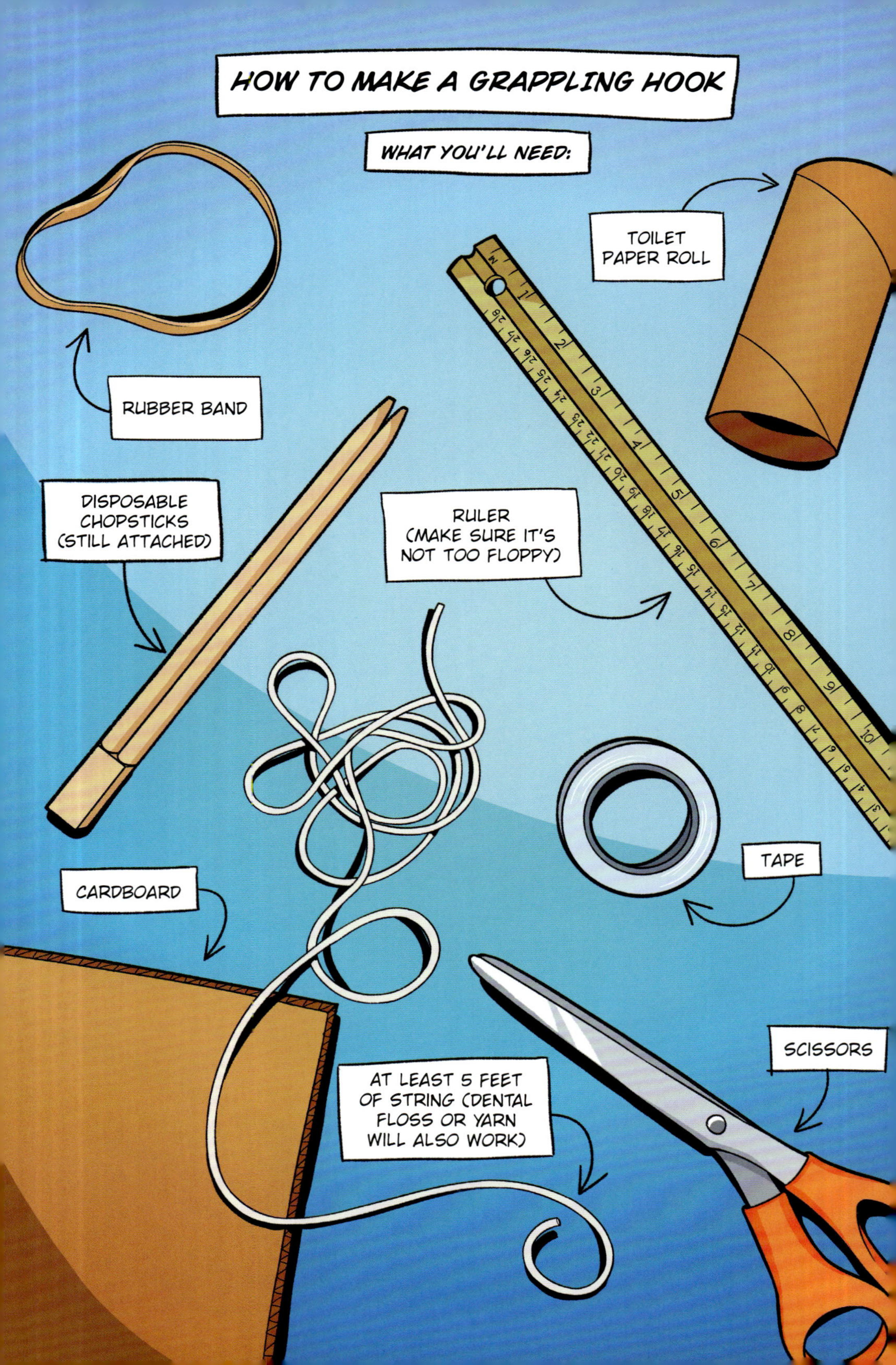
HOW TO MAKE A GRAPPLING HOOK
WHAT YOU'LL NEED:
TOILET PAPER ROLL
RUBBER BAND
DISPOSABLE CHOPSTICKS (STILL ATTACHED)
RULER (MAKE SURE IT'S NOT TOO FLOPPY)
TAPE
CARDBOARD
SCISSORS
AT LEAST 5 FEET OF STRING (DENTAL FLOSS OR YARN WILL ALSO WORK)

CUT THE TOILET PAPER ROLL AND USE SOME TAPE TO MAKE IT INTO A SMALLER TUBE.
1½ inches
2½ inches
TAPE THE TUBE TO THE RULER. IF YOUR RULER HAS A HOLE, TAPE THE TUBE CLOSER TO THAT END.
6½ inches
THE MEASUREMENTS ARE ALL APPROXIMATE—YOU CAN EXPERIMENT WITH THE DESIGN!
IF YOUR RULER HAS A HOLE, LOOP THE RUBBER BAND THROUGH IT TO ATTACH IT TO THE RULER.
IF YOUR RULER DOESN'T HAVE A HOLE, LOOP TWO RUBBER BANDS TOGETHER, THEN WRAP ONE OF THEM TIGHTLY AROUND THE RULER.
TAPE THE STRING TO THE END OF THE RULER OPPOSITE THE SIDE WITH THE RUBBER BAND, THEN PULL THE STRING THROUGH THE TUBE.

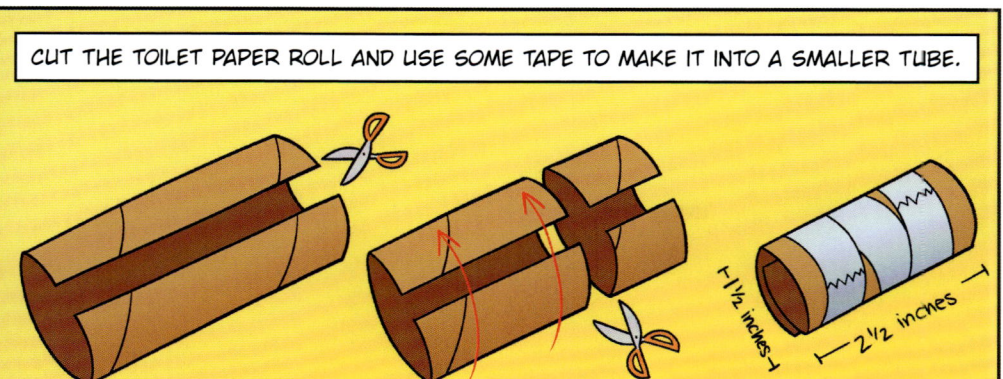

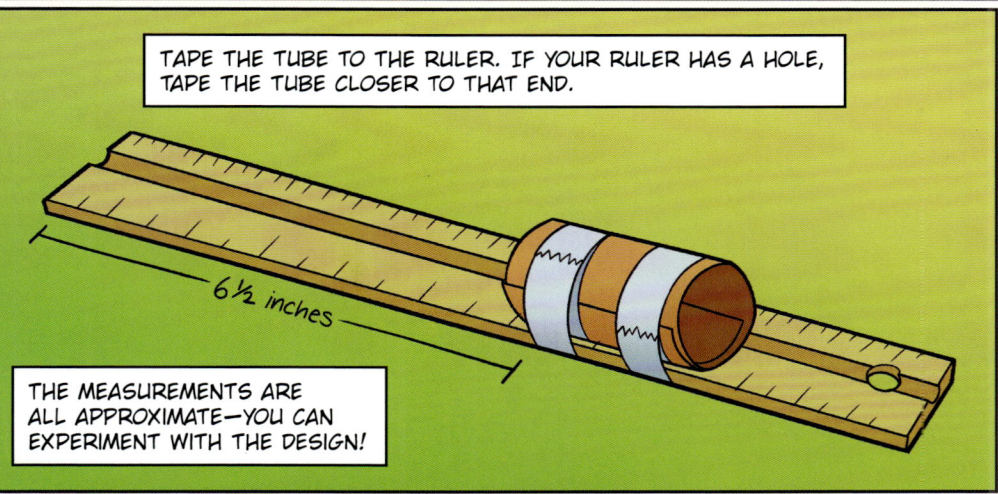

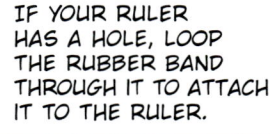

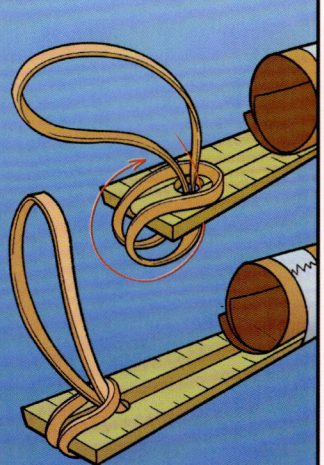

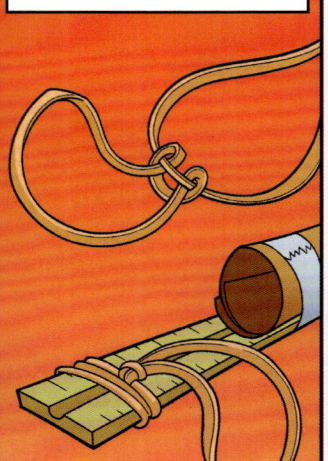

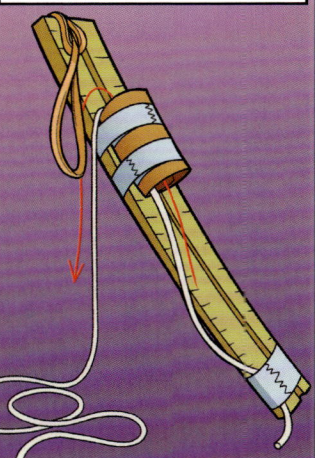

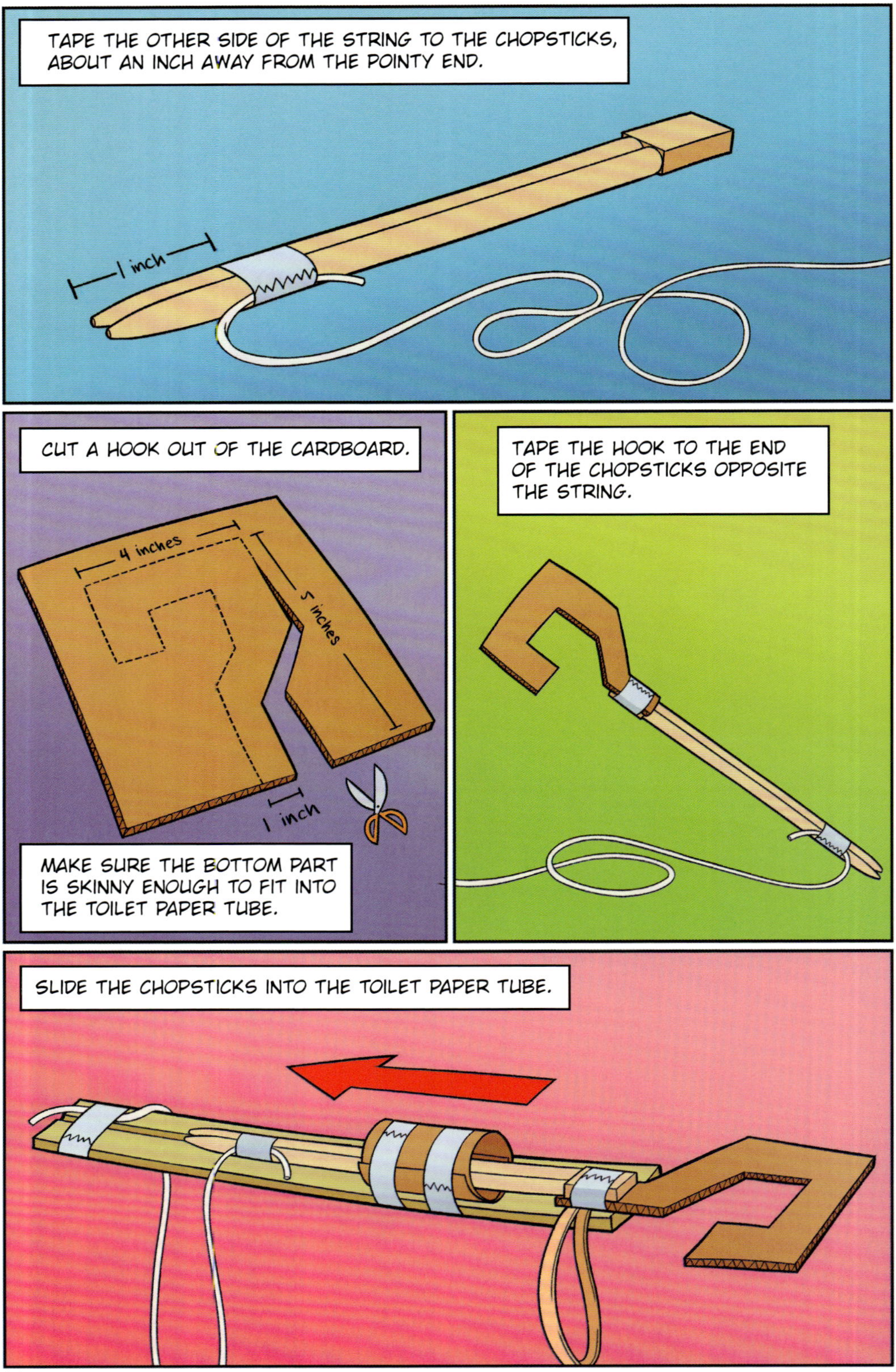
TAPE THE OTHER SIDE OF THE STRING TO THE CHOPSTICKS, ABOUT AN INCH AWAY FROM THE POINTY END.
1 inch
CUT A HOOK OUT OF THE CARDBOARD.
4 inches
5 inches
1 inch
MAKE SURE THE BOTTOM PART IS SKINNY ENOUGH TO FIT INTO THE TOILET PAPER TUBE.
TAPE THE HOOK TO THE END OF THE CHOPSTICKS OPPOSITE THE STRING.
SLIDE THE CHOPSTICKS INTO THE TOILET PAPER TUBE.

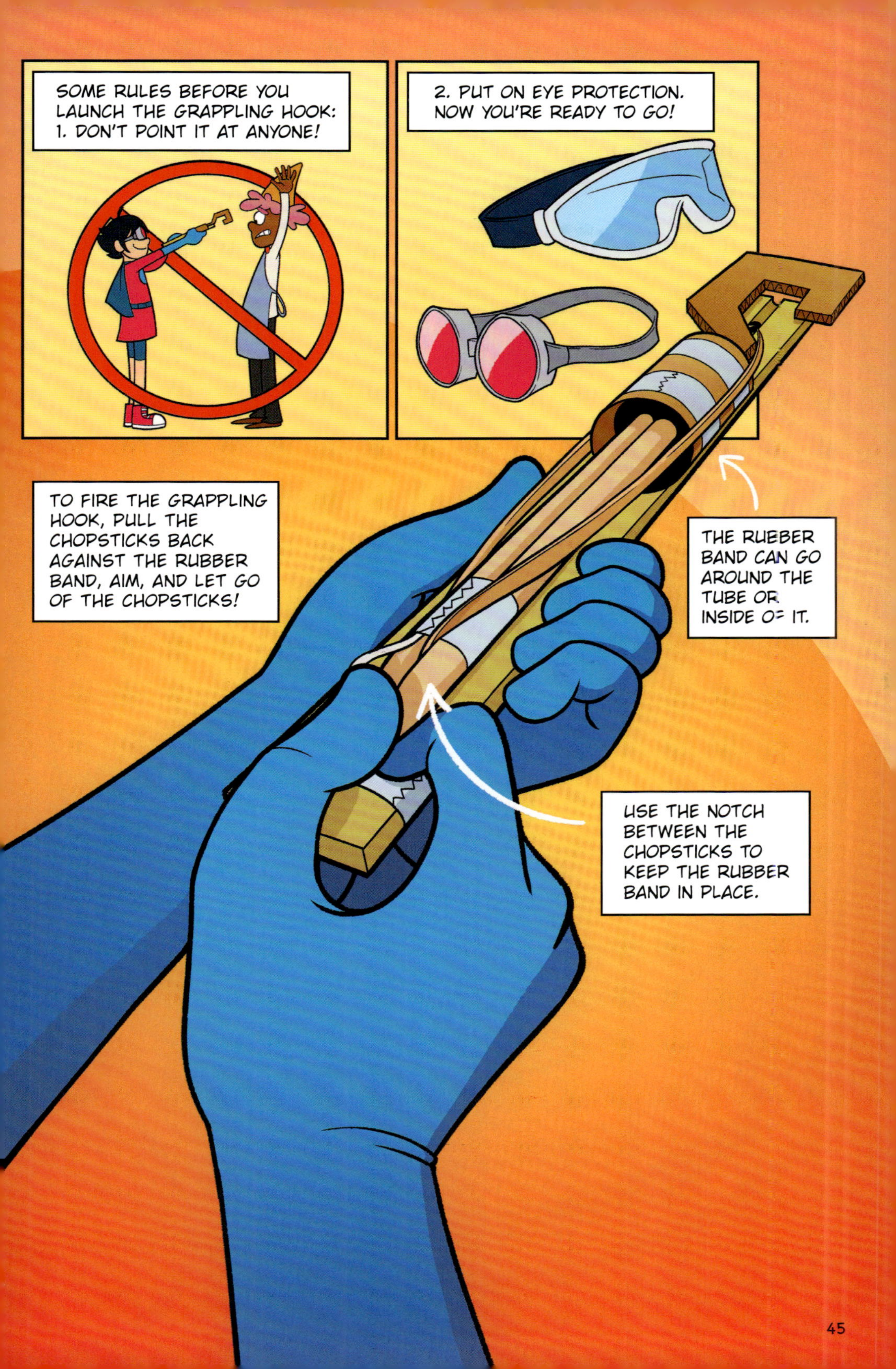
SOME RULES BEFORE YOU LAUNCH THE GRAPPLING HOOK:
1. DON'T POINT IT AT ANYONE!
2. PUT ON EYE PROTECTION. NOW YOU'RE READY TO GO!
TO FIRE THE GRAPPLING HOOK, PULL THE CHOPSTICKS BACK AGAINST THE RUBBER BAND, AIM, AND LET GO OF THE CHOPSTICKS!
THE RUBBER BAND CAN GO AROUND THE TUBE OR INSIDE OF IT.
USE THE NOTCH BETWEEN THE CHOPSTICKS TO KEEP THE RUBBER BAND IN PLACE.

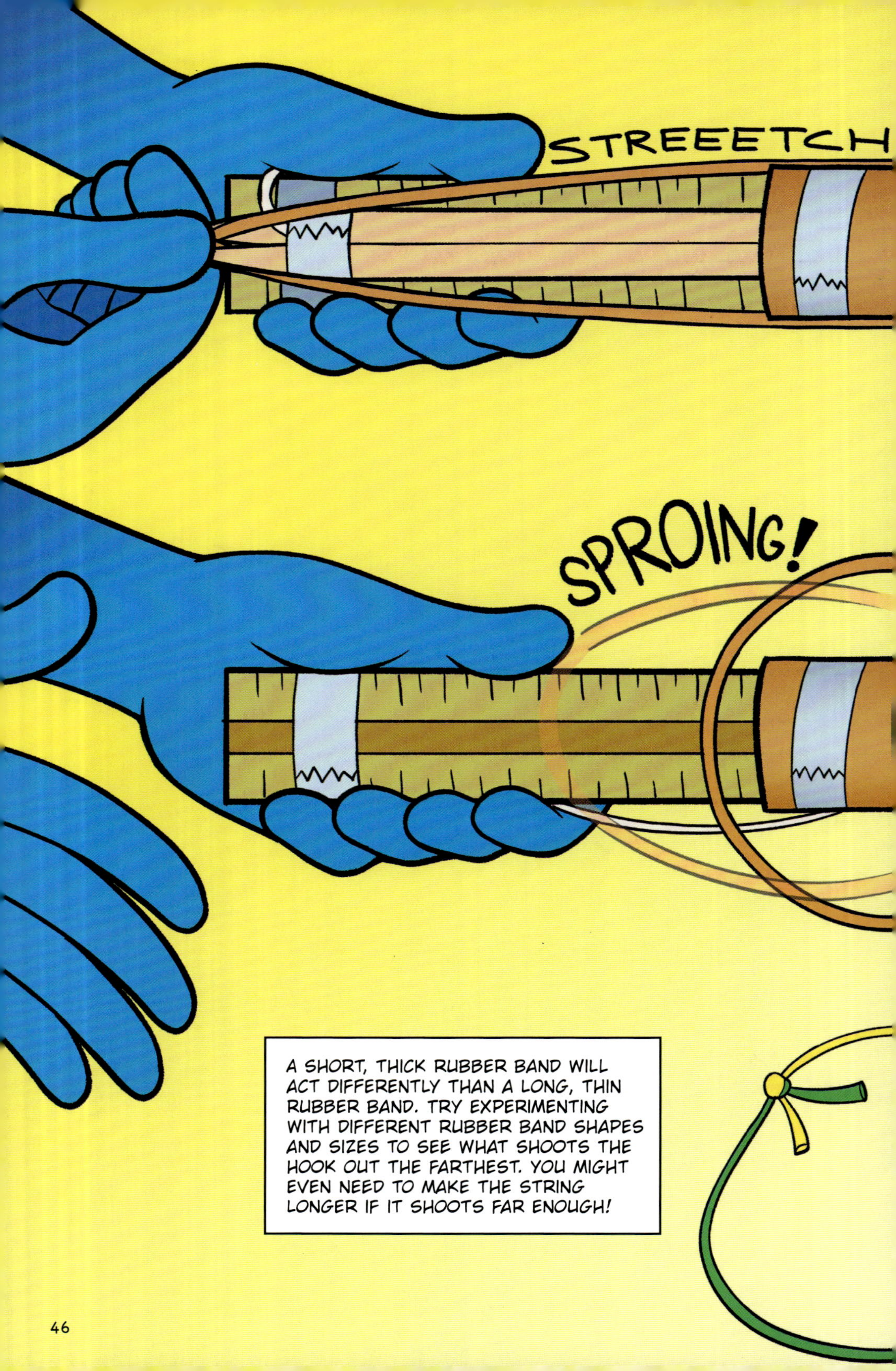
STREEETCH
SPROING!
A SHORT, THICK RUBBER BAND WILL ACT DIFFERENTLY THAN A LONG, THIN RUBBER BAND. TRY EXPERIMENTING WITH DIFFERENT RUBBER BAND SHAPES AND SIZES TO SEE WHAT SHOOTS THE HOOK OUT THE FARTHEST. YOU MIGHT EVEN NEED TO MAKE THE STRING LONGER IF IT SHOOTS FAR ENOUGH!

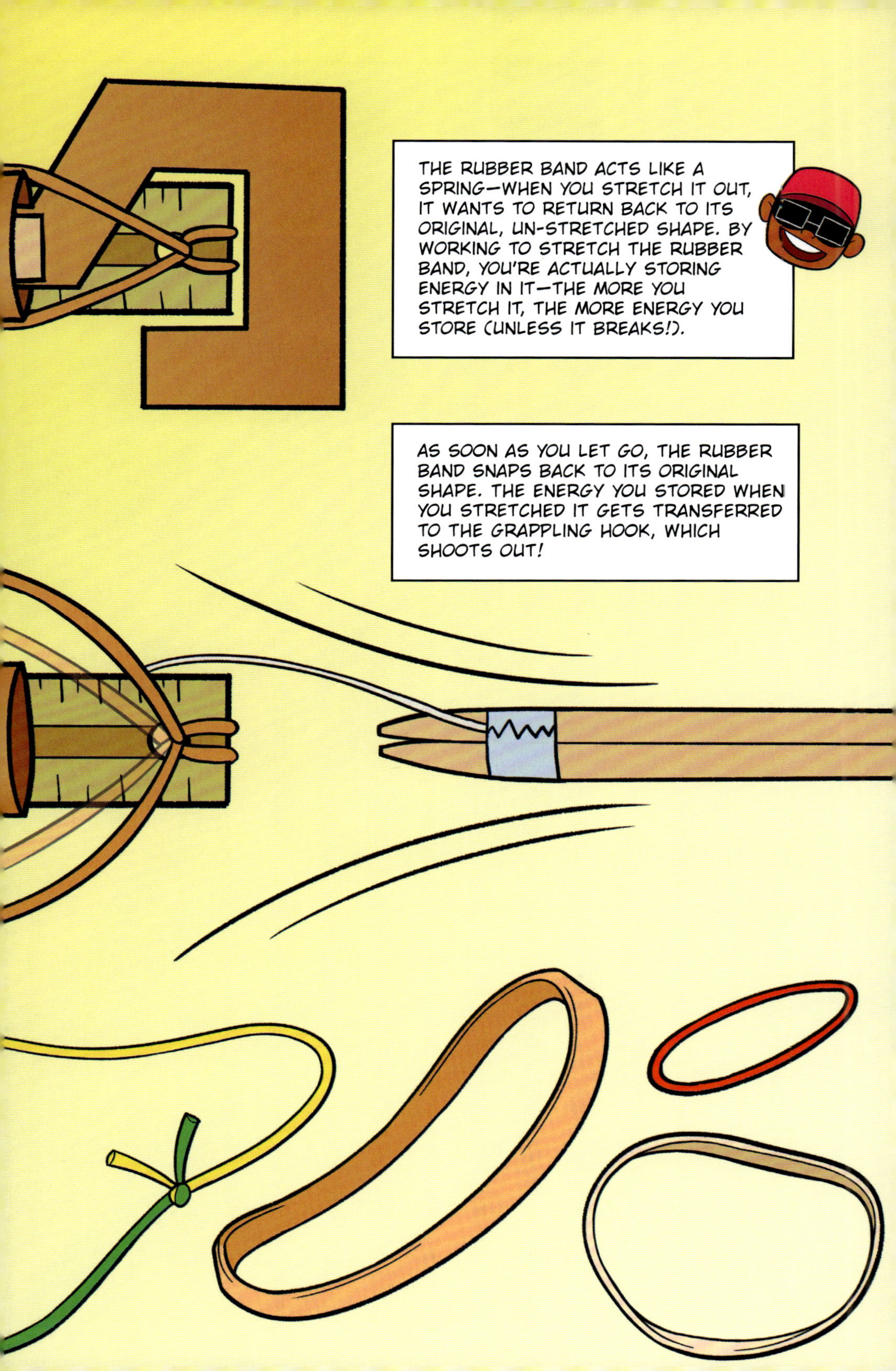
THE RUBBER BAND ACTS LIKE A SPRING—WHEN YOU STRETCH IT OUT, IT WANTS TO RETURN BACK TO ITS ORIGINAL, UN-STRETCHED SHAPE. BY WORKING TO STRETCH THE RUBBER BAND, YOU'RE ACTUALLY STORING ENERGY IN IT—THE MORE YOU STRETCH IT, THE MORE ENERGY YOU STORE (UNLESS IT BREAKS!).
AS SOON AS YOU LET GO, THE RUBBER BAND SNAPS BACK TO ITS ORIGINAL SHAPE. THE ENERGY YOU STORED WHEN YOU STRETCHED IT GETS TRANSFERRED TO THE GRAPPLING HOOK, WHICH SHOOTS OUT!

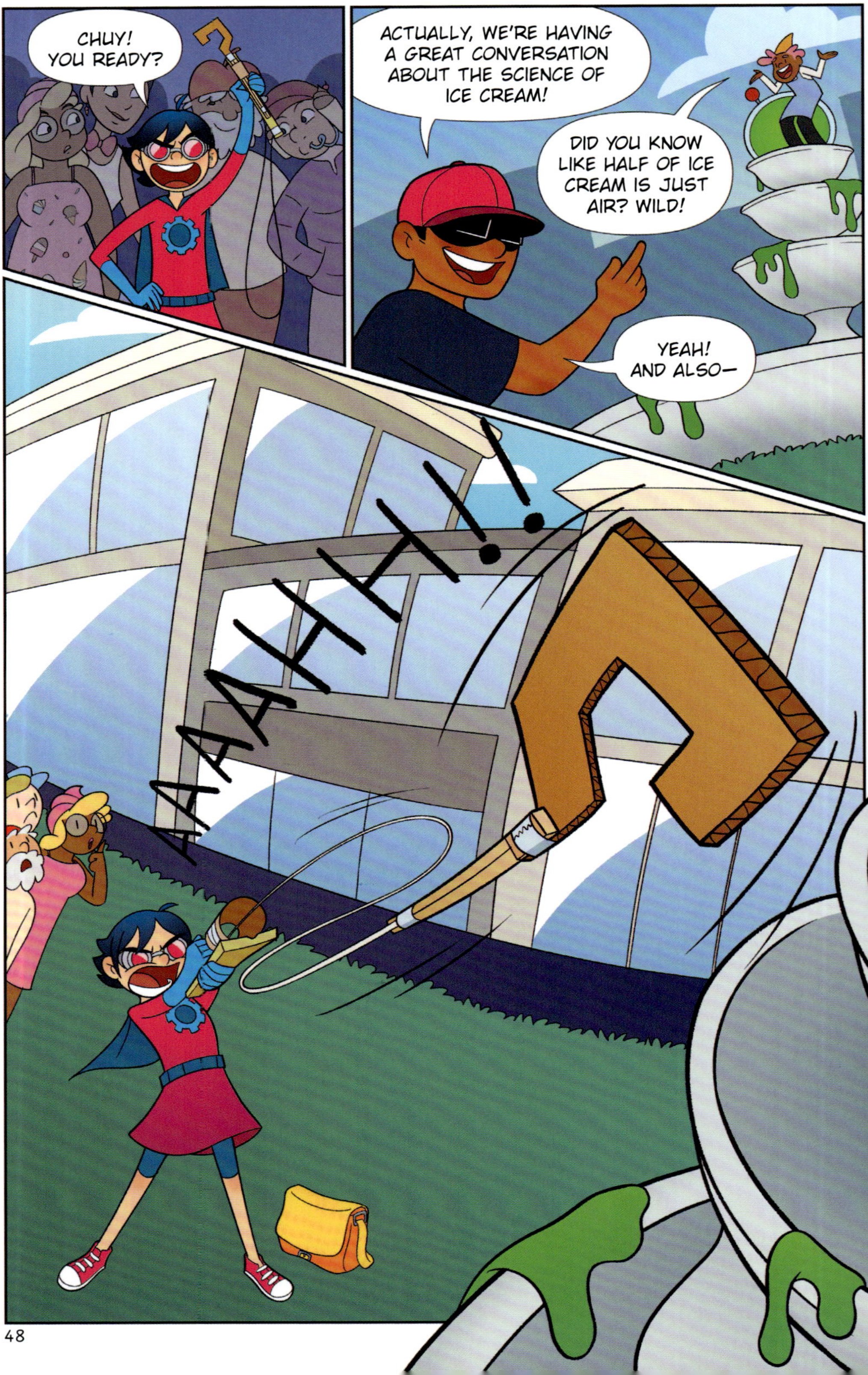
CHUY! YOU READY?
ACTUALLY, WE'RE HAVING A GREAT CONVERSATION ABOUT THE SCIENCE OF ICE CREAM!
DID YOU KNOW LIKE HALF OF ICE CREAM IS JUST AIR? WILD!
YEAH! AND ALSO—
AAAHHH!!

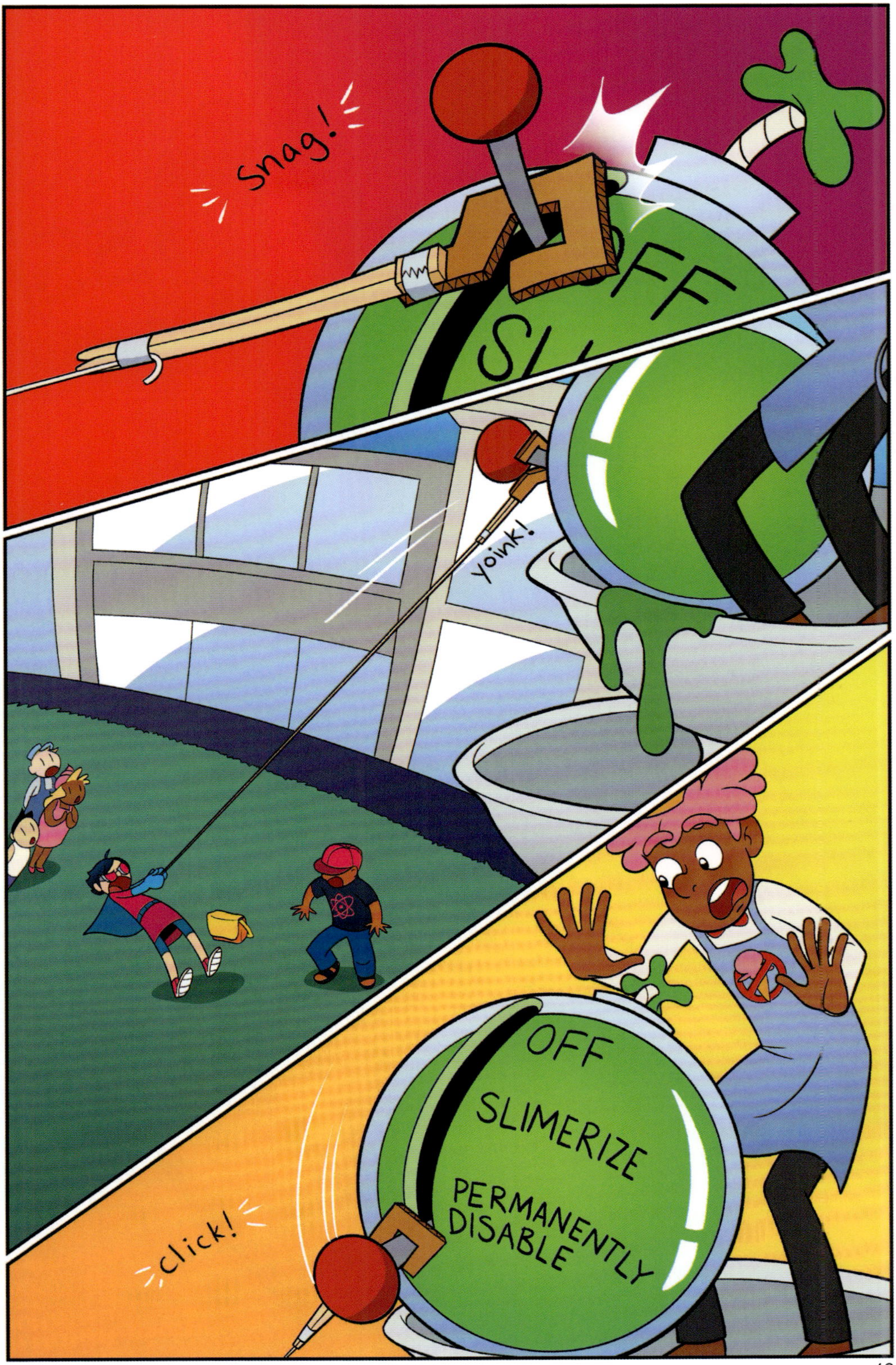
Snag!
OFF
SL
yoink!
OFF
SLIMERIZE
PERMANENTLY
DISABLE
click!

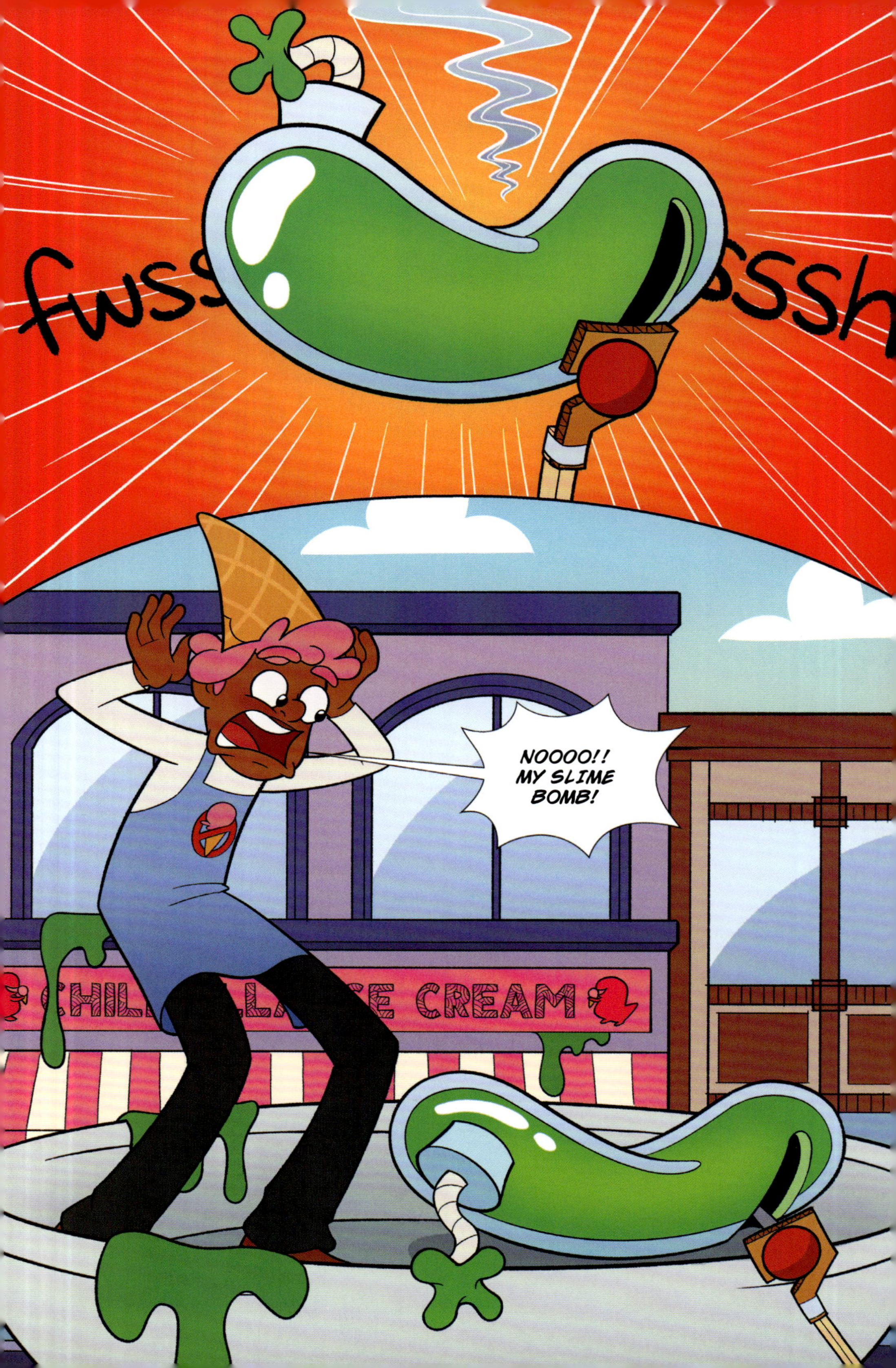
fwss
sssh
NOOOO!! MY SLIME BOMB!
CREAM

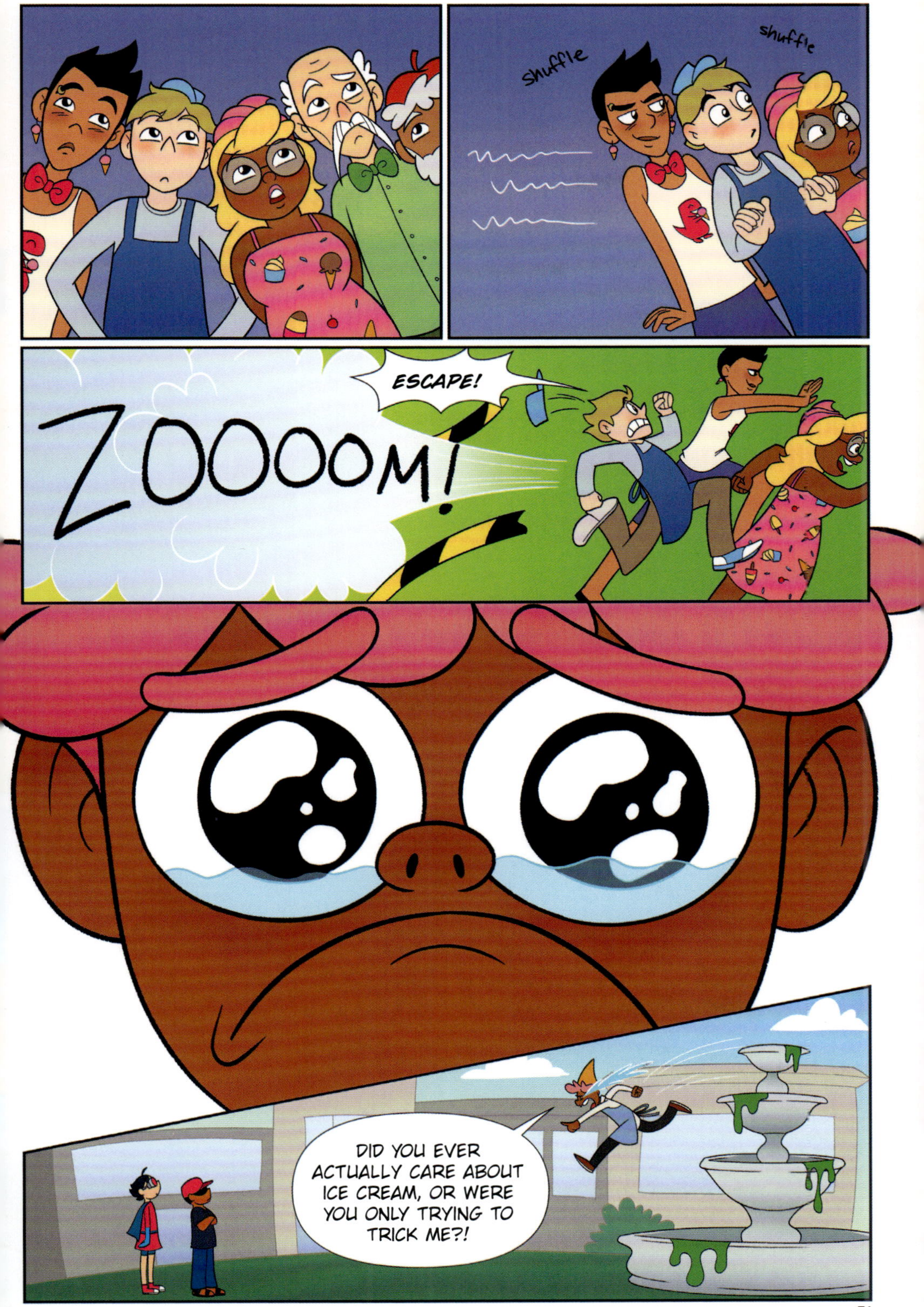
shuffle
shuffle
ESCAPE!
ZOOOOM!
DID YOU EVER ACTUALLY CARE ABOUT ICE CREAM, OR WERE YOU ONLY TRYING TO TRICK ME?!

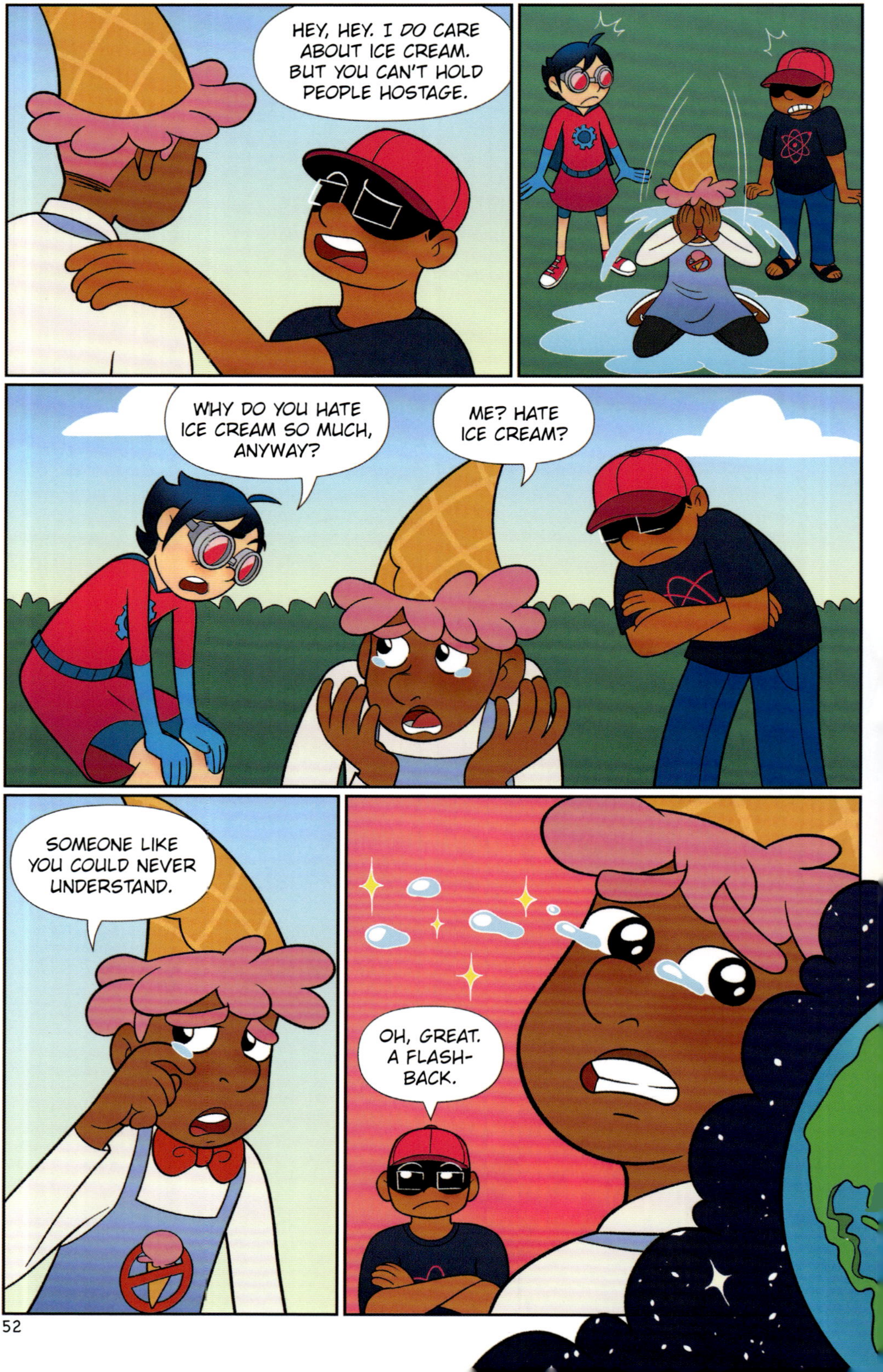
HEY, HEY. I DO CARE ABOUT ICE CREAM. BUT YOU CAN'T HOLD PEOPLE HOSTAGE.
WHY DO YOU HATE ICE CREAM SO MUCH, ANYWAY?
ME? HATE ICE CREAM?
SOMEONE LIKE YOU COULD NEVER UNDERSTAND.
OH, GREAT. A FLASH-BACK.

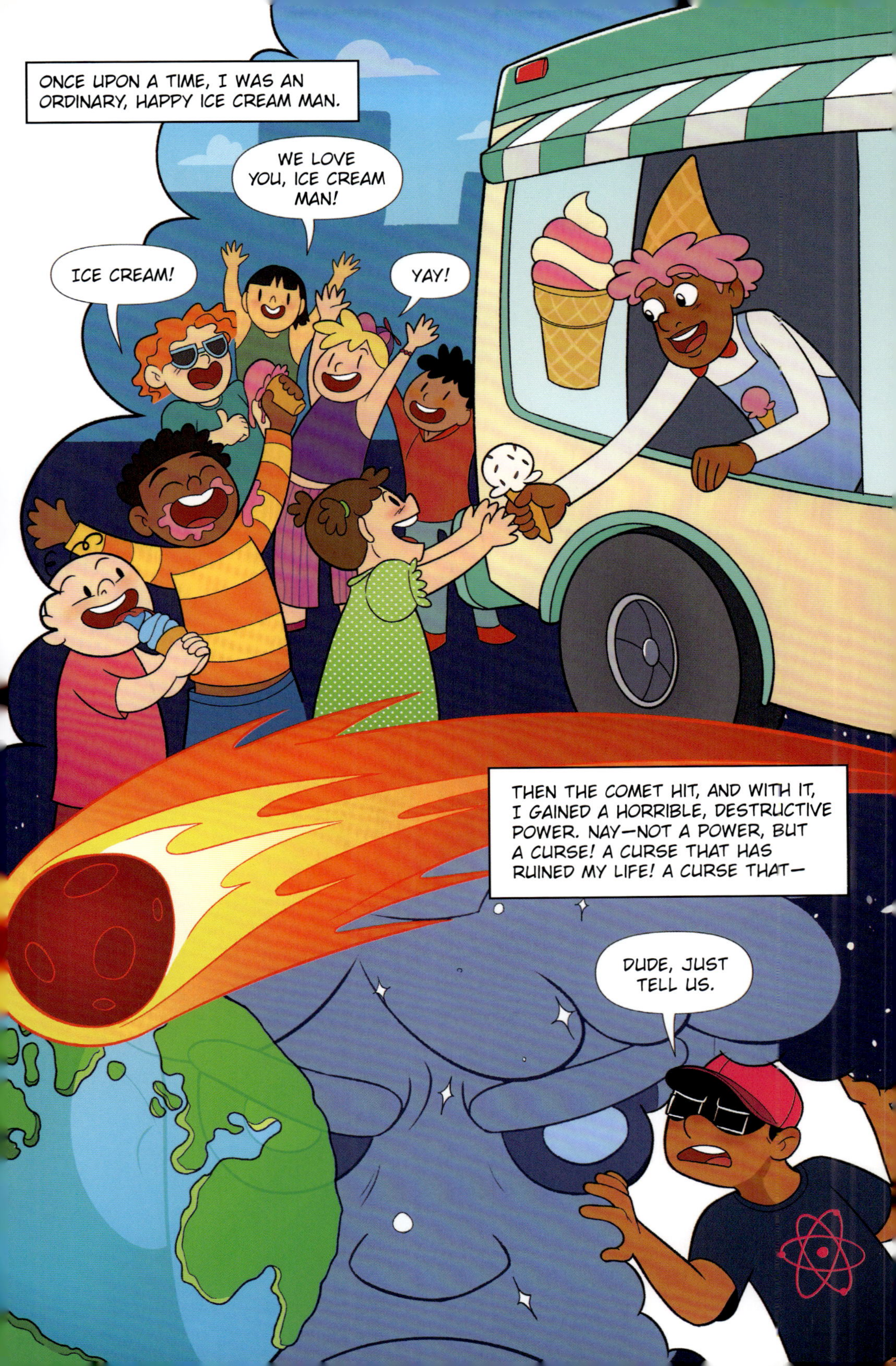
ONCE UPON A TIME, I WAS AN ORDINARY, HAPPY ICE CREAM MAN.
WE LOVE YOU, ICE CREAM MAN!
ICE CREAM!
YAY!
THEN THE COMET HIT, AND WITH IT, I GAINED A HORRIBLE, DESTRUCTIVE POWER. NAY—NOT A POWER, BUT A CURSE! A CURSE THAT HAS RUINED MY LIFE! A CURSE THAT—
DUDE, JUST TELL US.

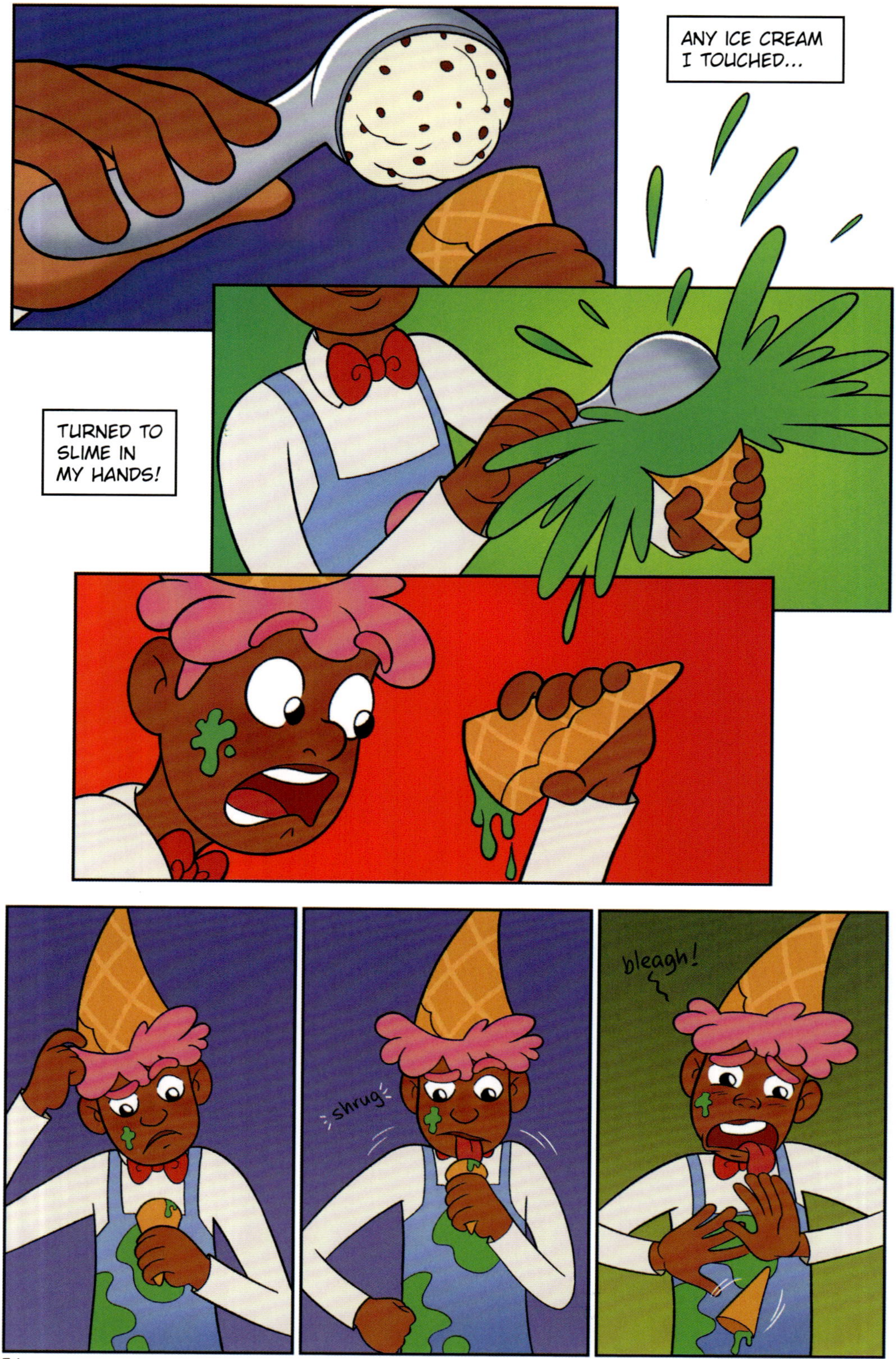
ANY ICE CREAM I TOUCHED...
TURNED TO SLIME IN MY HANDS!
shrug
bleagh!

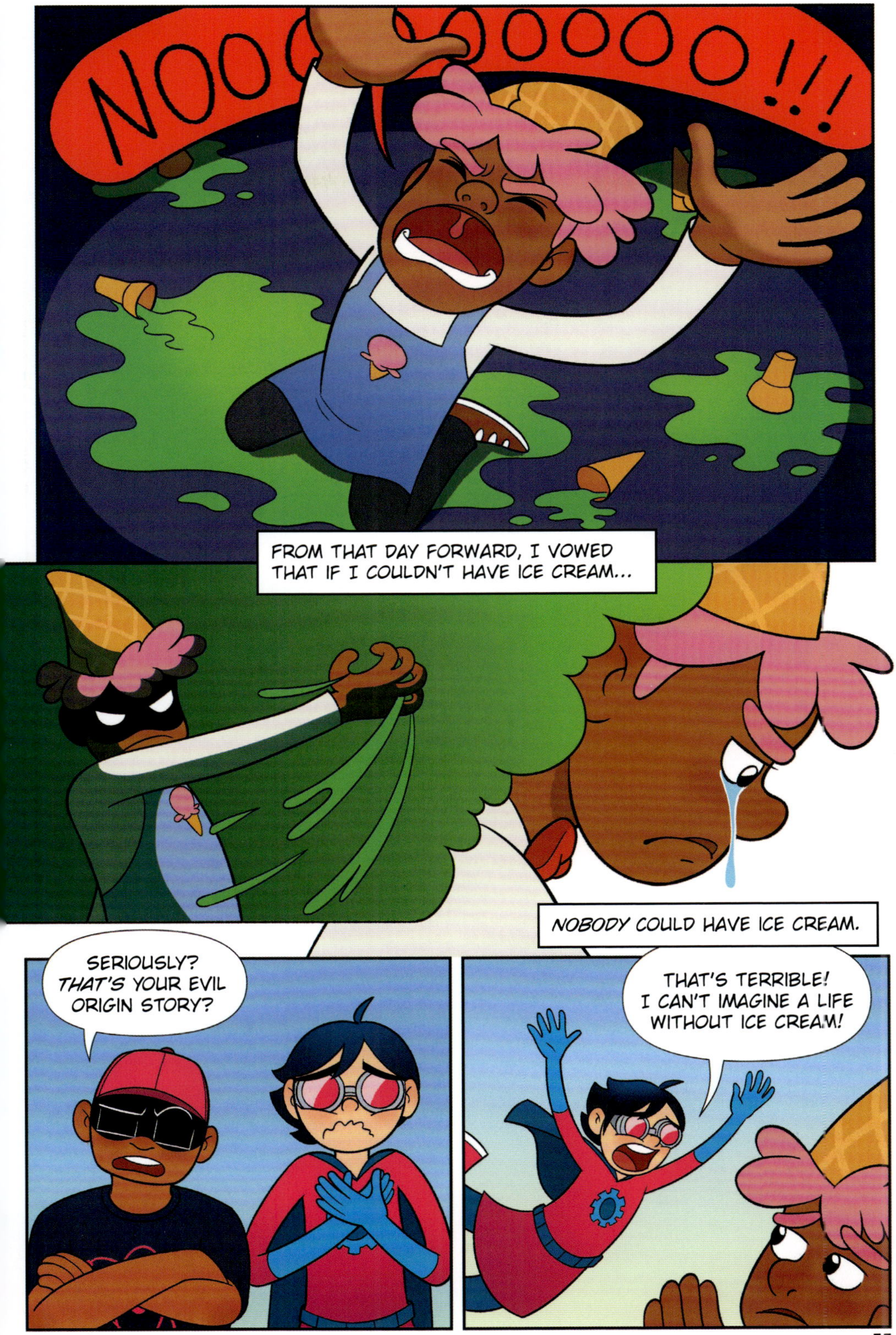
NOOOOOOOOO!!!
FROM THAT DAY FORWARD, I VOWED THAT IF I COULDN'T HAVE ICE CREAM...
NOBODY COULD HAVE ICE CREAM.
SERIOUSLY? *THAT'S* YOUR EVIL ORIGIN STORY?
THAT'S TERRIBLE! I CAN'T IMAGINE A LIFE WITHOUT ICE CREAM!

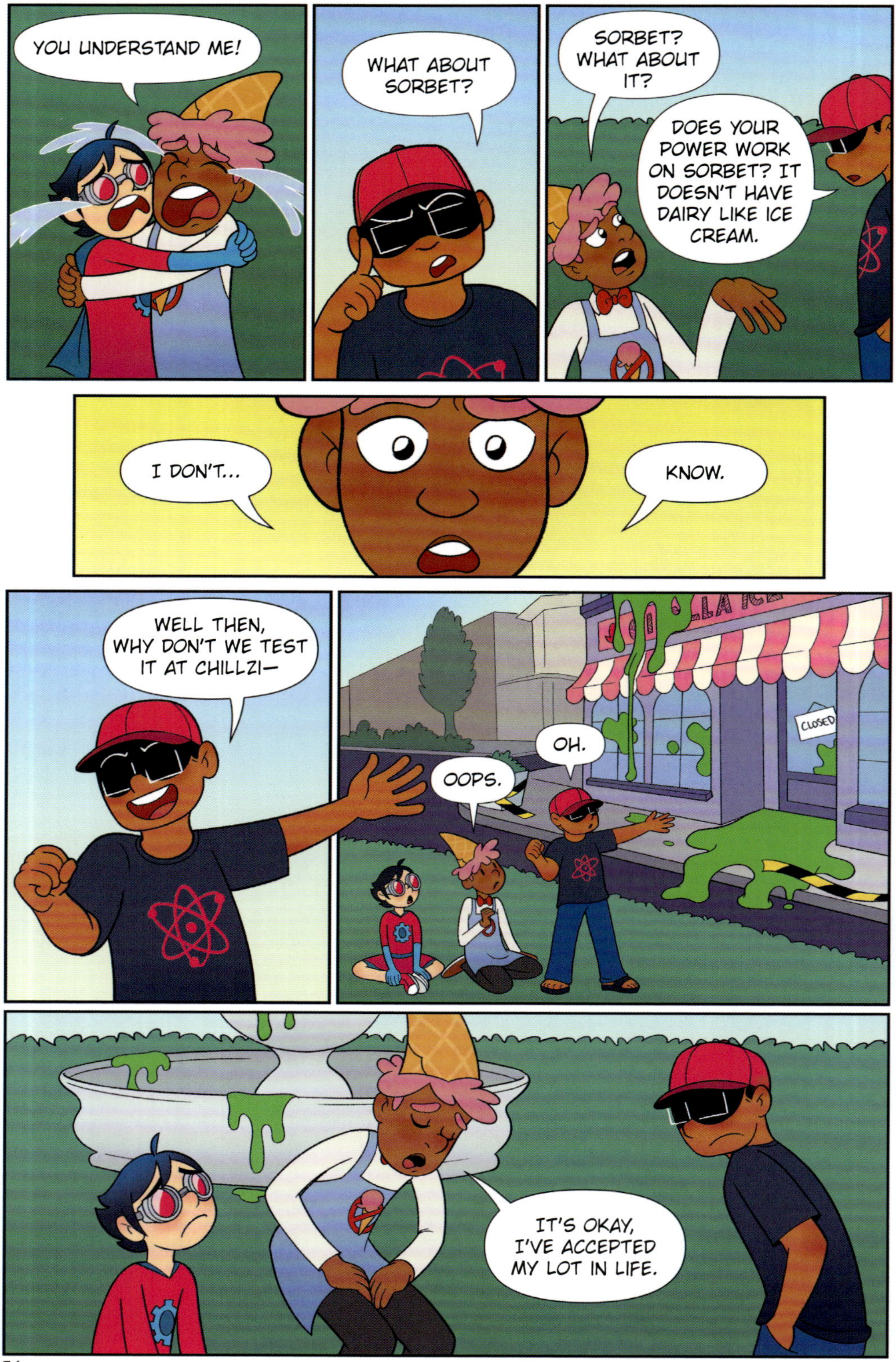
YOU UNDERSTAND ME!
WHAT ABOUT SORBET?
SORBET? WHAT ABOUT IT?
DOES YOUR POWER WORK ON SORBET? IT DOESN'T HAVE DAIRY LIKE ICE CREAM.
I DON'T...
KNOW.
WELL THEN, WHY DON'T WE TEST IT AT CHILLZI—
CLOSED
OH.
OOPS.
IT'S OKAY, I'VE ACCEPTED MY LOT IN LIFE.

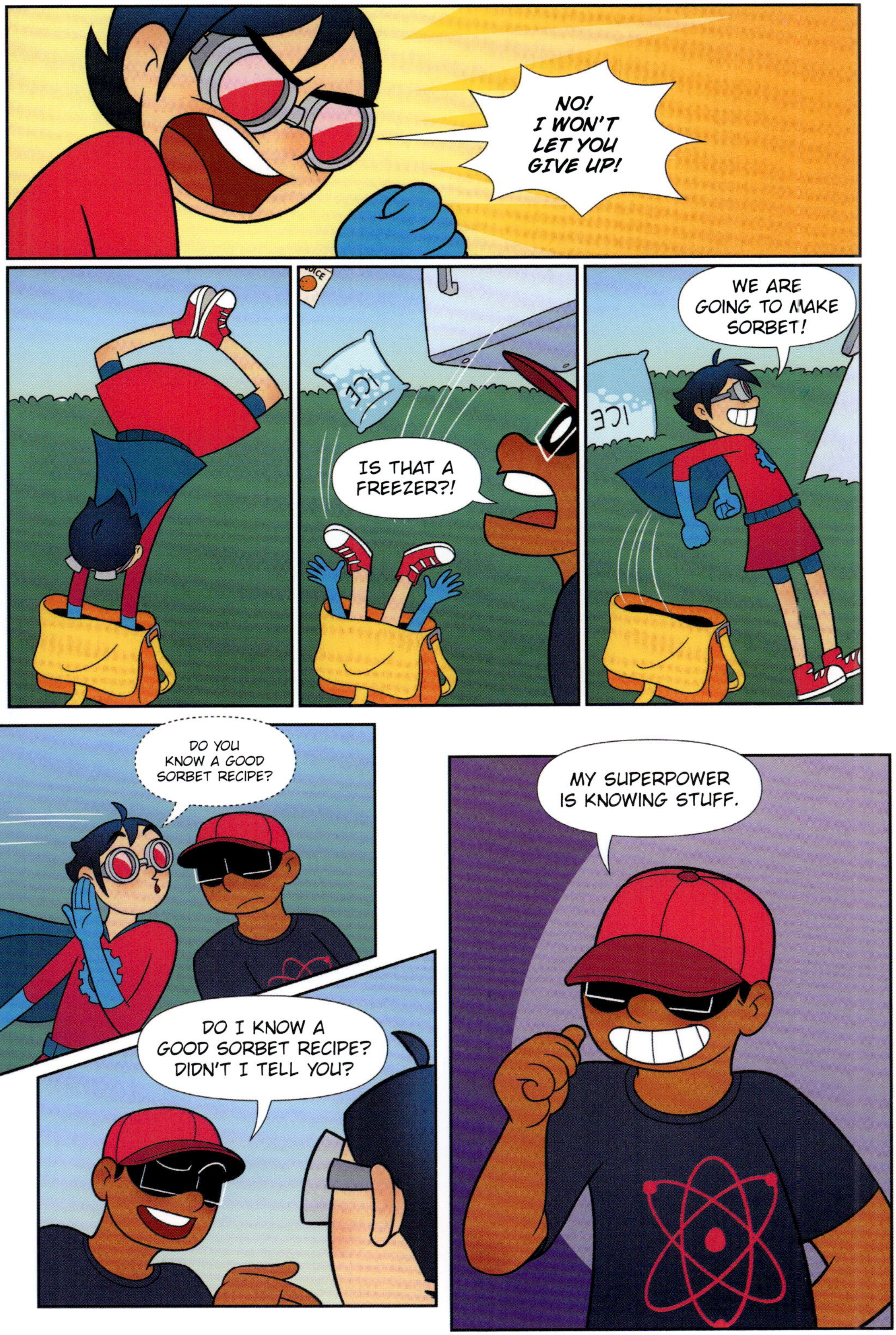
NO! I WON'T LET YOU GIVE UP!
IS THAT A FREEZER?!
WE ARE GOING TO MAKE SORBET!
DO YOU KNOW A GOOD SORBET RECIPE?
DO I KNOW A GOOD SORBET RECIPE? DIDN'T I TELL YOU?
MY SUPERPOWER IS KNOWING STUFF.

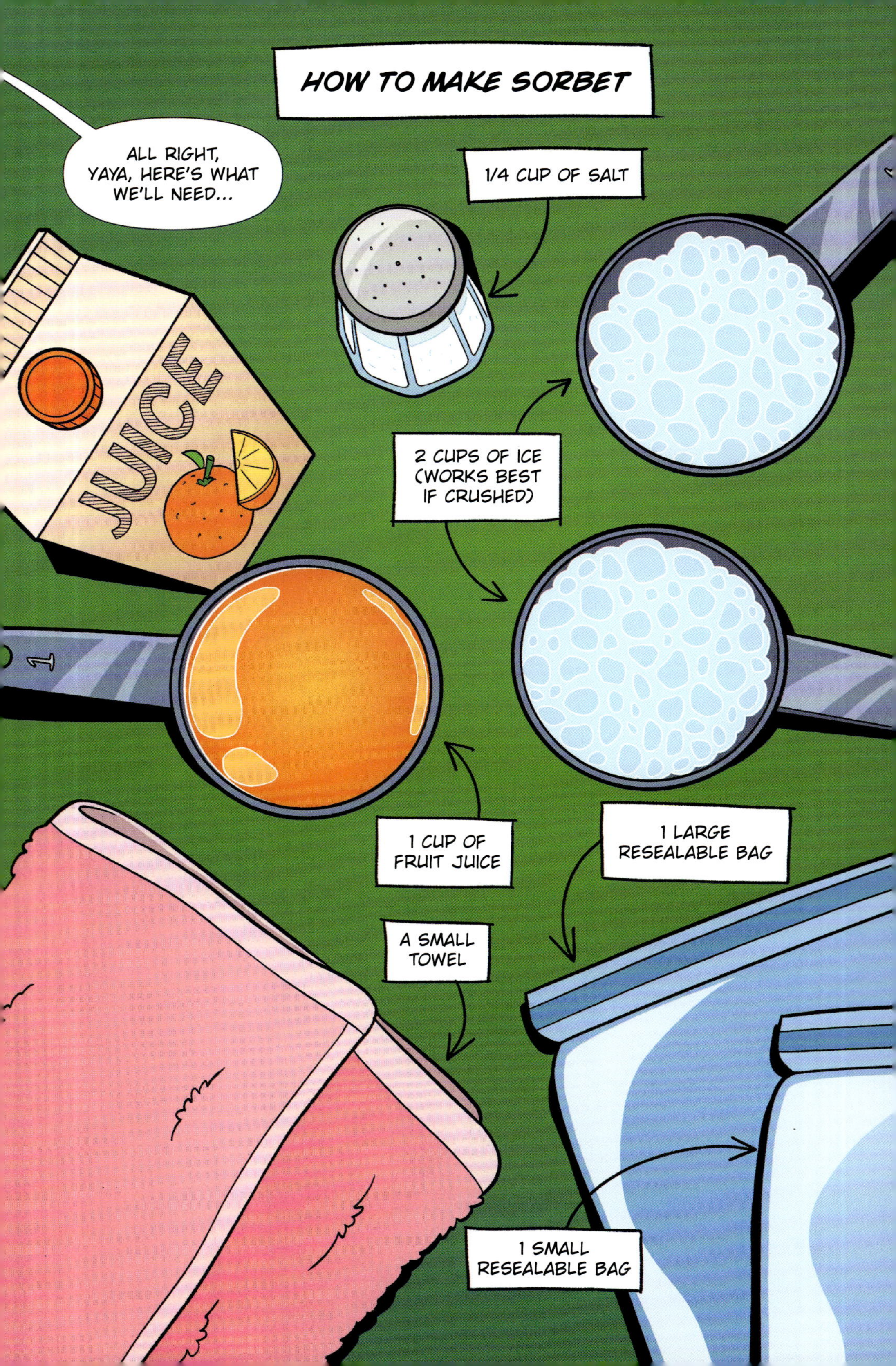
HOW TO MAKE SORBET
ALL RIGHT, YAYA, HERE'S WHAT WE'LL NEED...
1/4 CUP OF SALT
JUICE
2 CUPS OF ICE (WORKS BEST IF CRUSHED)
1 CUP OF FRUIT JUICE
1 LARGE RESEALABLE BAG
A SMALL TOWEL
1 SMALL RESEALABLE BAG

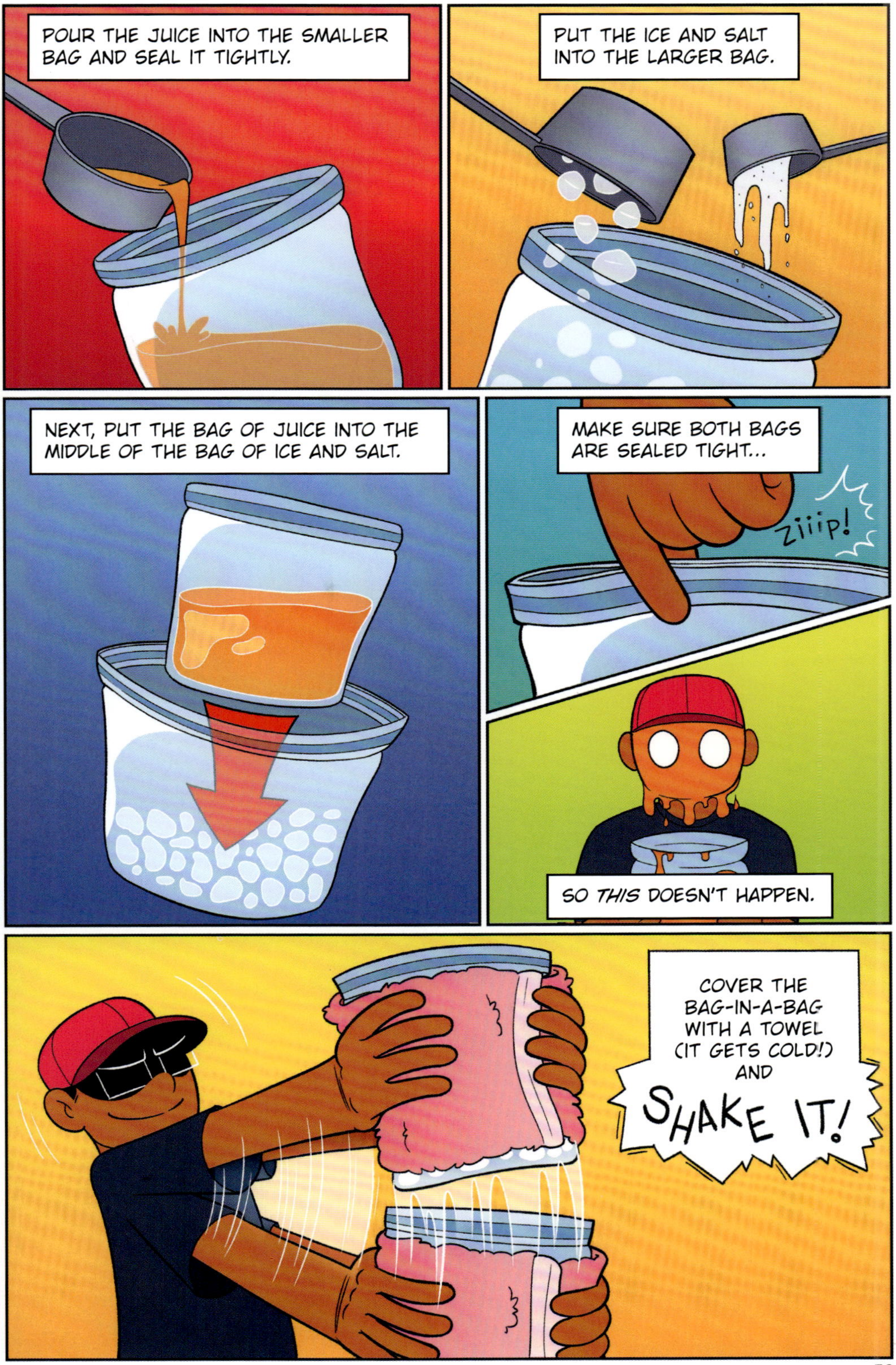

POUR THE JUICE INTO THE SMALLER BAG AND SEAL IT TIGHTLY.
PUT THE ICE AND SALT INTO THE LARGER BAG.
NEXT, PUT THE BAG OF JUICE INTO THE MIDDLE OF THE BAG OF ICE AND SALT.
MAKE SURE BOTH BAGS ARE SEALED TIGHT...
ZIIIP!
SO *THIS* DOESN'T HAPPEN.
COVER THE BAG-IN-A-BAG WITH A TOWEL (IT GETS COLD!) AND
SHAKE IT!

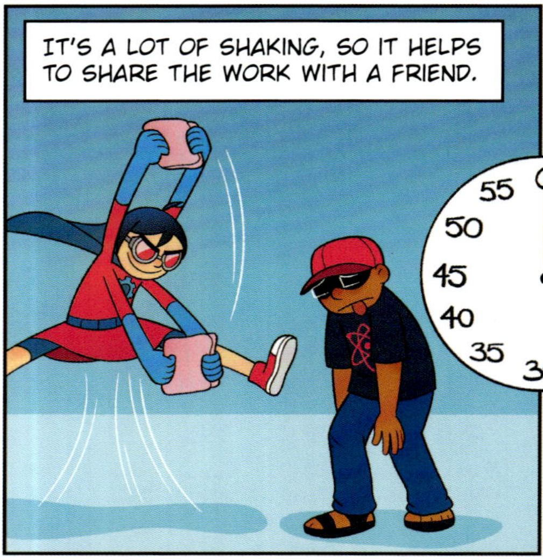
IT'S A LOT OF SHAKING, SO IT HELPS TO SHARE THE WORK WITH A FRIEND.

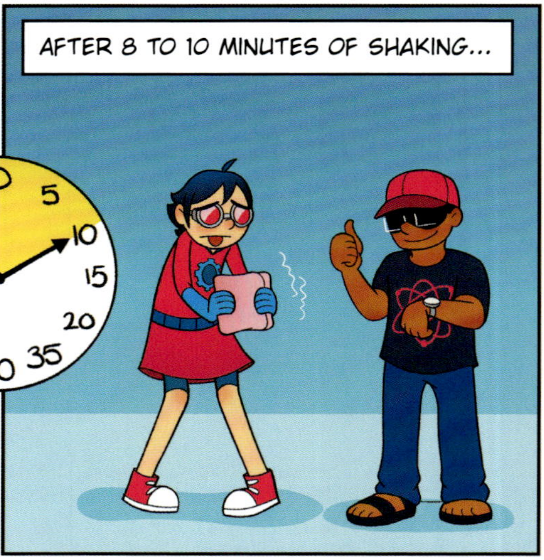
AFTER 8 TO 10 MINUTES OF SHAKING...

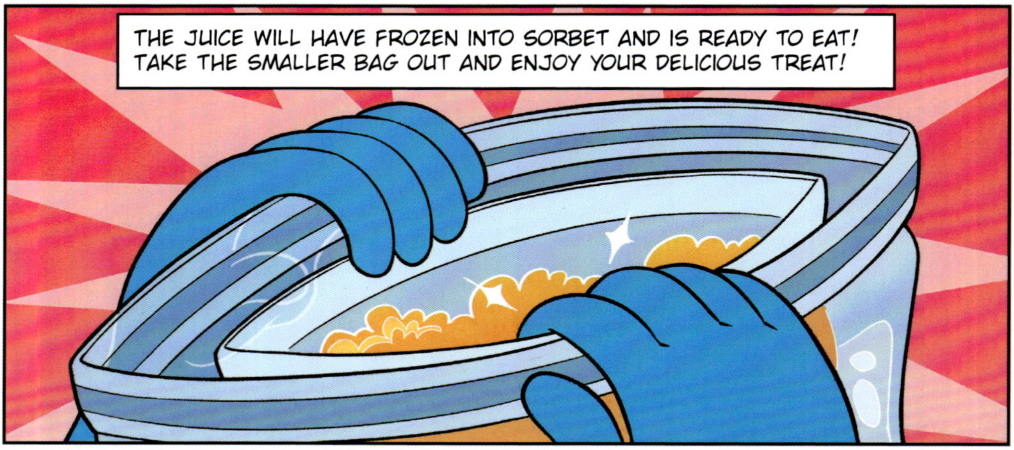
THE JUICE WILL HAVE FROZEN INTO SORBET AND IS READY TO EAT! TAKE THE SMALLER BAG OUT AND ENJOY YOUR DELICIOUS TREAT!

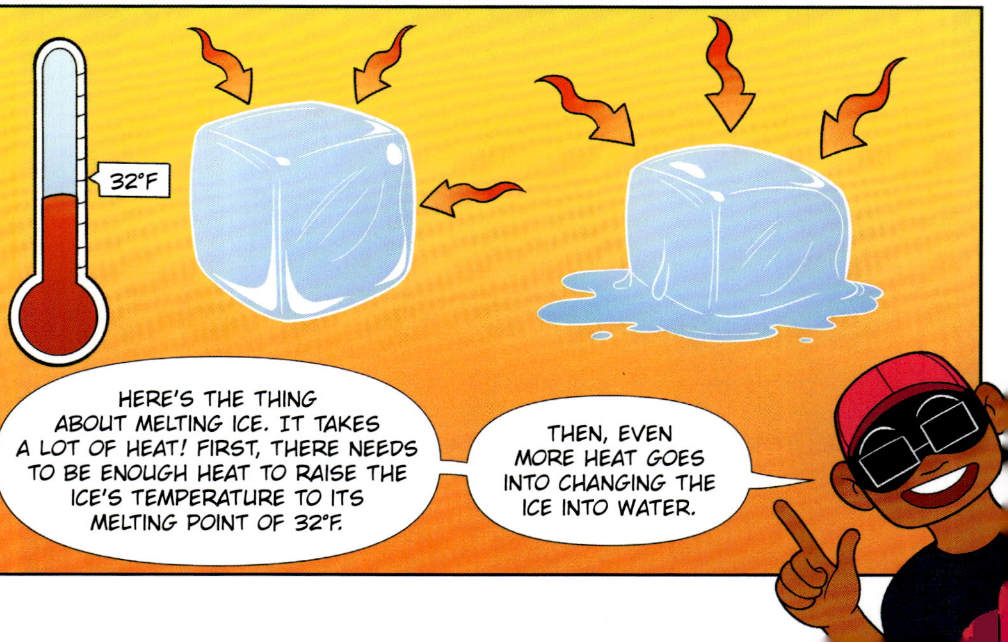
32°F
HERE'S THE THING ABOUT MELTING ICE. IT TAKES A LOT OF HEAT! FIRST, THERE NEEDS TO BE ENOUGH HEAT TO RAISE THE ICE'S TEMPERATURE TO ITS MELTING POINT OF 32°F.
THEN, EVEN MORE HEAT GOES INTO CHANGING THE ICE INTO WATER.

WHERE IS ALL THAT HEAT COMING FROM?

THE JUICE!

(SOME OF THE HEAT ALSO COMES FROM YOUR HANDS, THE TOWEL, AND THE AIR AROUND THE ICE.)

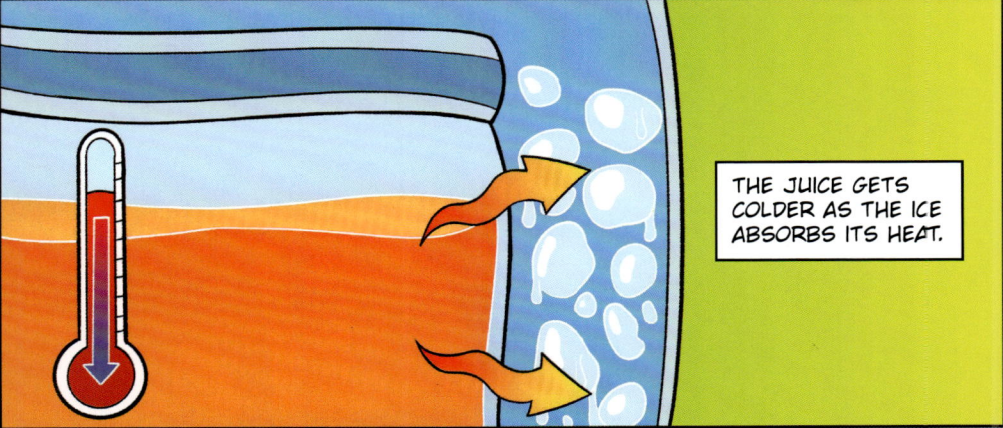

THE JUICE GETS COLDER AS THE ICE ABSORBS ITS HEAT.

WHEN YOU ADD SALT TO THE ICE, IT MELTS AT A TEMPERATURE LOWER THAN 32°F.

THAT MEANS THE MELTY SALTWATER MIX IS COLDER THAN REGULAR ICE WATER WOULD BE.

THIS SALTWATER MIX IS SO COLD, HEAT LEAVES THE JUICE, WHICH FREEZES INTO SORBET!

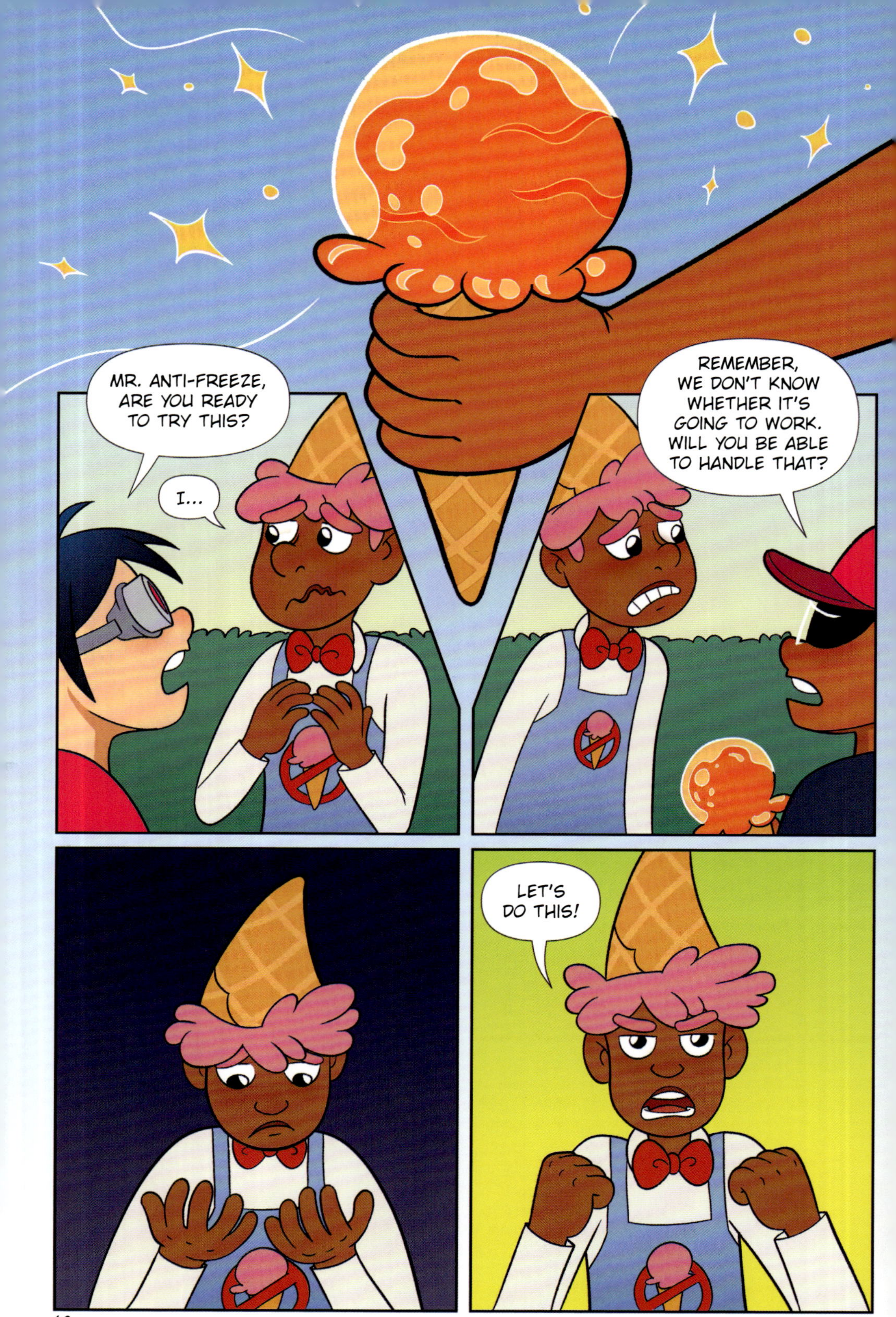
MR. ANTI-FREEZE, ARE YOU READY TO TRY THIS?
I...
REMEMBER, WE DON'T KNOW WHETHER IT'S GOING TO WORK. WILL YOU BE ABLE TO HANDLE THAT?
LET'S DO THIS!

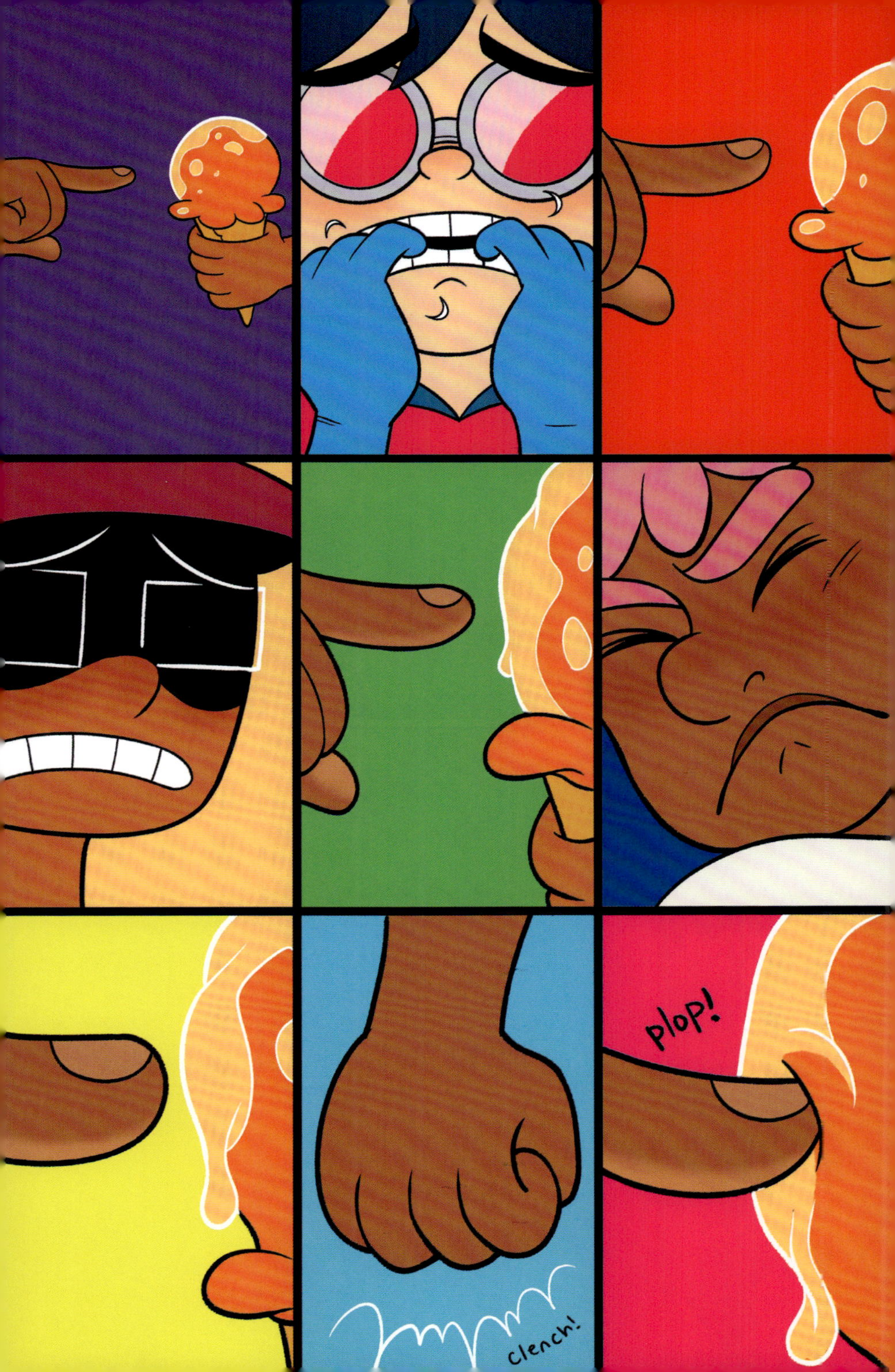
Clench!
plop!

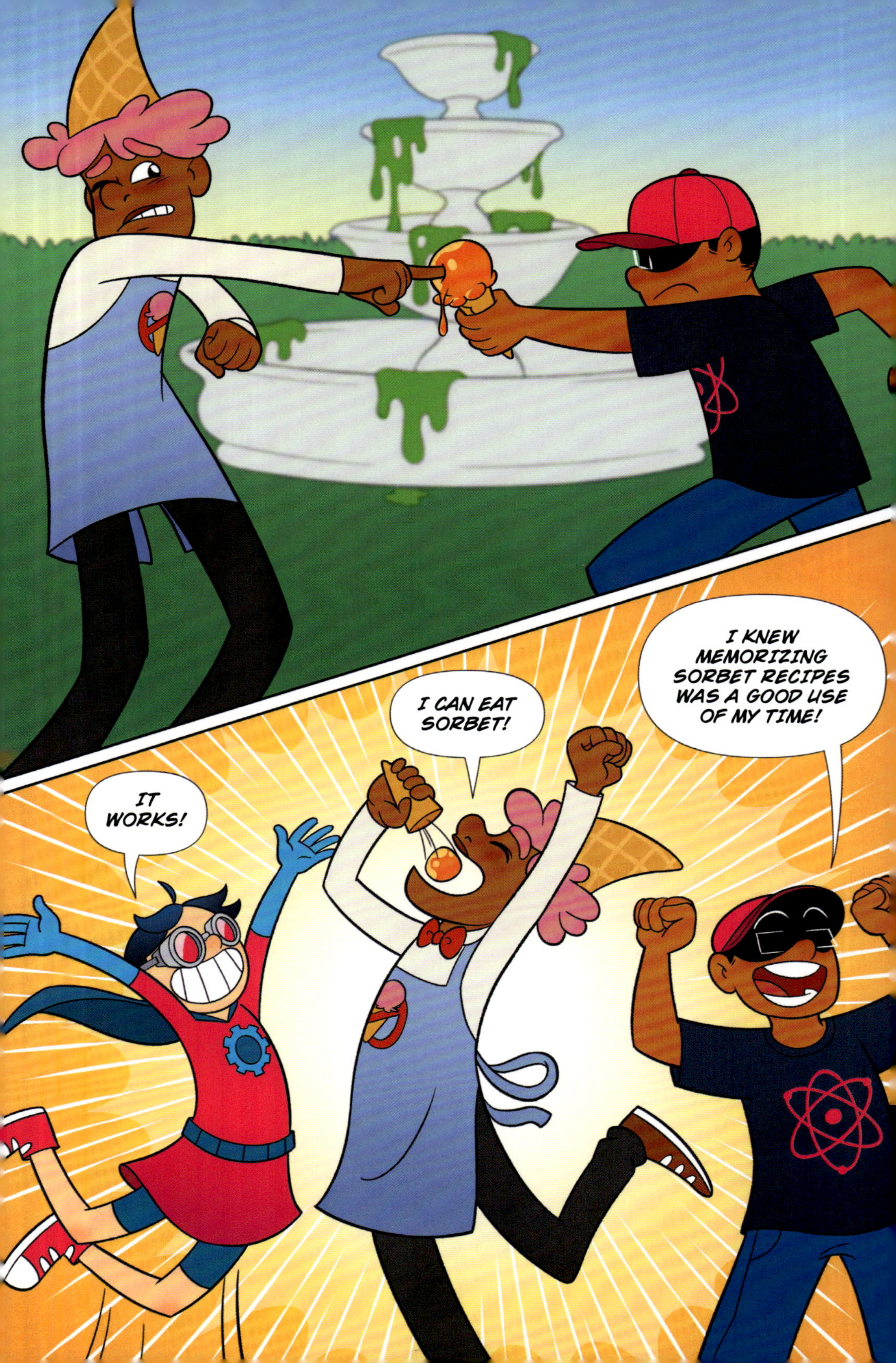
IT WORKS!
I CAN EAT SORBET!
I KNEW MEMORIZING SORBET RECIPES WAS A GOOD USE OF MY TIME!

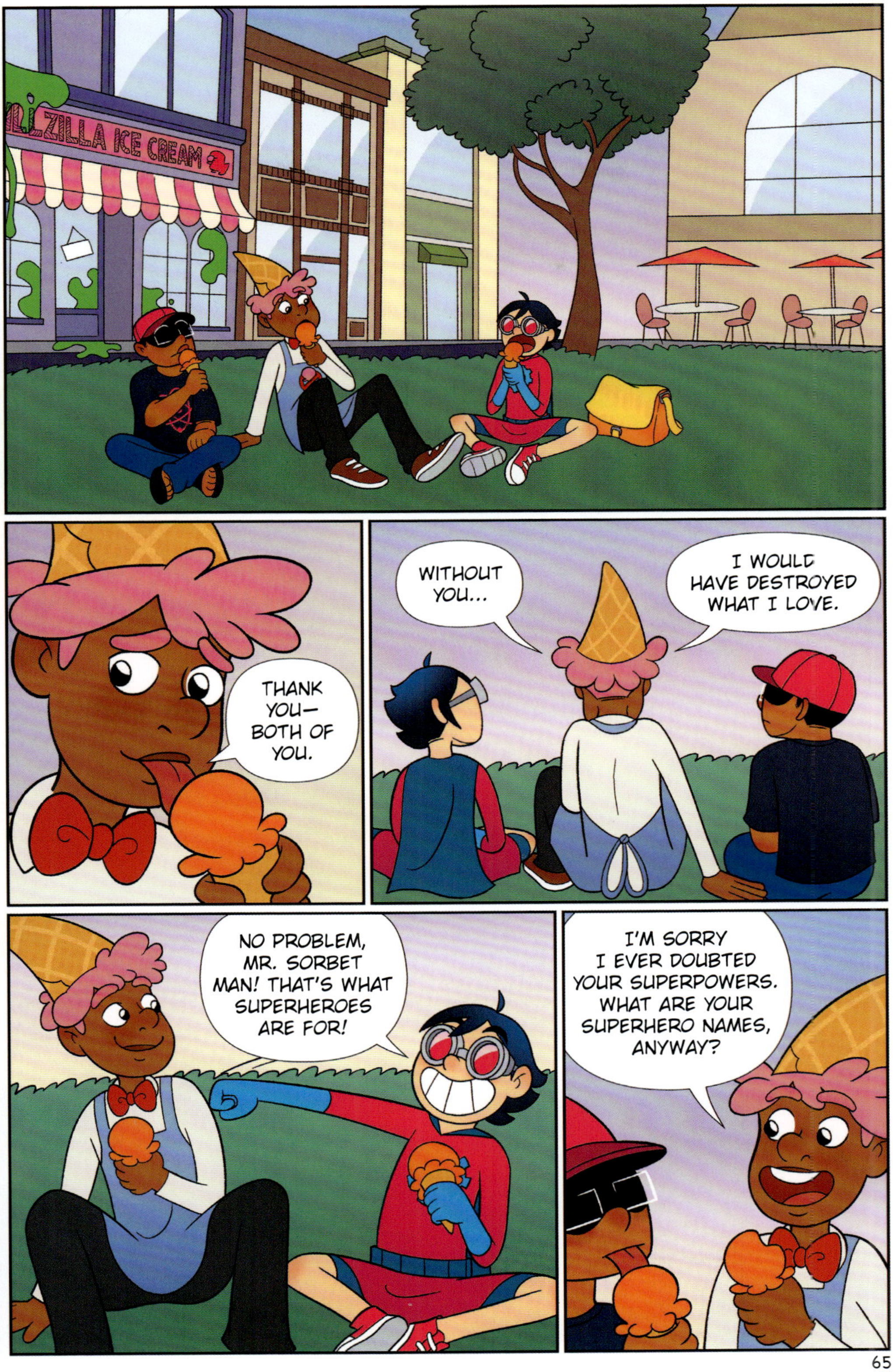
ZILLA ICE CREAM
THANK YOU— BOTH OF YOU.
WITHOUT YOU...
I WOULD HAVE DESTROYED WHAT I LOVE.
NO PROBLEM, MR. SORBET MAN! THAT'S WHAT SUPERHEROES ARE FOR!
I'M SORRY I EVER DOUBTED YOUR SUPERPOWERS. WHAT ARE YOUR SUPERHERO NAMES, ANYWAY?

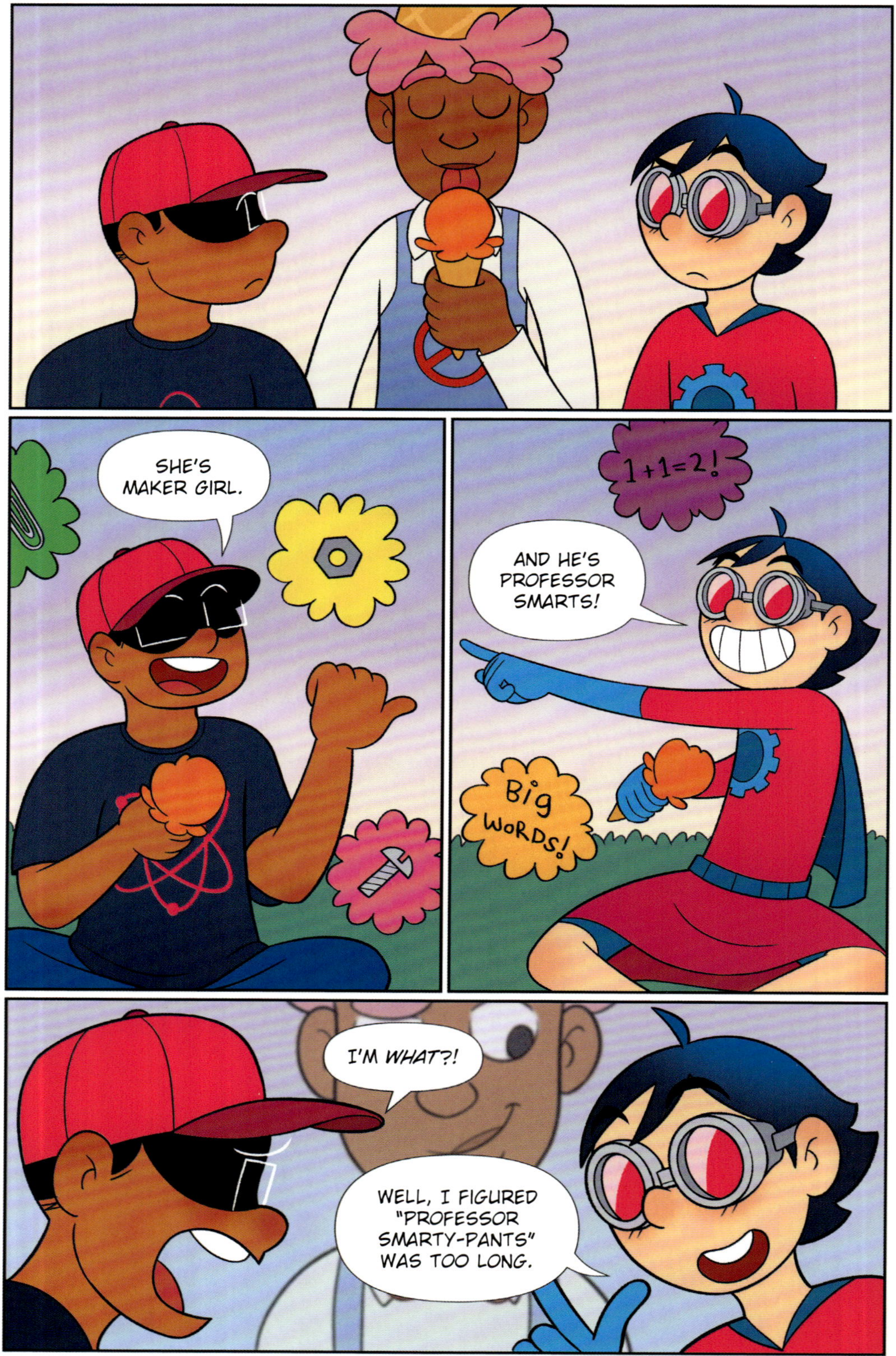
SHE'S MAKER GIRL.
AND HE'S PROFESSOR SMARTS!
1+1=2!
Big WORDS!
I'M WHAT?!
WELL, I FIGURED "PROFESSOR SMARTY-PANTS" WAS TOO LONG.

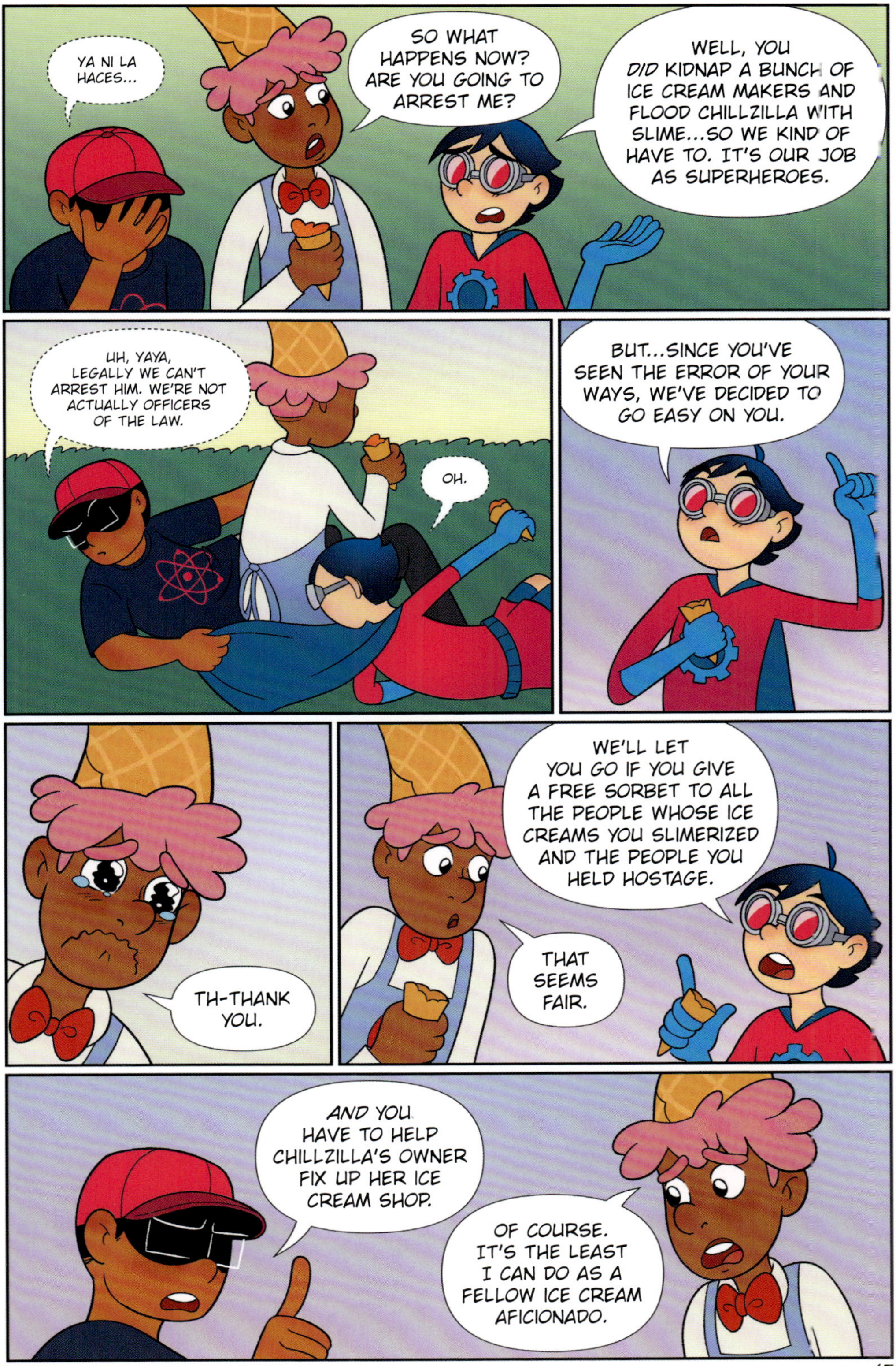
YA NI LA HACES...
SO WHAT HAPPENS NOW? ARE YOU GOING TO ARREST ME?
WELL, YOU *DID* KIDNAP A BUNCH OF ICE CREAM MAKERS AND FLOOD CHILLZILLA WITH SLIME...SO WE KIND OF HAVE TO. IT'S OUR JOB AS SUPERHEROES.
UH, YAYA, LEGALLY WE CAN'T ARREST HIM. WE'RE NOT ACTUALLY OFFICERS OF THE LAW.
OH.
BUT...SINCE YOU'VE SEEN THE ERROR OF YOUR WAYS, WE'VE DECIDED TO GO EASY ON YOU.
TH-THANK YOU.
WE'LL LET YOU GO IF YOU GIVE A FREE SORBET TO ALL THE PEOPLE WHOSE ICE CREAMS YOU SLIMERIZED AND THE PEOPLE YOU HELD HOSTAGE.
THAT SEEMS FAIR.
AND YOU HAVE TO HELP CHILLZILLA'S OWNER FIX UP HER ICE CREAM SHOP.
OF COURSE. IT'S THE LEAST I CAN DO AS A FELLOW ICE CREAM AFICIONADO.

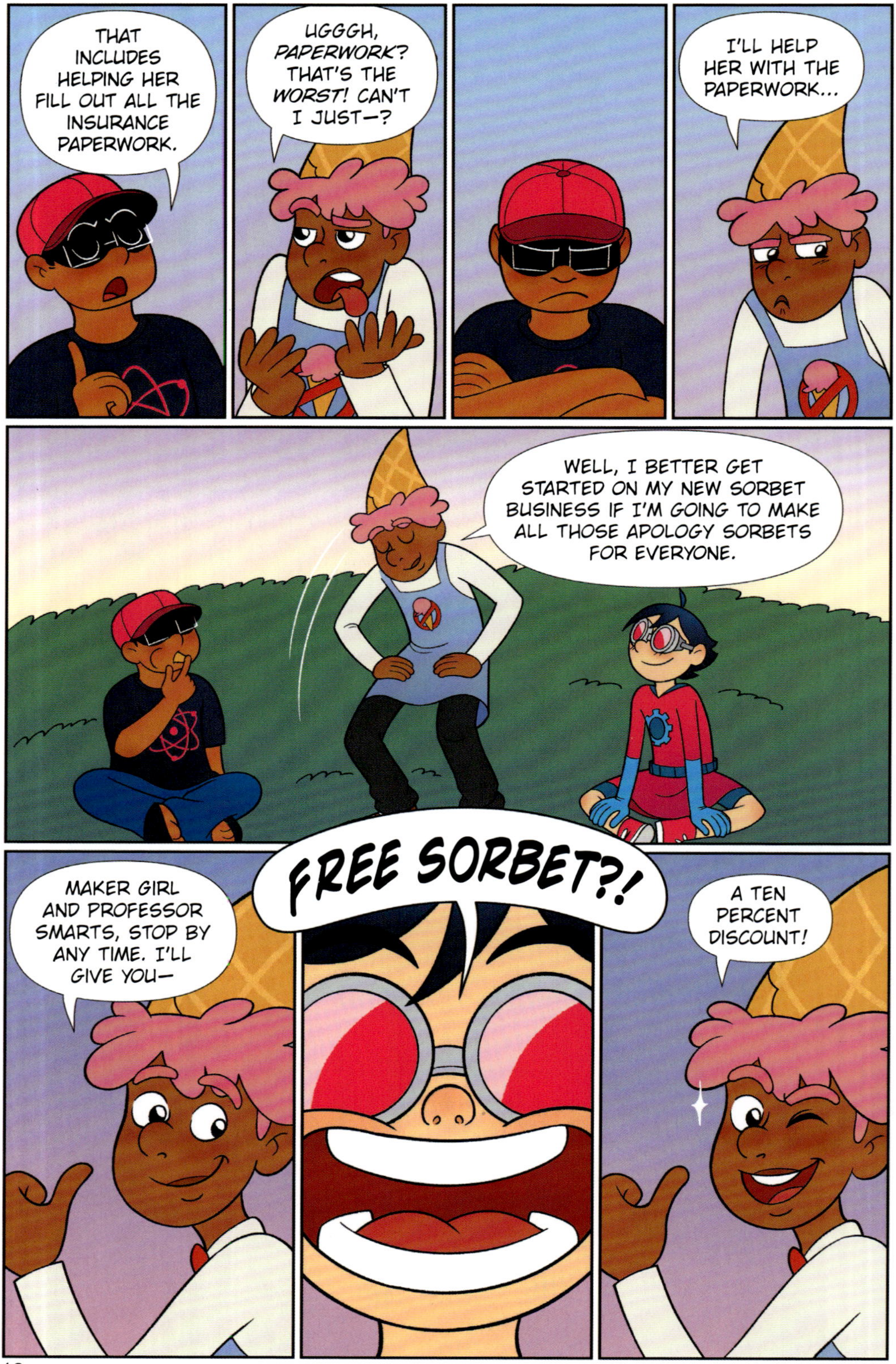
THAT INCLUDES HELPING HER FILL OUT ALL THE INSURANCE PAPERWORK.
UGGGH, *PAPERWORK?* THAT'S THE *WORST!* CAN'T I JUST—?
I'LL HELP HER WITH THE PAPERWORK...
WELL, I BETTER GET STARTED ON MY NEW SORBET BUSINESS IF I'M GOING TO MAKE ALL THOSE APOLOGY SORBETS FOR EVERYONE.
MAKER GIRL AND PROFESSOR SMARTS, STOP BY ANY TIME. I'LL GIVE YOU—
FREE SORBET?!
A TEN PERCENT DISCOUNT!

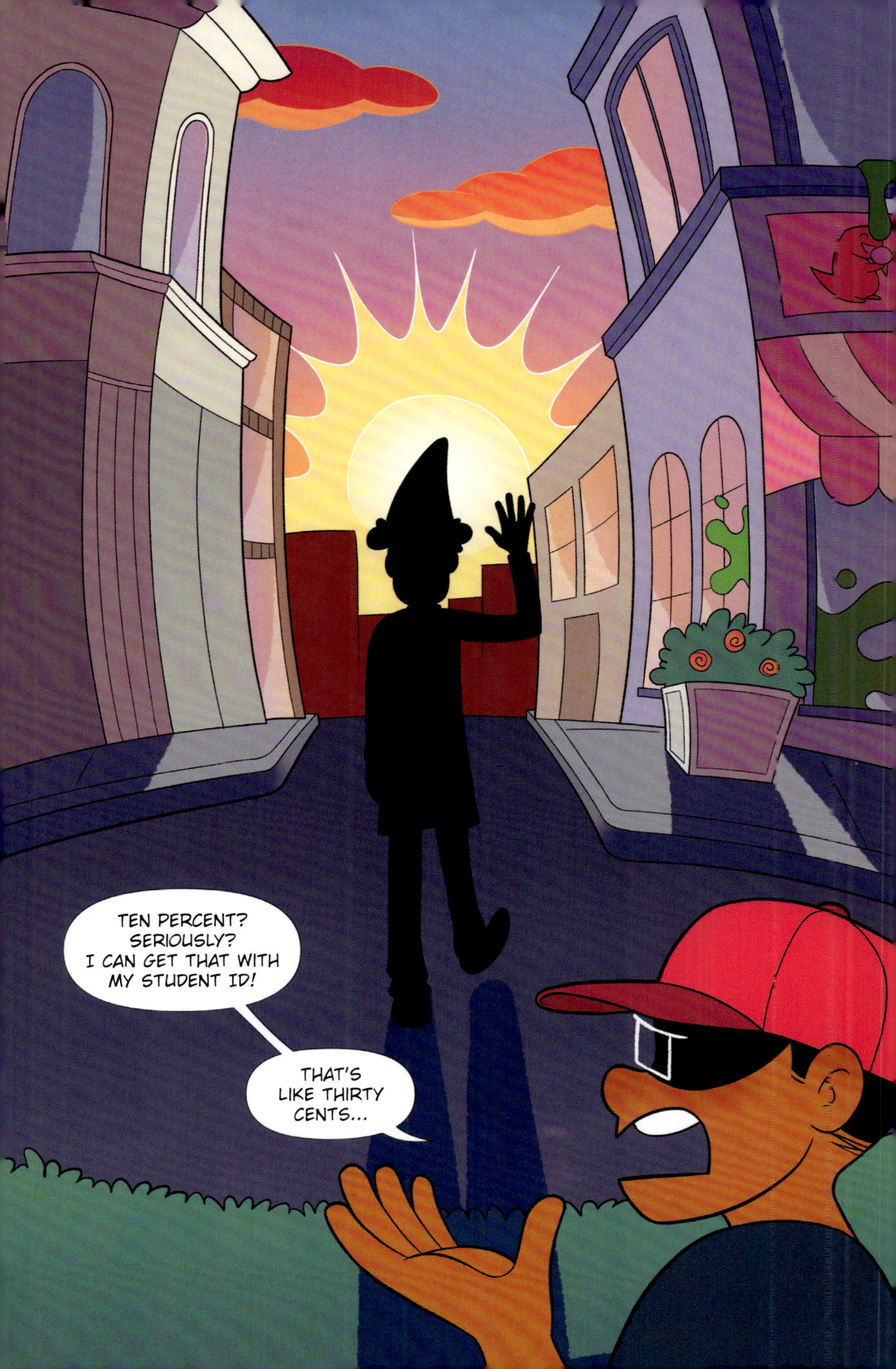
TEN PERCENT? SERIOUSLY? I CAN GET THAT WITH MY STUDENT ID!
THAT'S LIKE THIRTY CENTS...

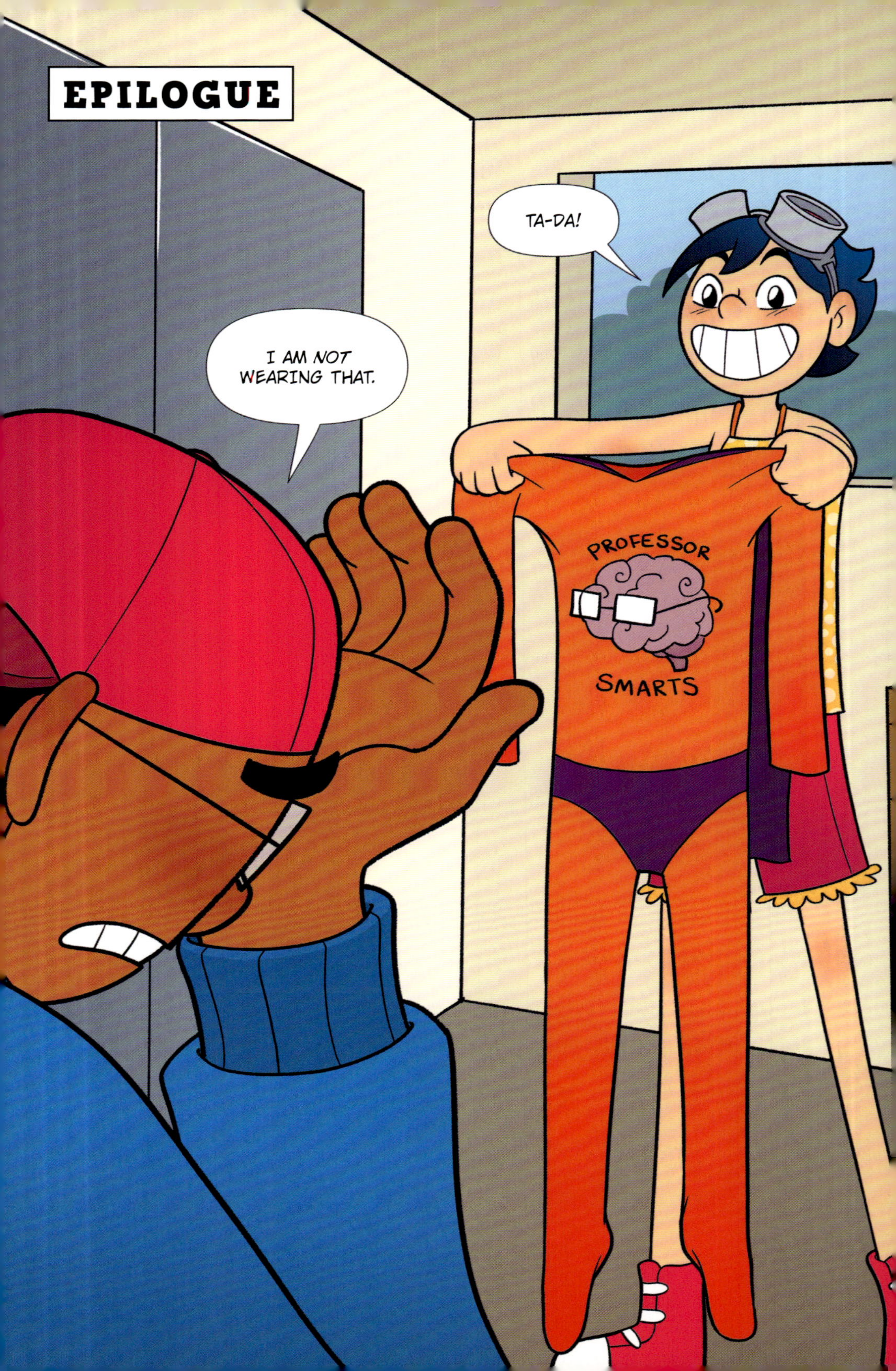
EPILOGUE
TA-DA!
I AM NOT WEARING THAT.
PROFESSOR SMARTS

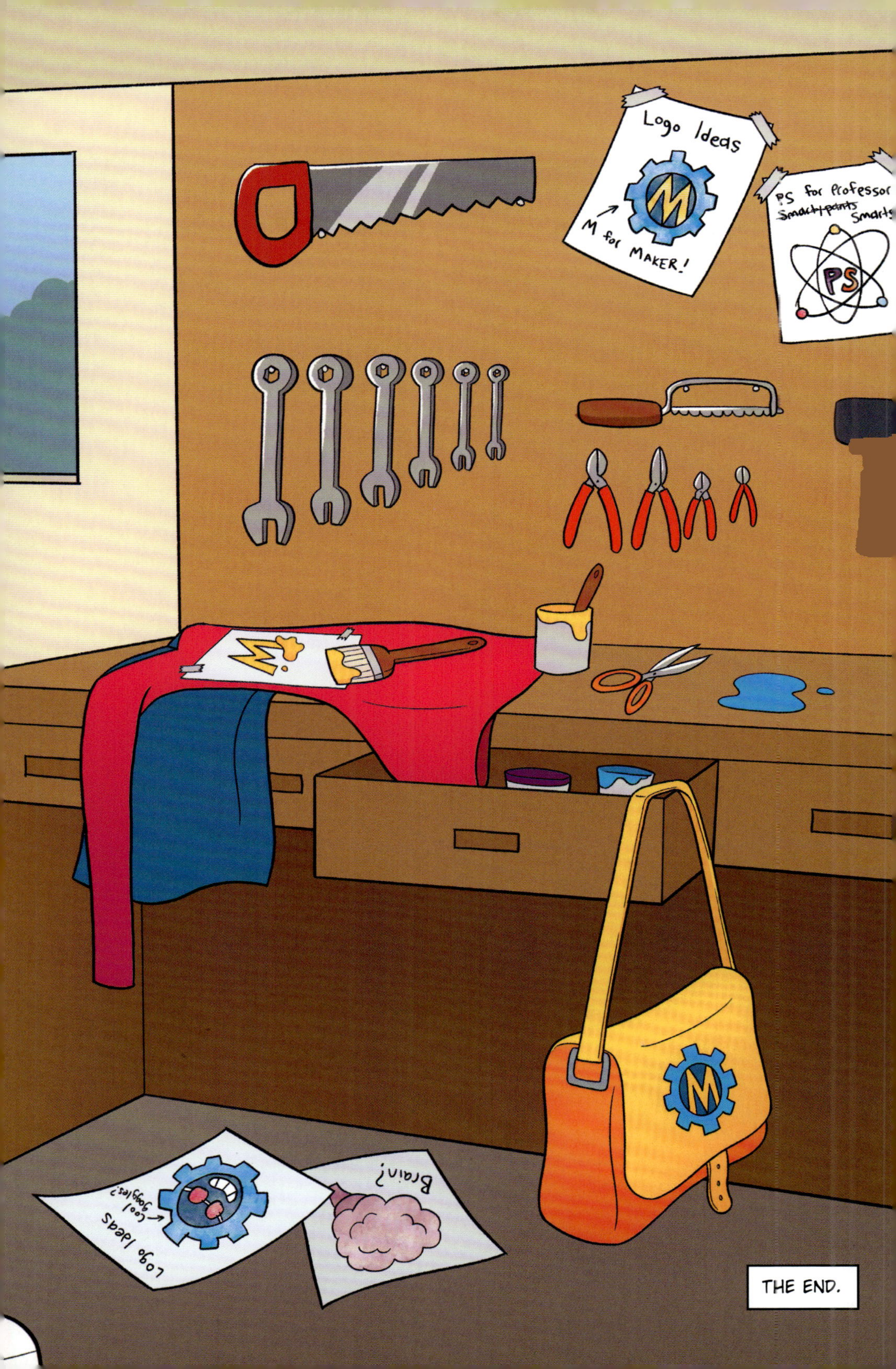
Logo Ideas
M for MAKER!
PS for Professor Smartypants Smarts
PS
Logo Ideas
Cool goggles?
Brain?
THE END.

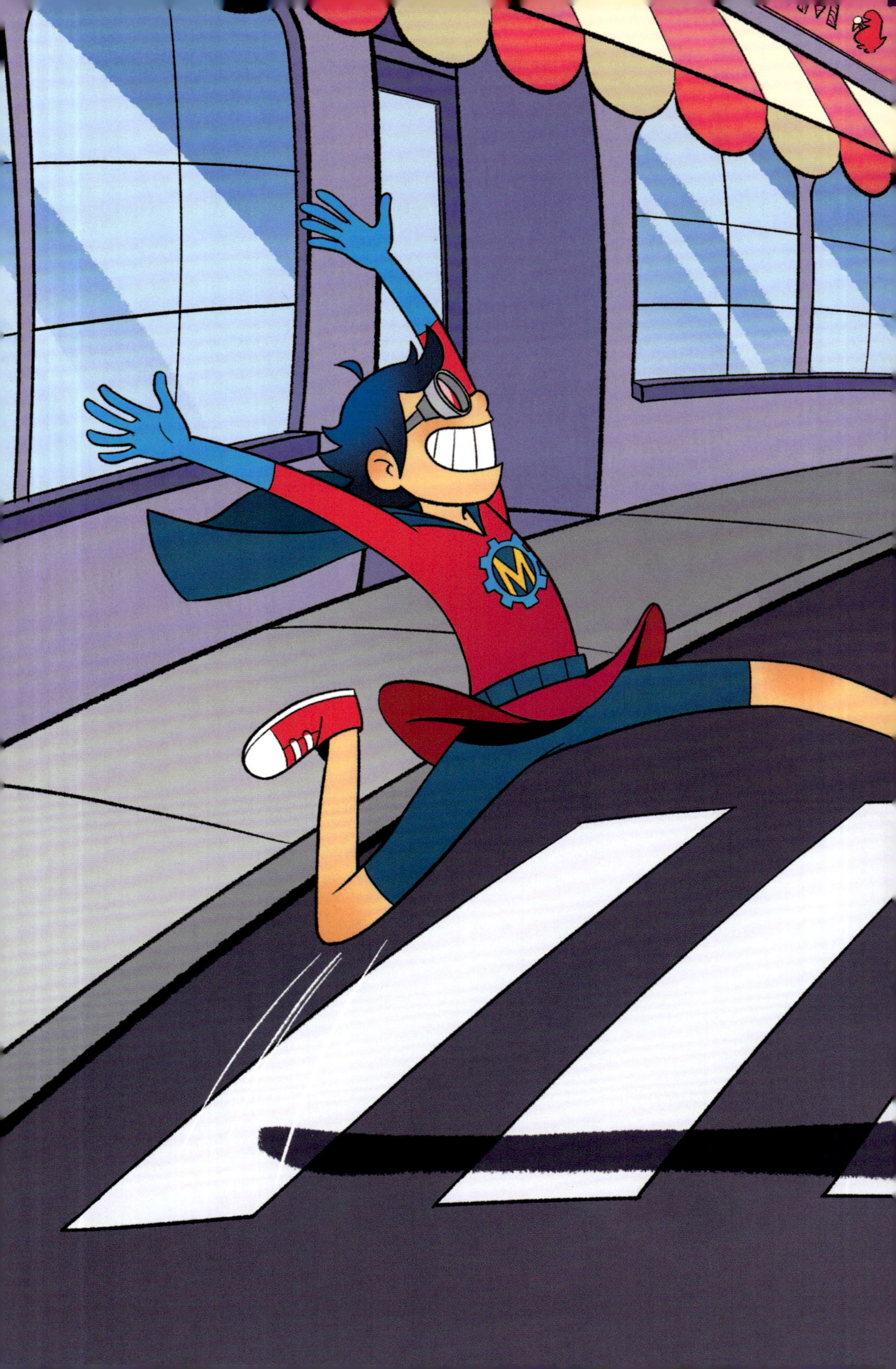

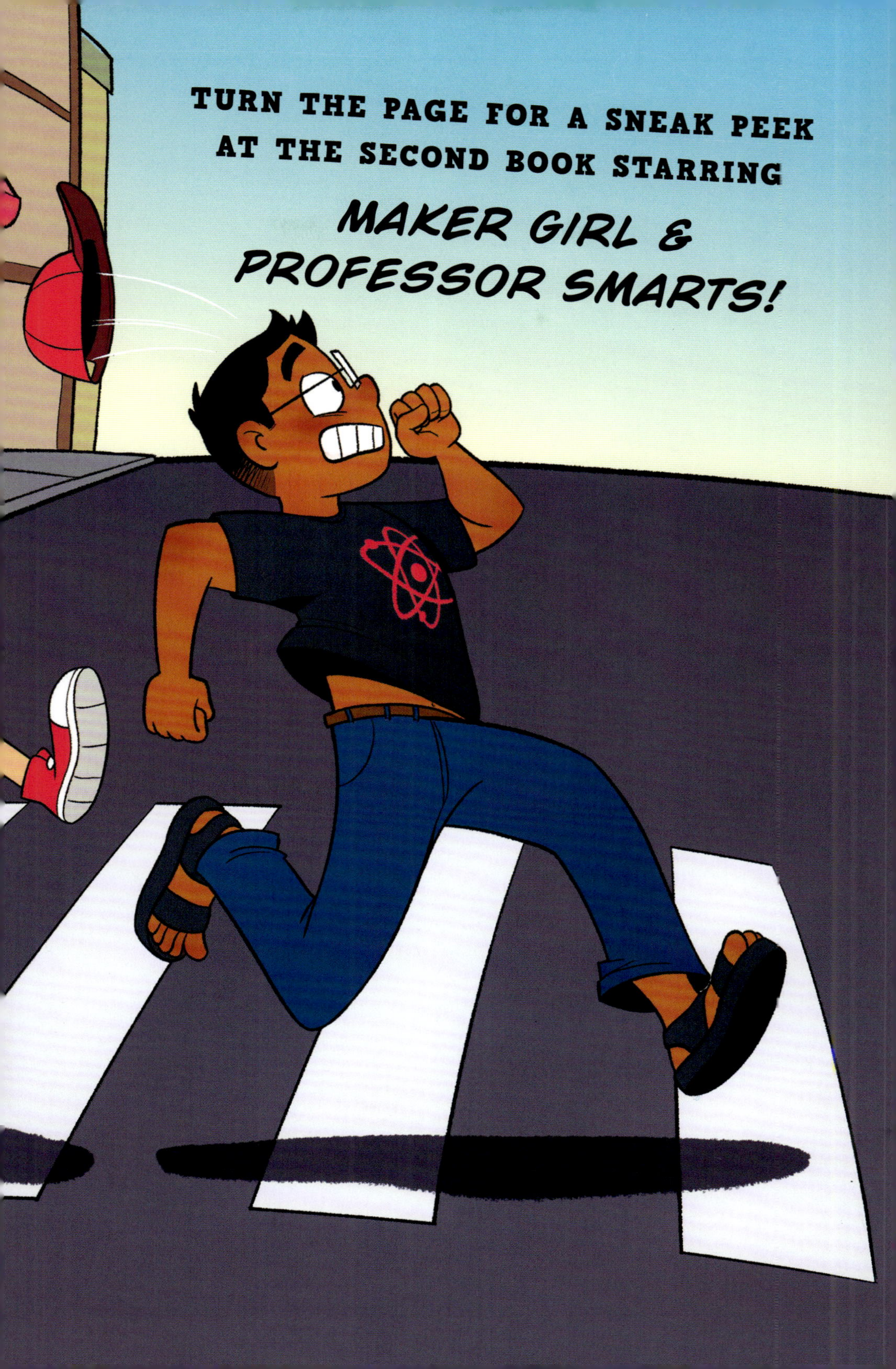
TURN THE PAGE FOR A SNEAK PEEK
AT THE SECOND BOOK STARRING
MAKER GIRL &
PROFESSOR SMARTS!

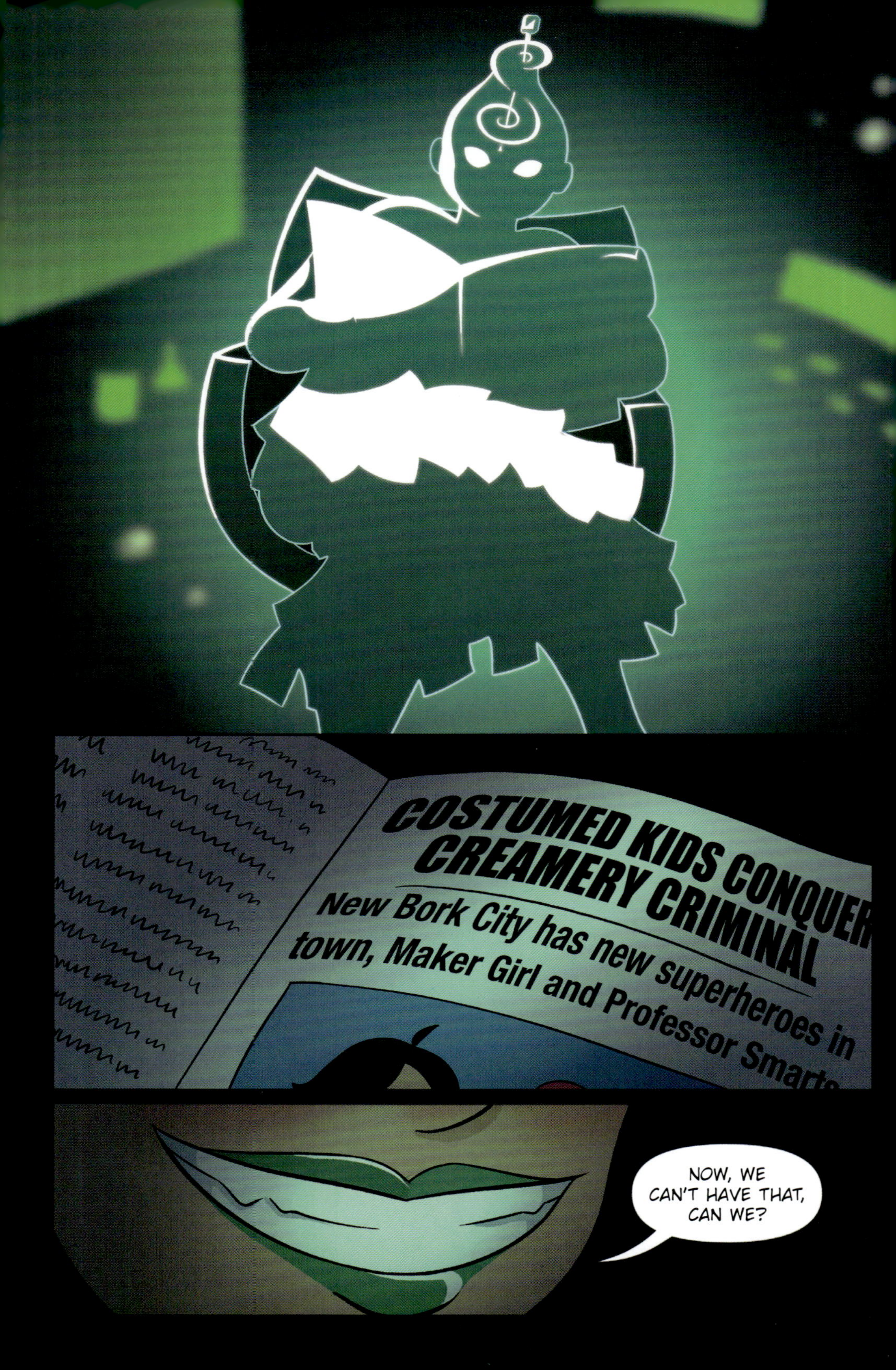
COSTUMED KIDS CONQUER CREAMERY CRIMINAL
New Bork City has new superheroes in town, Maker Girl and Professor Smart
NOW, WE CAN'T HAVE THAT, CAN WE?

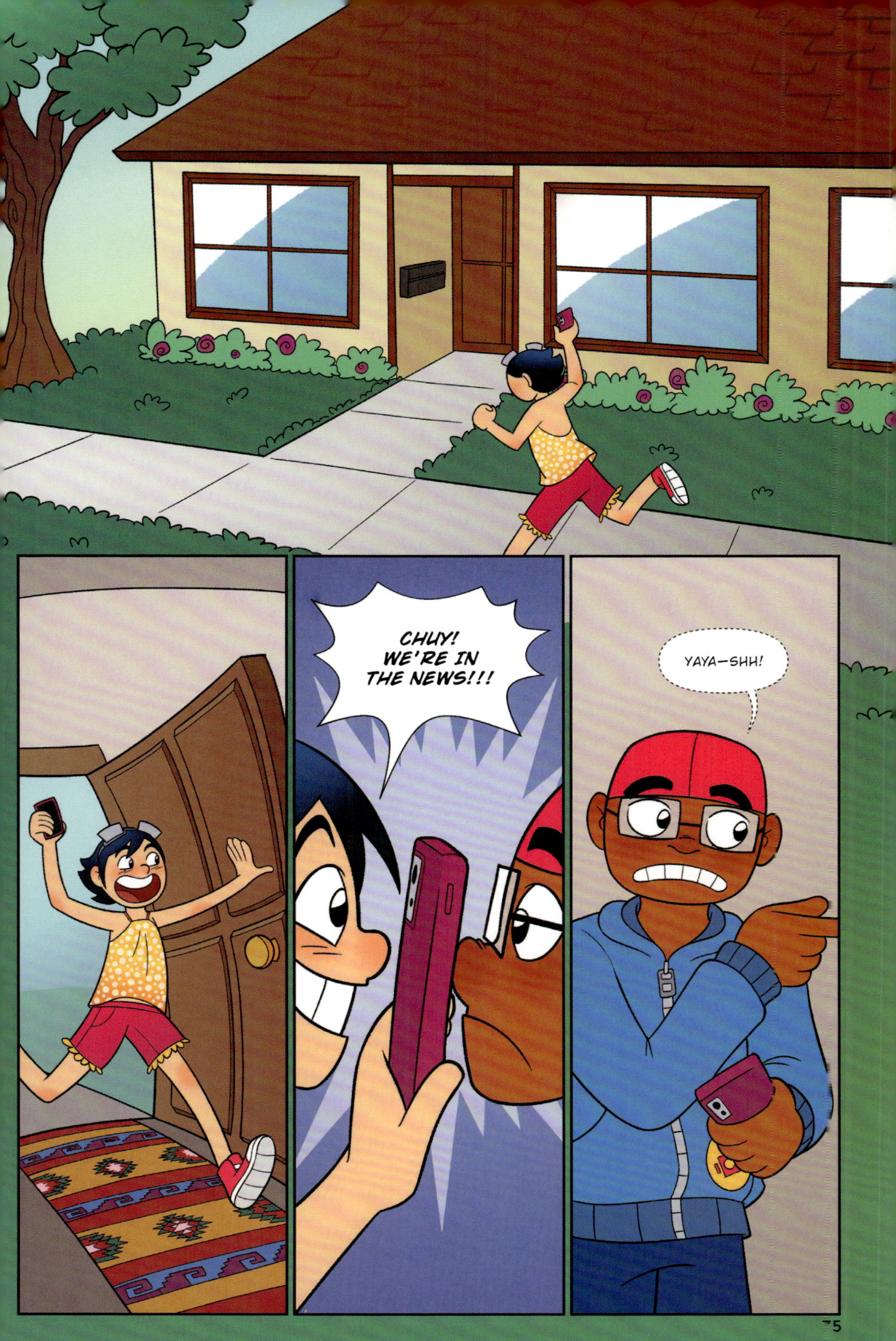
CHUY! WE'RE IN THE NEWS!!!
YAYA—SHH!

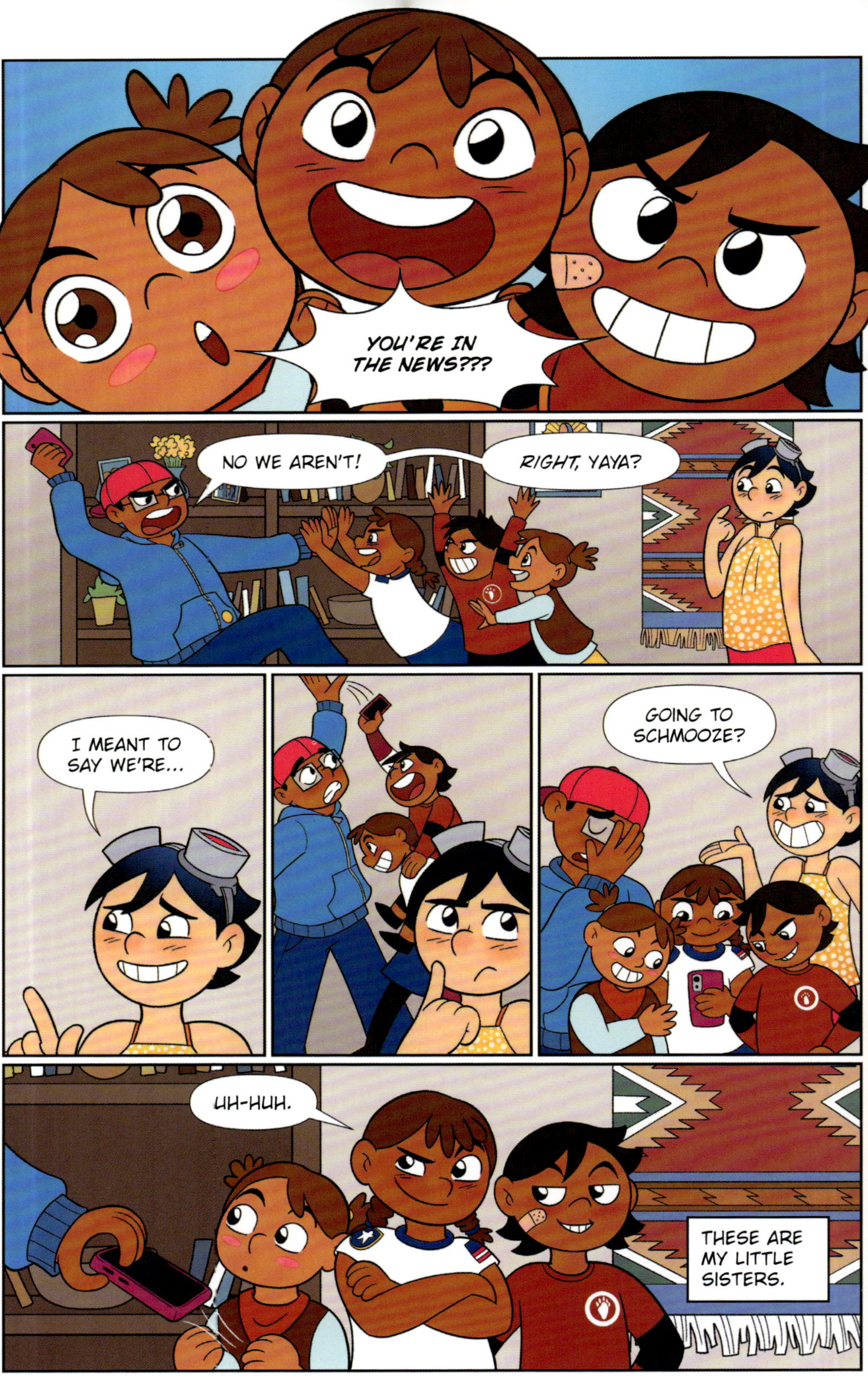
YOU'RE IN THE NEWS???
NO WE AREN'T!
RIGHT, YAYA?
I MEANT TO SAY WE'RE...
GOING TO SCHMOOZE?
UH-HUH.
THESE ARE MY LITTLE SISTERS.

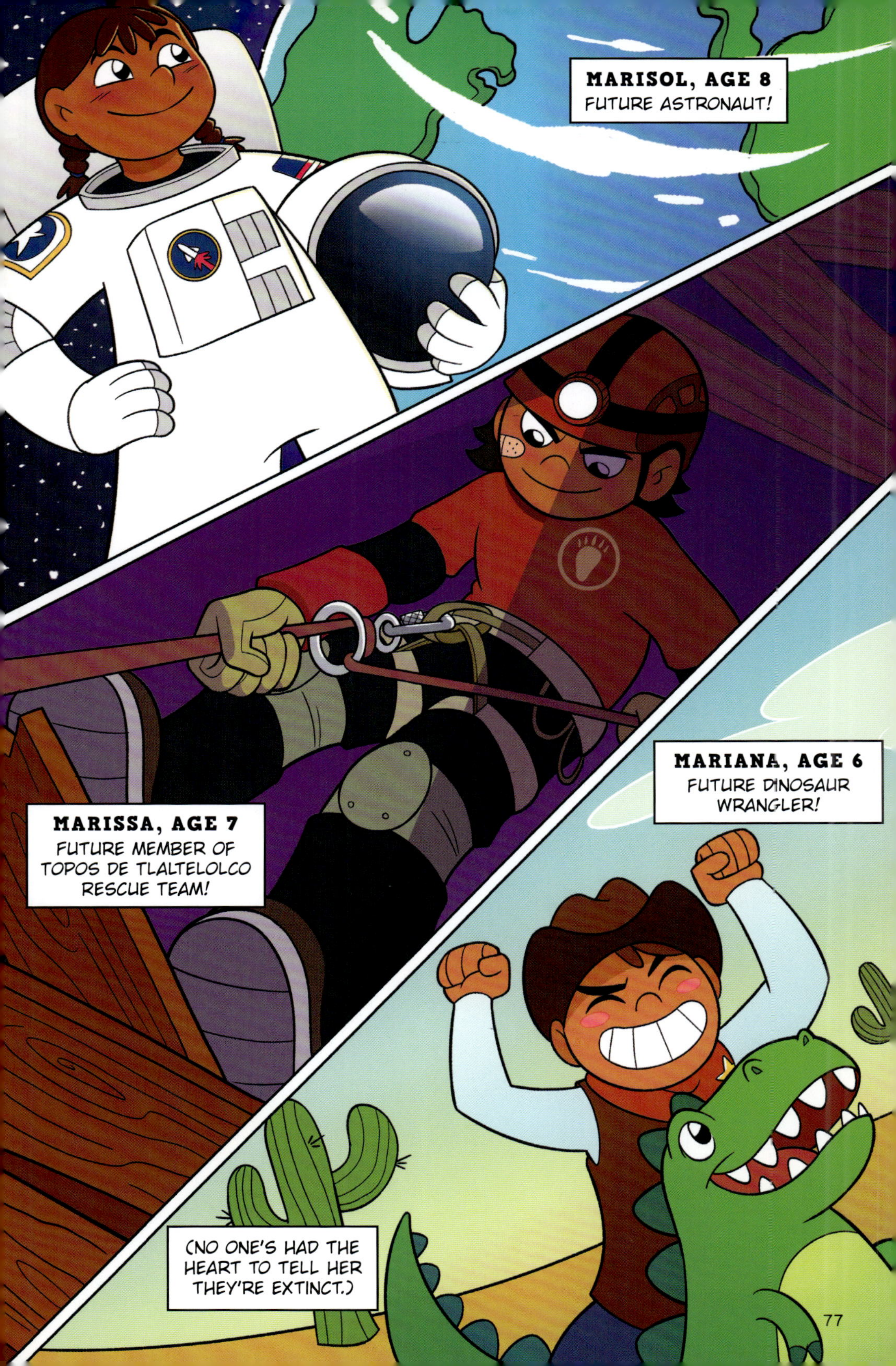
MARISOL, AGE 8
FUTURE ASTRONAUT!
MARISSA, AGE 7
FUTURE MEMBER OF TOPOS DE TLALTELOLCO RESCUE TEAM!
MARIANA, AGE 6
FUTURE DINOSAUR WRANGLER!
(NO ONE'S HAD THE HEART TO TELL HER THEY'RE EXTINCT.)

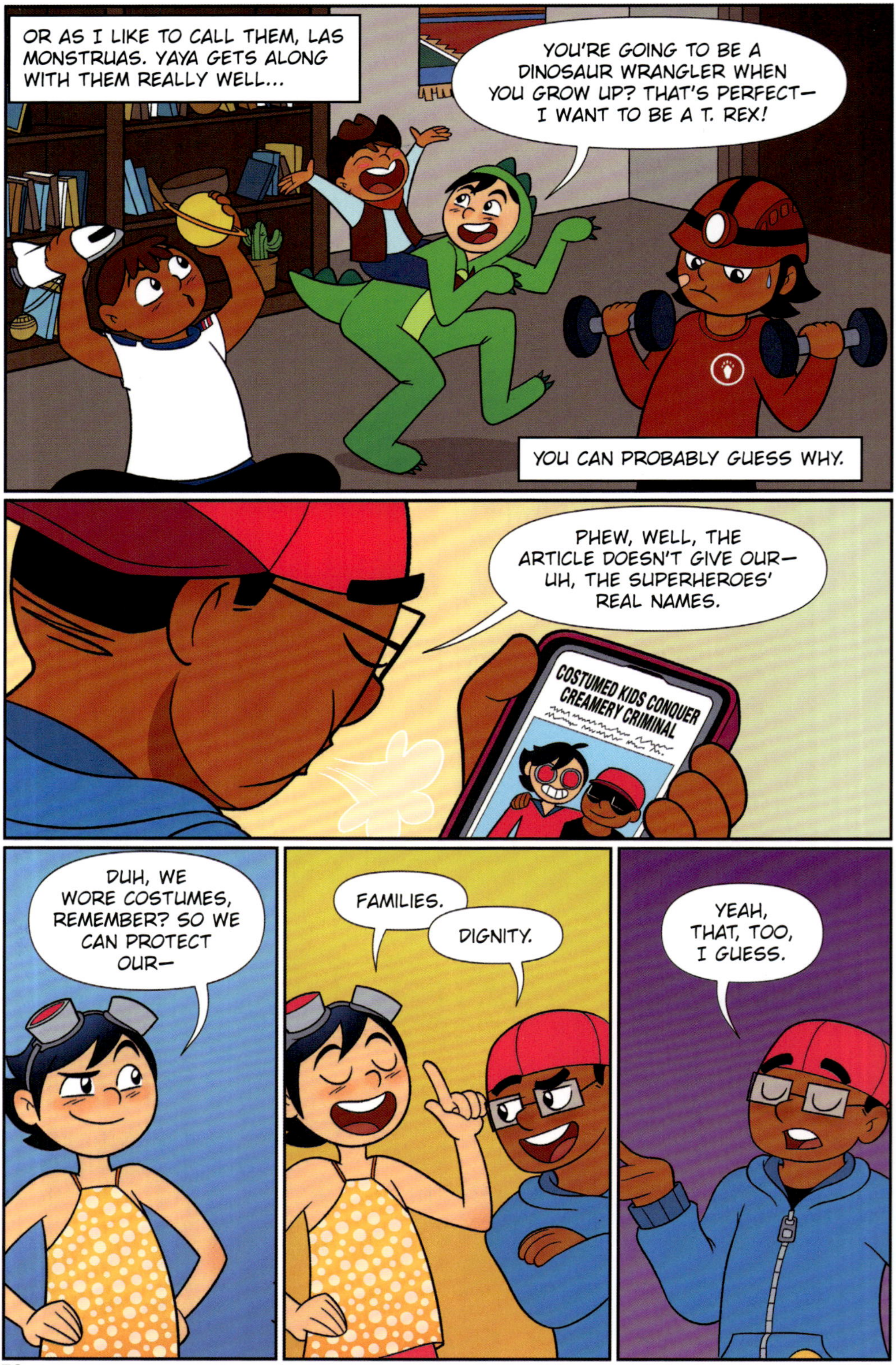
OR AS I LIKE TO CALL THEM, LAS MONSTRUAS. YAYA GETS ALONG WITH THEM REALLY WELL...
YOU'RE GOING TO BE A DINOSAUR WRANGLER WHEN YOU GROW UP? THAT'S PERFECT— I WANT TO BE A T. REX!
YOU CAN PROBABLY GUESS WHY.
PHEW, WELL, THE ARTICLE DOESN'T GIVE OUR— UH, THE SUPERHEROES' REAL NAMES.
COSTUMED KIDS CONQUER CREAMERY CRIMINAL
DUH, WE WORE COSTUMES, REMEMBER? SO WE CAN PROTECT OUR—
FAMILIES.
DIGNITY.
YEAH, THAT, TOO, I GUESS.

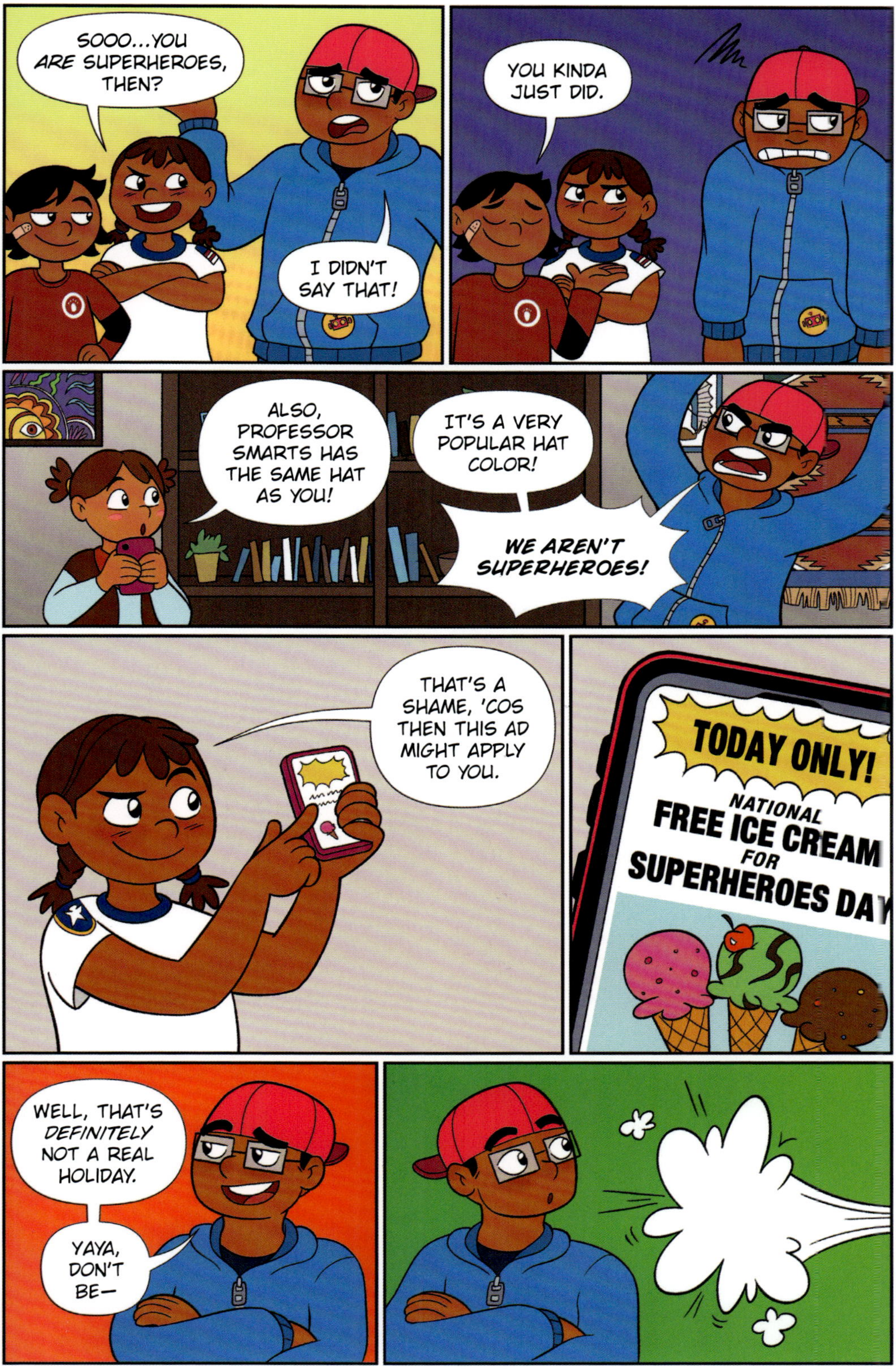
SOOO...YOU *ARE* SUPERHEROES, THEN?
I DIDN'T SAY THAT!
YOU KINDA JUST DID.
ALSO, PROFESSOR SMARTS HAS THE SAME HAT AS YOU!
IT'S A VERY POPULAR HAT COLOR!
WE AREN'T SUPERHEROES!
THAT'S A SHAME, 'COS THEN THIS AD MIGHT APPLY TO YOU.
TODAY ONLY!
NATIONAL
FREE ICE CREAM
FOR
SUPERHEROES DAY
WELL, THAT'S *DEFINITELY* NOT A REAL HOLIDAY.
YAYA, DON'T BE—

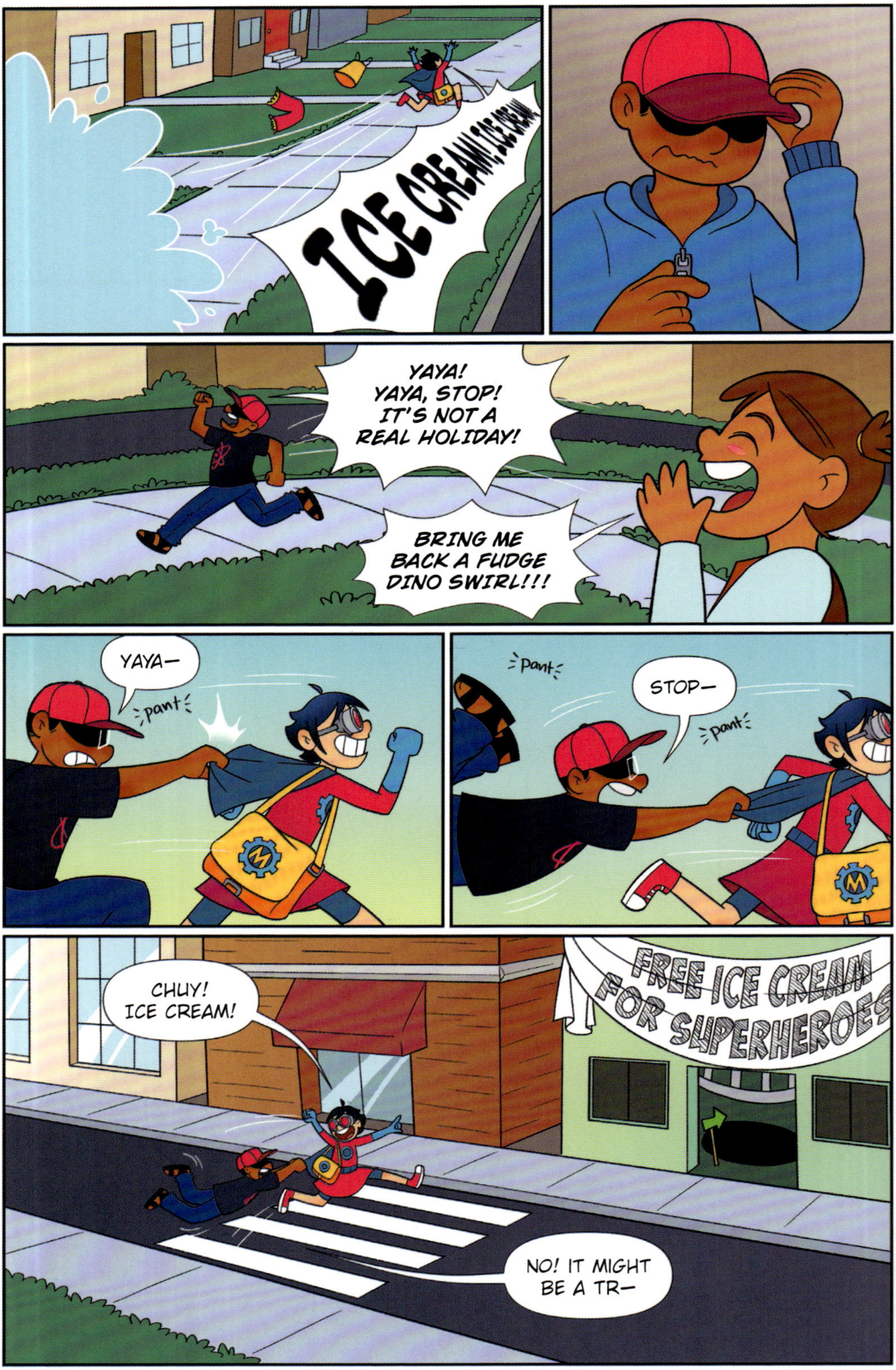
ICE CREAM! ICE CREAM!
YAYA! YAYA, STOP! IT'S NOT A REAL HOLIDAY!
BRING ME BACK A FUDGE DINO SWIRL!!!
YAYA—
pant
STOP—
pant
pant
CHUY! ICE CREAM!
FREE ICE CREAM FOR SUPERHEROES
NO! IT MIGHT BE A TR—

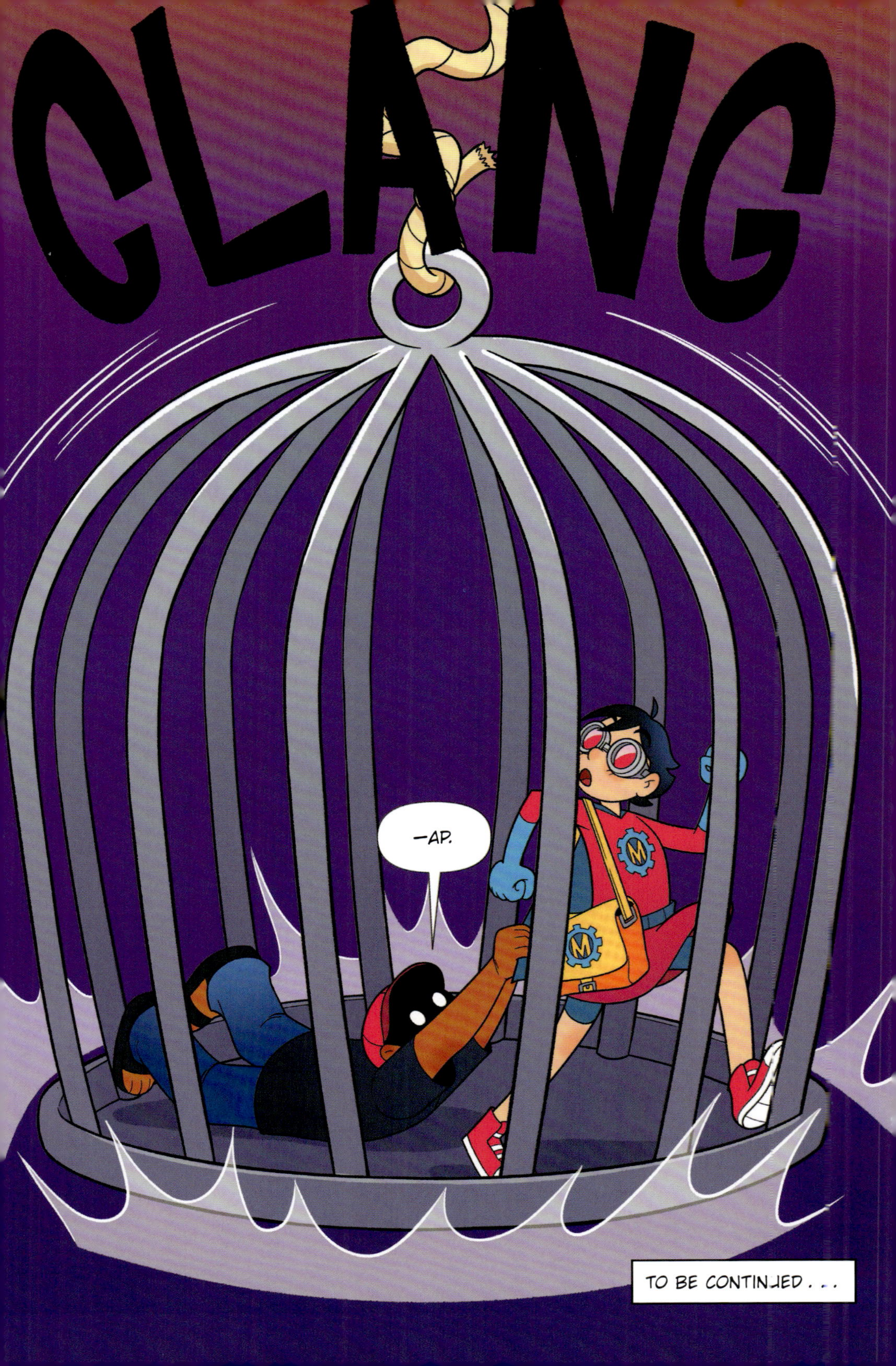
CLANG
—AP.
TO BE CONTINUED . . .

MEET YAYA!

SUPERHERO NAME: MAKER GIRL

REAL NAME: YAEL LEVY

AGE: 12

SUPERPOWER: MAKING STUFF!

FAVORITE FOOD: ICE CREAM

FAVORITE COLOR: ANYTHING BRIGHT

HOBBIES: MAKING STUFF, OBVIOUSLY

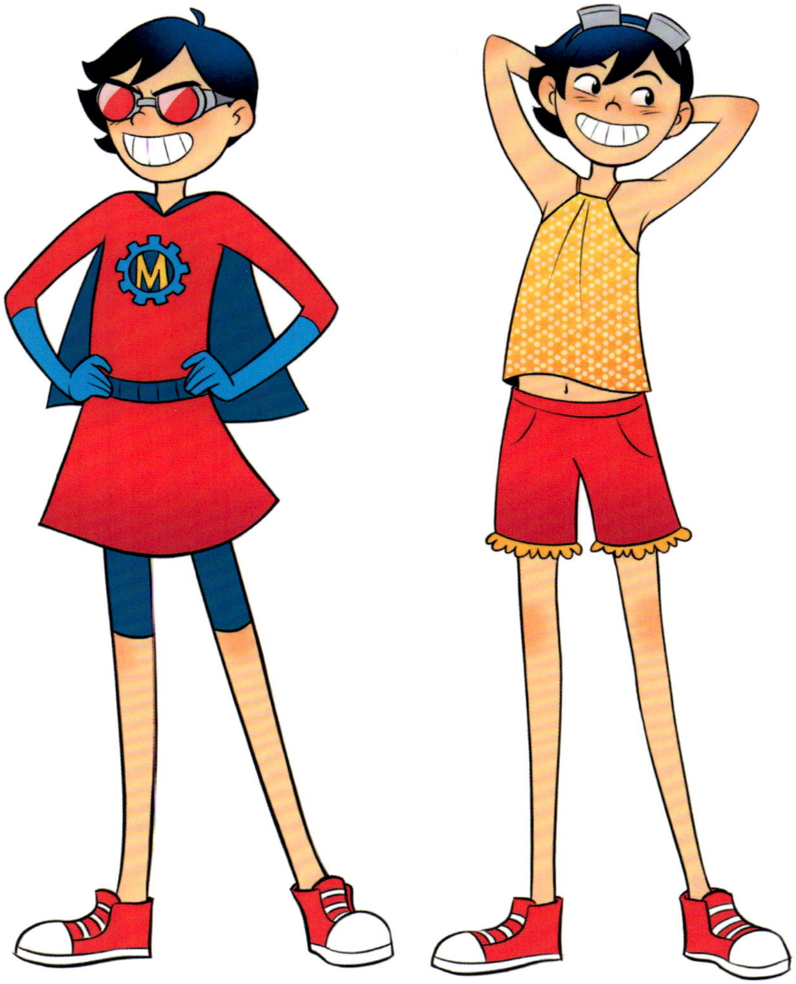
M

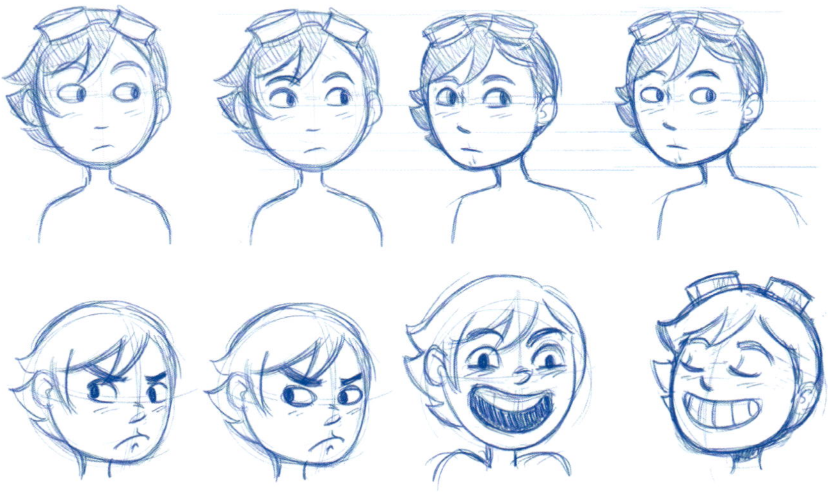

EARLY SKETCHES OF YAYA EXPERIMENTED WITH DIFFERENT EYE SHAPES.

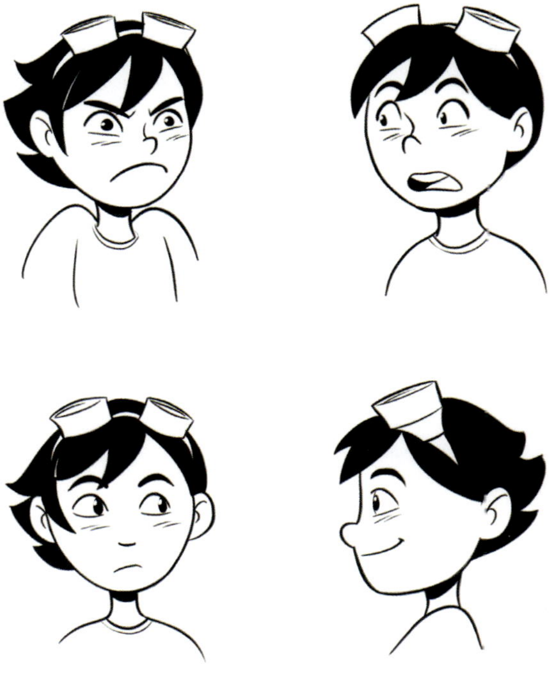

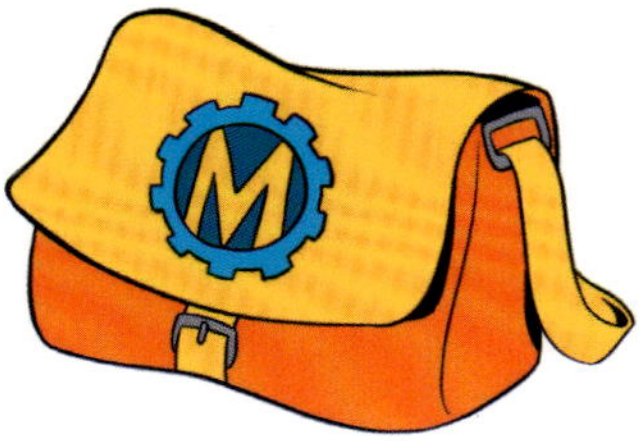

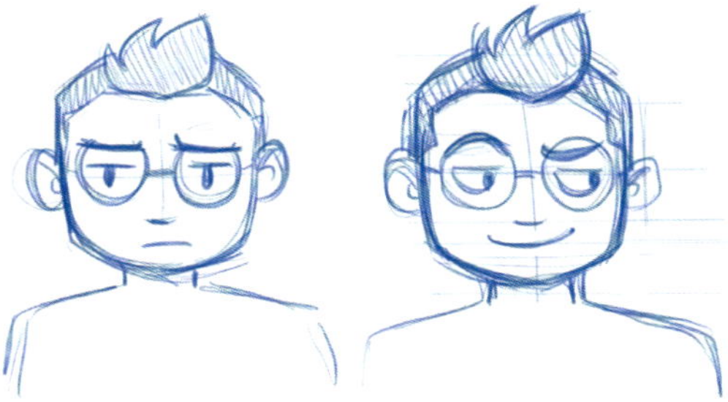

IN THE EARLY SKETCHES OF CHUY, HIS HEAD WAS LESS SQUARE, BUT THE SQUARE HEAD MADE FOR BETTER CONTRAST WITH YAYA'S ROUND HEAD.

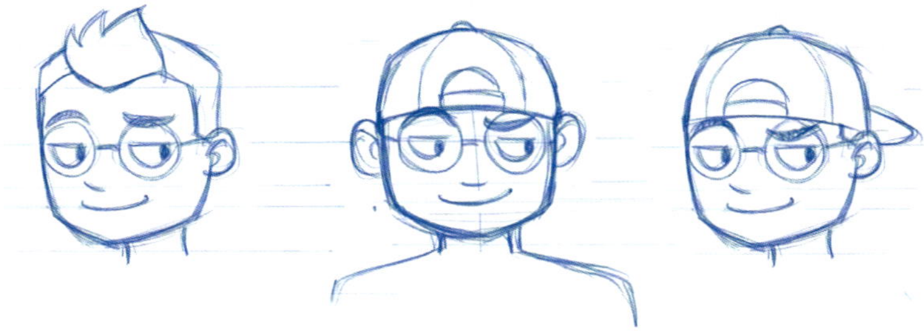

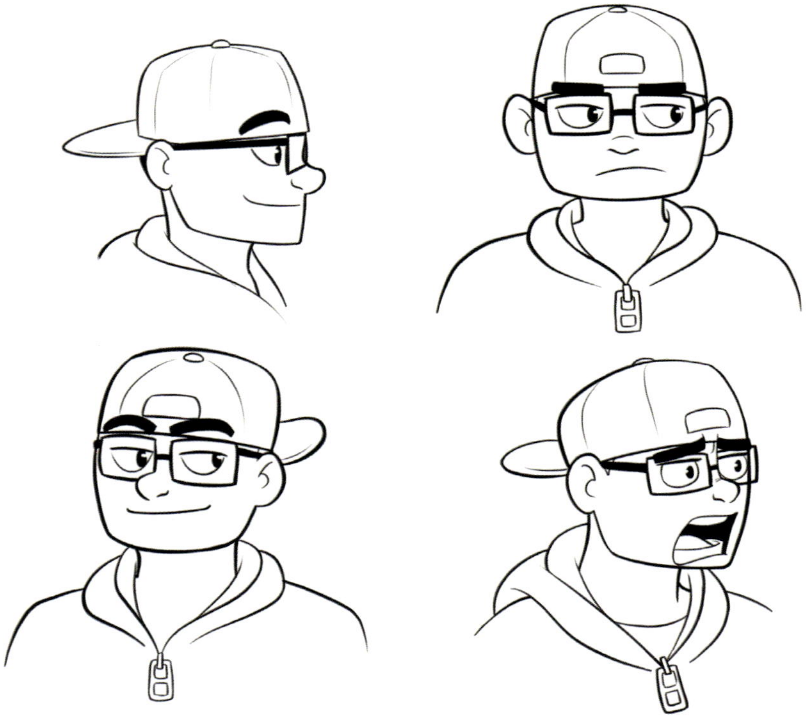

MEET CHUY!

SUPERHERO NAME: PROFESSOR SMARTS

REAL NAME: JESÚS REYES

AGE: 12

SUPERPOWER: KNOWING STUFF!

HOBBIES: MEMORIZING TEXTBOOKS, WINNING ALL THE COMPETITIONS

PET PEEVES: BEING WRONG, SUPERPOWERS THAT BREAK THE LAWS OF PHYSICS, UNNECESSARILY EXTRAVAGANT ICE CREAM FLAVORS

WANT TO MAKE STUFF OR KNOW STUFF? HERE ARE SOME AMAZING FREE RESOURCES!

INSTRUCTABLES
https://www.instructables.com

Here you'll find people who love to make stuff! Their website has step-by-step instructions for everything from interactive cakes to fully functioning paper robots.

MAKE: COMMUNITY
https://make.co

This association is responsible for tons of maker resources, including an online maker camp, a project library, and in-person maker faires! They also publish a magazine series and instructional books.

THE EXPLORATORIUM'S TINKERING STUDIO
https://www.exploratorium.edu/tinkering

This studio is based inside San Francisco's famous science museum. Their website includes projects and activities that showcase their playful approach to combining art, science, and technology.

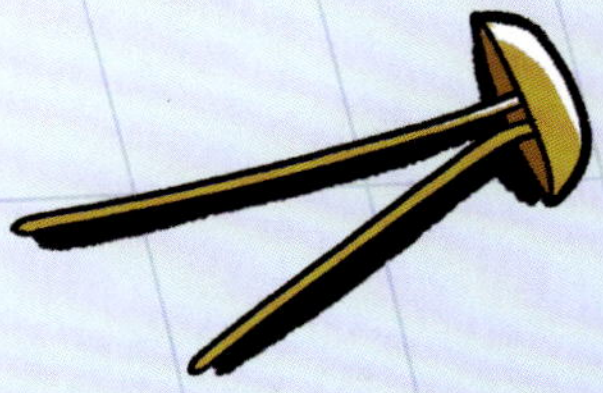

NATIONAL GEOGRAPHIC KIDS

https://kids.nationalgeographic.com

THIS WEBSITE HAS INFORMATION ON EVERYTHING FROM MUMMIES TO MARS—PERFECT FOR PEOPLE WHO WANT TO KNOW STUFF!

OLOGY

https://www.amnh.org/explore/ology

THIS SCIENCE WEBSITE FROM THE AMERICAN MUSEUM OF NATURAL HISTORY COVERS TOPICS FROM A VARIETY OF DIFFERENT "-OLOGIES" (LIKE BIOLOGY AND PALEONTOLOGY) AS WELL AS FIELDS OF STUDY THAT DON'T END WITH "OLOGY" (LIKE ASTRONOMY AND PHYSICS)!

NASA

https://www.nasa.gov/learning-resources/for-kids-and-students

WHO DOESN'T LOVE SPACE? NASA'S WEBSITE HAS GAMES, VIDEOS, AND ACTIVITIES WHERE YOU CAN LEARN NOT JUST ABOUT SPACE BUT ABOUT OUR HOME PLANET AS WELL!

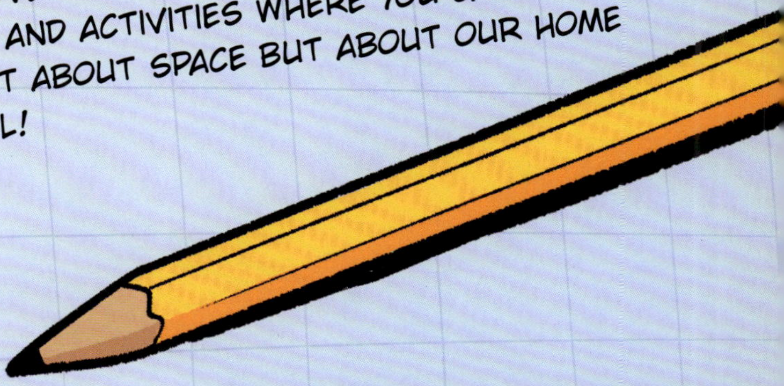

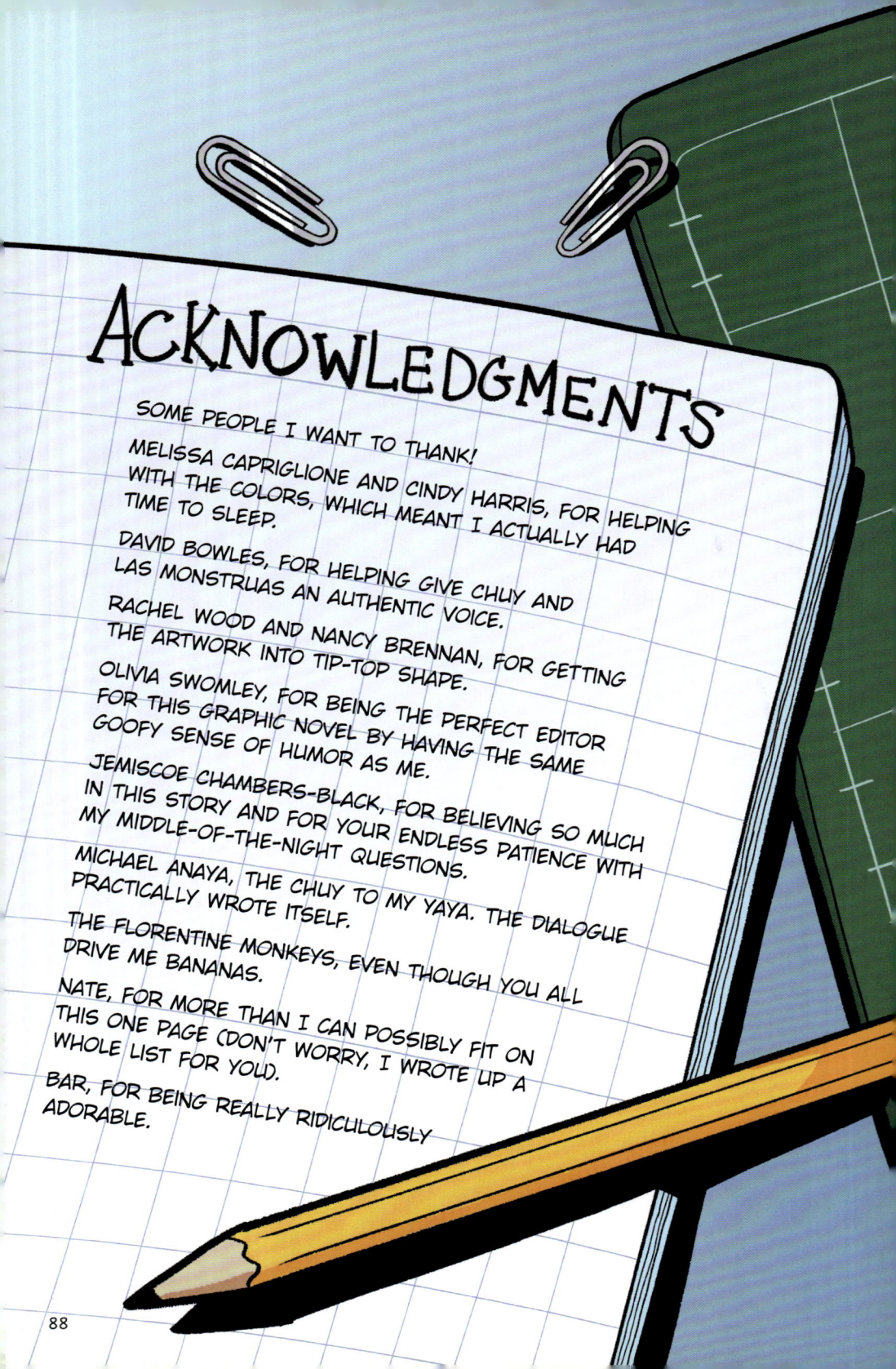

ACKNOWLEDGMENTS

Some people I want to thank!

Melissa Capriglione and Cindy Harris, for helping with the colors, which meant I actually had time to sleep.

David Bowles, for helping give Chuy and Las Monstruas an authentic voice.

Rachel Wood and Nancy Brennan, for getting the artwork into tip-top shape.

Olivia Swomley, for being the perfect editor for this graphic novel by having the same goofy sense of humor as me.

Jemiscoe Chambers-Black, for believing so much in this story and for your endless patience with my middle-of-the-night questions.

Michael Anaya, the Chuy to my Yaya. The dialogue practically wrote itself.

The Florentine Monkeys, even though you all drive me bananas.

Nate, for more than I can possibly fit on this one page (don't worry, I wrote up a whole list for you).

Bar, for being really ridiculously adorable.

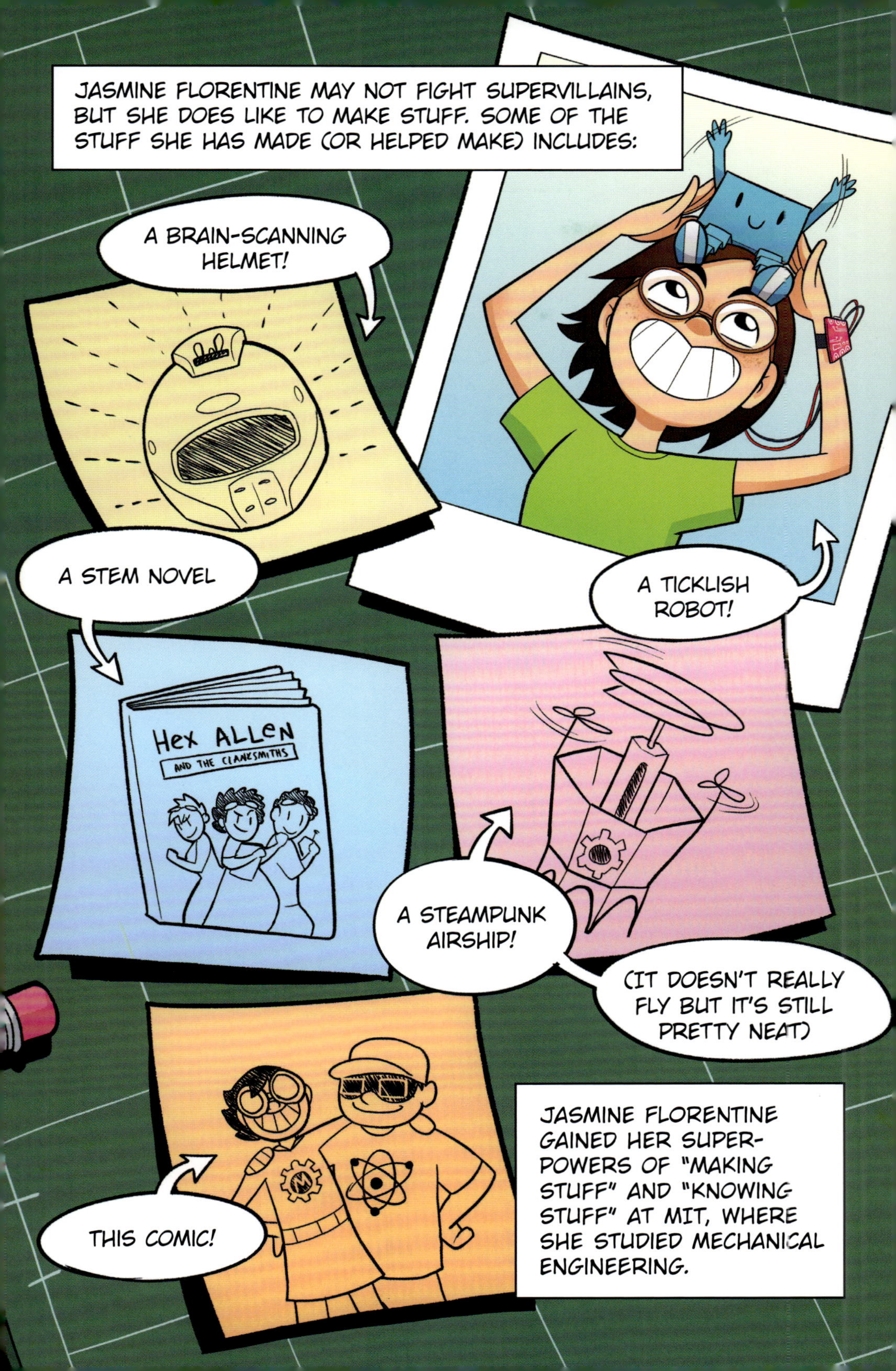

JASMINE FLORENTINE MAY NOT FIGHT SUPERVILLAINS, BUT SHE DOES LIKE TO MAKE STUFF. SOME OF THE STUFF SHE HAS MADE (OR HELPED MAKE) INCLUDES:
A BRAIN-SCANNING HELMET!
A TICKLISH ROBOT!
A STEM NOVEL
Hex ALLEN
AND THE CLANKSMITHS
A STEAMPUNK AIRSHIP!
(IT DOESN'T REALLY FLY BUT IT'S STILL PRETTY NEAT)
THIS COMIC!
JASMINE FLORENTINE GAINED HER SUPER-POWERS OF "MAKING STUFF" AND "KNOWING STUFF" AT MIT, WHERE SHE STUDIED MECHANICAL ENGINEERING.

This is a work of fiction. Names, characters, places, and incidents are either products of the author's imagination or, if real, are used fictitiously.

Copyright © 2025 by Jasmine Florentine
Flatting by Melissa Capriglione and Cindy Harris

All rights reserved. No part of this book may be reproduced, transmitted, or stored in an information retrieval system in any form or by any means, graphic, electronic, or mechanical, including photocopying, taping, and recording, without prior written permission from the publisher.

The MIT Press, the ≡mit Kids Press colophon, and MIT Kids Press are trademarks of The MIT Press, a department of the Massachusetts Institute of Technology, and used under license from The MIT Press. The colophon and MIT Kids Press are registered in the US Patent and Trademark Office.

First edition 2025

Library of Congress Catalog Card Number pending
ISBN 978-1-5362-2764-2 (hardcover)
ISBN 978-1-5362-3958-4 (paperback)

25 26 27 28 29 30 CCP 10 9 8 7 6 5 4 3 2 1

Printed in Shenzhen, Guangdong, China

This book was typeset in CCWildWords.
The illustrations were created digitally.

MIT Kids Press
an imprint of Candlewick Press
99 Dover Street
Somerville, Massachusetts 02144

mitkidspress.com
www.candlewick.com

EU Authorized Representative: HackettFlynn Ltd., 36 Cloch Choirneal, Balrothery, Co. Dublin, K32 C942, Ireland. EU@walkerpublishinggroup.com

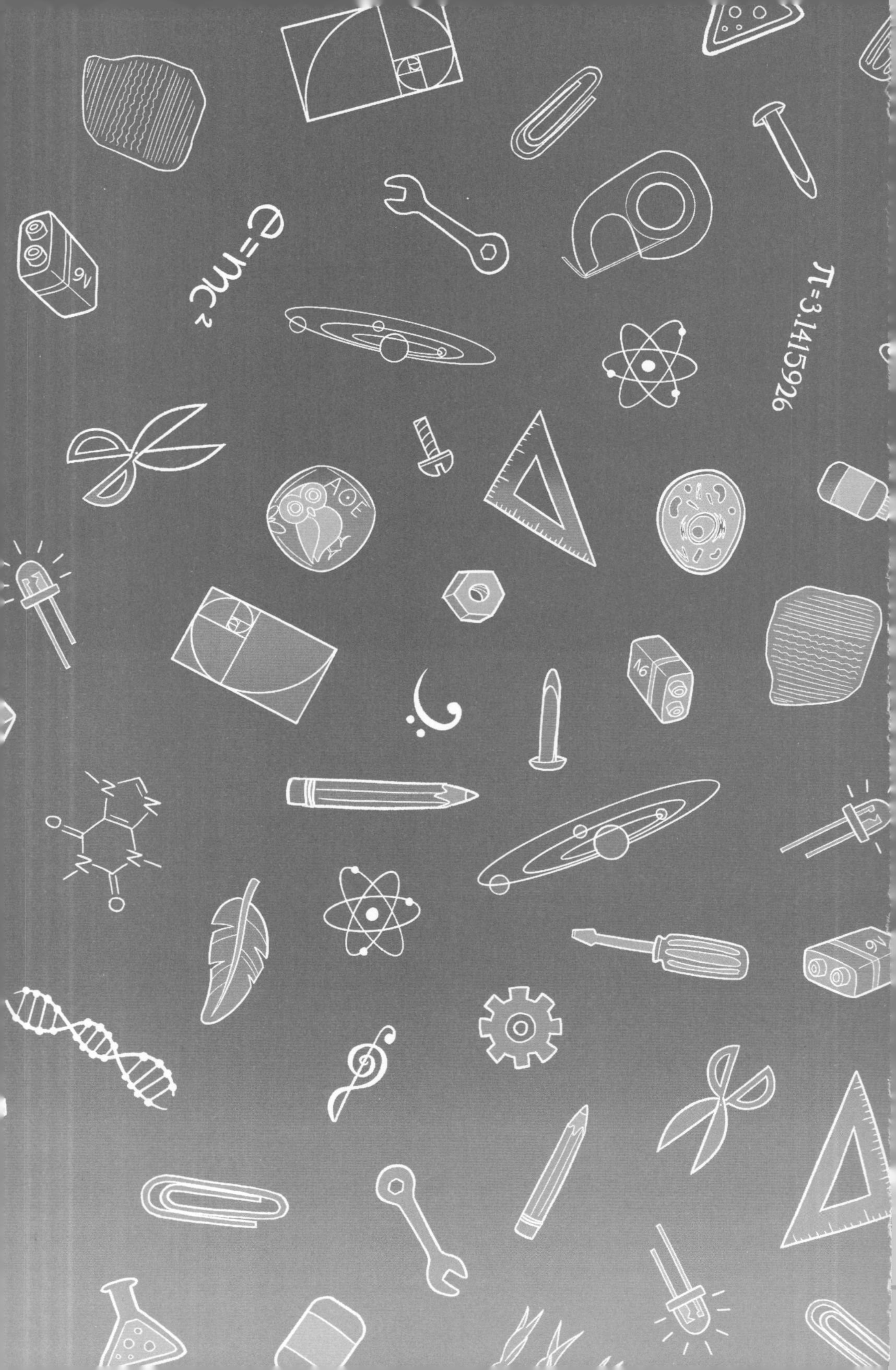
e=mc²
π=3.1415926